WAVES

Stephen Brooke

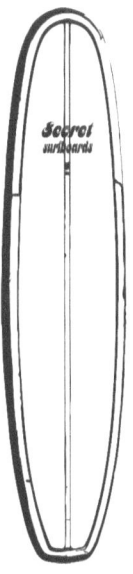

Arachis Press 2016

Waves ©2016 Stephen Brooke

ISBN 978-1-937745-39-4

Arachis Press
4803 Peanut Road
Graceville, FL 32440
http://arachispress.com

Chapter 1

"Did you realize your tenth anniversary is coming up?" asked Michelle.

"We haven't been together *that* long," I replied. "And you can't start counting till we're officially married anyway." That was intended as a hint. I very much wanted to be officially married to Michelle Jackson. Or Michelle Sandor. She changed her mind about which to use, day to day.

As long as she eventually became Michelle Carrol, it didn't matter to me.

"Of the shop." The woman sounded just a tad exasperated. I undoubtedly gave her reason to be. "You opened this place in February of Ninety-One."

Charlie looked up from her homework, spread across the round kitchen table. "Do you want me to paint a sign?" she asked. "Oh, I know. A commemorative surfboard!"

That really was not a bad idea at all. But I would have to shape one before she could paint on it. "Draw something up," I told her, "if you have time. Passing your test comes first."

Charlie was studying for her GED exam at the local branch of the community college, over in Scott City. She nodded. "Will do, Shaper." She looked back into the book opened in front of her. "I think I could have done this without taking the course. Pass the test, I mean."

I only nodded. I was inclined to agree.

"Ted is rubbing off on you," came from Michelle. "Don't start thinking you can do everything on your own. Now clear those books off the table so we can eat."

SHAPER

Michelle was cooking tonight. I was willing to make that concession from time to time; I couldn't expect the girls to eat my bland vegetarian meals every night. Not that I had ever actually prepared large evening meals for myself, being more inclined to 'forage' through the day. This was just one of many changes my routine had undergone over the past three weeks.

Well, more than three, if you think about it. Things had started to change the day Janice Bell had come into my shop with Charlie in tow, months ago. Jan would have started her classes this week, wouldn't she? Her last semester at the community college.

"Wake up, Shaper."

"Miles away again," remarked Michelle, shaking her head. "Stir-fry is ready." She set the big saute pan in the center of the table. One of my pans — the few kitchen items that had come with her and Charlie were mostly still in boxes, out in my workshop. There just wasn't much space for them in here. "And here's the rice," she added, setting the bowl down. It was white rice but that's okay. Sometimes, anyway.

There were shrimp mixed in with the veggies. I'm willing to eat those; anything without a backbone is my rule. Except maybe squid and such. They're just a little too intelligent for me to be comfortable with them on the menu.

Charlie liberally dosed her plateful with soy sauce, then sprinkled on more salt. "This close to the beach we probably breathe in about all the salt we need," I informed her.

"And you swallow a lot of it every time you surf!" came her giggling response. "Maybe you get way more than you need, too."

4

"Maybe," I agreed.

"Jane says the motel still is not on the market," Michelle informed me, as she shoveled rice onto her plate. Jane Warner was the local post mistress. Moreover, her husband was in the real estate business.

"So there was probably a sale lined up already before they forced you out of your lease." Michelle and her daughter had come to Cully Beach to open and possibly buy the *Easy Breezes* motel.

She nodded slowly and took a sip of iced tea before replying. "That's what Dick thinks. It wouldn't have occurred to me."

"Mom's an innocent," proclaimed Charlie.

"Your mom had too many other things to worry about at the time." That was certainly true. Drug smugglers, a dead ex-husband, an alcoholic daughter — and me, I guess. "You could still sue them, you know," I told Michelle. "Sammy thought you had a legitimate claim." I had convinced her to at least allow my attorney to send a letter to the owners.

"No. I'm well rid of that place. And I kind of like living with you." That was nice to hear.

"Except you need more room," chimed in Charlie.

"Oh, I was thinking of turning your bedroom into sales space." I seriously had been considering just that change before the pair moved in. It had been only an unused spare bedroom then.

She shrugged. "I could sleep in your workshop." Charlie spent a lot of time back there anyway. In warmer weather it might be an okay place to sleep, but not now. It wasn't exactly airtight.

"If you and I don't start contributing around here, we're all likely to be sleeping in the van," stated Michelle. "And don't object, Ted. You can't keep on paying the bills for all three of us."

I probably could, but it would be tight.

"John thinks he can get me a shift at the coffee shop," Charlie said. That would be *Coastal Coffee*, where her boyfriend was a manager.

"Sure you would want John-boy as your boss?" I asked.

Charlie smirked. "It would let me keep an eye on him."

Chapter 2

The poetic temperament's a very nice temperament...but it's an old maid's temperament.

Bernard Shaw wrote that. He could have been describing me, except I wasn't alive then. I was the guy who idealized 'woman' but could never make things work out with one. Ted Carrol truly was a bit of an old maid.

I do prefer doing things at a set time, in a set way. Having Michelle and Charlie move in upset my carefully arranged apple cart. But change is inevitable, right? One thing that did not change was my early morning routine. I still got up around Five, turned on the coffee maker, and then walked across the street to check the surf.

It was cold — not unexpected in January — but quite still and clear, the sky thick with stars. There was no hint yet of the sun over the Atlantic. I crossed A-1-A at the corner by the Bells's house-slash-boutique and continued down the road next to the deserted and quite dark *Easy Breezes*. Even the security light was out.

No waves to speak of, not that I expected any. But the ocean can sometimes serve up a surprise, so I always check. Plus, as I said, it is my routine.

However, in the past few months that routine had twice led me to happen upon dead bodies. I was hopeful that would not repeat itself in this new year. Or this new century and new millennium, I could say. It had brought some mighty big changes to my life. I headed back through the chill morning air, back to a warm kitchen and hot coffee.

Now this anniversary of the surf shop — chances are I would not even have thought of it. Yes, I should do some sort of celebration or promotion or something. Mark the occasion in some way. I stood in front of the *Cully Beach Surf Shop*, this modest little 'Florida house' that had been converted into a place of business. My place. Had that been enough for me?

I once thought it was. Obviously, I had been much mistaken. I went on up the drive and in the back door, into the kitchen.

No one up yet. I poured myself a cup of coffee and contemplated breakfast. Hmm, grits, I think, and a soft-boiled egg or two. I thought that was a good choice on a cold morn but the girls would most certainly turn up both their noses at such fare. Some water was set to boil and I rummaged in the fridge for eggs. Things were no longer in the places I was accustomed to keeping them.

Other things were in their place now, things I would never have bought myself. Also, as a concession to Charlie's problems with alcohol, I no longer kept beer or wine in my refrigerator. That, of course, was of no concern at breakfast time.

A door closed quietly somewhere down the hall. Probably Charlie claiming the bathroom. She was almost always up before her mom. I'd have to get that promised indoor shower for them eventually. No one liked showering out back in the cold at this time of year, though I had done it for ten years.

Grits were bubbling. In go the eggs. Let everything sit for three or four minutes. I carried my cup up into the shop. Kind of cool in there. No point in heating that space overnight. Hmm, a blinking light on the answering machine. Just one call.

"Hi Ted, it's Pat. Wanted to let you know that Betty and I plan to come over next month. She gets the Presidents Day weekend off, y'know. Um, that's the — Seventeenth through the Nineteenth. Talk at you more later!"

That would be just the time to have my anniversary celebration, wouldn't it? A holiday weekend would work nicely. About five weeks away so I had plenty of time to get ready.

Charlie stood in the kitchen when I returned, pouring herself a cup of coffee. "'Morning, Shaper," she mumbled, and wrinkled up her nose. "Do I smell onions?"

"In the grits," I told her. "Do you think I should add garlic too?"

She only grimaced, fixed herself a bowl of cold cereal, and settled down across the table from me, as I stirred the egg yolks into my grits. "Pat and Betty are coming over next month," I said, between mouthfuls. She liked Pat, and his artwork.

"Does he have a show?"

"Nah, just vacation time. School is closed for the holiday." Betty taught elementary kids. "I'm going to do our anniversary thing that weekend, I think."

A door banged. "Mom's up," Charlie said, "or we have clumsy burglars in the place."

"We need a dog to discourage them. Is John going to give you a puppy?"

The girl sighed. "I don't think it would be safe here, do you? We're so close to the highway."

"Yeah, maybe so. Unless it were a little indoor dog."

SHAPER

We both noticed the lights at the same moment. Someone had pulled into the driveway. Charlie was on her feet and peeking through a window before I even got moving. "It's a police car," she whispered. I'm not sure why she felt the need to whisper. "A big one, a whatchacallit."

"An SUV?"

"Yeah. That would be Chief Cotton, wouldn't it?"

"Uh-huh." Everyone else on the force drove sedans. Or bicycles. "What the heck is he doing up so early?"

Only one way to find out. His vehicle was pulled in behind Michelle's minivan. She parked that on the street during the day but we thought it best to keep it in the drive at night. I stepped out the back door and gave the chief a wave. "Come on in, Bill, and have some coffee. It's too cold to stand around out here!" It was getting light by now and the sun would be above the horizon in a few more minutes.

Charlie had disappeared by the time we came back in. Probably felt the need to be more presentable though she didn't seem to care how she looked around me.

"I figured you would be wide awake by now," said Cotton. "I know you rise with the sun."

"Before the sun at this time of year. Anything on your mind, or just a social call?"

"Lots on my mind, Ted, but none of it stuff you need to hear. I was just cruising and thinking. I do that sometimes before going to the station — look over this town I'm supposed to be protecting." He gave me a rather wry smile. "I kind of stopped on a whim."

"Any time, Bill." I got up to start another pot of coffee going. "As long as it is after Five."

"And before Nine. I know you turn in early too." He glanced toward the short hallway opening from the other end of the kitchen. "Or has that changed?"

I laughed. "Some." I turned on the machine and returned to the table. It began to chug as the water heated.

"Maybe I need a change, too," said Bill Cotton. He hesitated a moment and then continued, "I'm thinking of retiring."

I must have looked skeptical. Bill wasn't that old after all — mid-Fifties maybe?

"Yeah, retiring. I could take a decent pension right now. And, well, the city council has been hinting that they want a younger man in the job."

I thought about the officers I knew. There were some good men and women but were any ready to be chief? "There's no one on the force who could take your place. Not right now." In a few years, maybe.

He agreed. "They would have to hire outside. I suspect there are those who want a clean sweep of the department. Our mayor, included." Bill rose. "Thanks for the coffee and the time. I appreciate it." He started for the door and then turned to me, and added, "Something is going on, Ted. I haven't told anyone else but I am sure something shady is going down at city hall."

Chapter 3

There was surf later that week. It was nice to know that Michelle or Charlie could look after the shop if I played hooky, that I would not need to depend on the part-time high school kids I had always hired. But Michelle was right about the two of them getting jobs, if only for their own self-esteem.

Hiring kids was good for the shop, as well. It kept me connected to the surfing community. I couldn't tell you how many boards I had sold because a friend or parent of an employee came into the place. Anyway, I was typically done with the waves and back at the shop by the official opening time of Ten AM. The kids I hired mostly came in after school, giving me a few afternoon hours to work on board building or other chores.

I was getting my board into the truck, ready to head for the pier, when Charlie came out, keys in hand.

"I'll move the van," she said. It was blocking my way in the narrow drive.

"Want to come along?"

"Surfing? No way, Shaper. Not until the water gets warmer!"

"Oh, I was thinking you might want to sit in the coffee shop and make eyes at John while I surfed."

The girl did not deign to answer but got into the old Dodge. It started, which was always a bit of a surprise to me. One or the other of our ancient vehicles was bound to fail one of these days. Charlie waved at me as I backed out and then she hurried back into the warmth of the kitchen.

I didn't know if her boyfriend actually had a shift on this Thursday morning. As a student at the community college, John's schedule might have shifted to accommodate his classes. Like Jan Bell, the boy was in his last semester at the local campus and would have to continue his education elsewhere next year. That might be hard on Charlie — she hadn't had much stability in her life up until now and John Brody was about as stable a kid as I knew. And Jan, her best friend here, would be leaving too.

I briefly wondered if young Miss Bell had chosen a major yet. Then I was pulling into a parking space just south of the pier and looking over the waves. Hardly worth the drive, were they? Small lines coming from the north, with a bit of side-wind. Oh well, I had ridden far worse.

No one else out, at least not yet. I slipped into double wet-suits, that is a sleeveless 'Long John' over a long-sleeved jacket. That much rubber wasn't necessary most of the time but the water gets mighty cold in January, even in Florida. It was a good thing I had brought the old longboard too. I could paddle it up on my knees and not have water flowing through the suit with every stroke.

I needed a new longboard. In time. Too many other projects at the moment, including building the commemorative board. Make it a give-away? Maybe. I stroked into my first wave and gave it no more thought. They weren't great waves but any day with surf beats any day without it.

"It's mighty cold for surfing, isn't it, Ted?" came a voice as I showered off. I think the water streaming from the shower there on the boardwalk was even colder than the Atlantic I had just left.

"And you out riding around in shorts, Jim?" I asked, turning to face Jaime Trejo, bicycle cop, and his partner. "Hey, Dave, they have you back on wheels?" I shook the water off and carried my board toward the truck. They followed behind me, pushing their mountain bikes.

"Now and again," replied Officer David Blake. "Johnson is under the weather."

"Flu," added Trejo. Both policemen wore bike shorts but were also encased in parkas. I was wondering whether to strip off my own wet-suits or drive the six blocks home in them. Simpler to stay wrapped in neoprene, maybe, especially with this wind picking up.

Did they want something? Even if we were friends, having a couple cops following me made me a tad nervous. "I'll ride on south," said Jim. "Catch up when you can." He pedaled away, leaving me with Dave. So it was Blake that wanted something.

"Um, Ted, the Bells are good friends of yours, right?"

"My best friends." What kind of trouble was Rick in now?

"Do you —" He looked distinctly embarrassed but blurted it on out. "Do you think you could be at their house tomorrow evening? Maybe around Six or so?"

"Yeah, I suppose so. Michelle and I go over there a lot. Charlie too. She's best buds with their daughter."

"Janice. I know. I asked her out."

That was unexpected. And maybe a tad funny. "Ah! And you want me to vouch for your outstanding character." Not that Rick had much need to be protective of his daughter. She was probably the most responsible person in the family.

"Something like that. I'm, well, older than the guys their daughter usually dates. I don't know how they might take that."

I gave the officer a good looking-over. "You're what, about twenty-five? That's not very old, man, believe me."

"Twenty-four, actually, for another month. But still, it is a bit of an age difference, you know?

"Hey, I'll try to be there and give moral support." It wasn't like I had anything else planned. "But maybe you could do something for me, too." I laid out the gist of my conversation with Bill Cotton a couple days earlier. "I consider the chief a friend," I told him. "I don't know if he needs any support in all this, but I'd appreciate it if you could keep an eye open. Jim, too. Might as well tell him."

Dave nodded soberly. "I've noticed some things. Thanks for letting me know what's going on." Then he smiled. "See you tomorrow night!" he called as he pedaled off after his partner.

Chapter 4

Valentine's Day was coming. I had ignored that holiday for many years. Now things were different.

Maybe it would be a good time to ask Michelle to marry me, I thought, as I sat waiting for her in the kitchen. Or would it be too soon? I really considered us married already, 'in the eyes of God and Nature,' from the moment we had agreed to be together, just as I had considered Michelle to be divorced from the late Bradley Jackson as soon as both had agreed to sign the papers. Legality lags behind reality, at times.

So, even if our partnership wasn't legally recognized, I reckon if two people agree to live together as man and wife, it is a marriage. The government has nothing to do with that. But as with any other sort of partnership, a legal contract is a sound idea. It's just good business to have something in writing. That's what civil marriage provides.

In fact, we could marry in the Church. With her former husband deceased, there was no longer any divorced status to get in the way of that. Both her former husbands. I assumed she had been married to Charlie's father, not that it mattered one way or the other.

Hmm, I hoped she wouldn't be expecting a ring. That wasn't going to happen.

Was this evening going to happen? "Ready to go?" I called.

Michelle yelled something back from the bathroom. As the door remained closed, I guessed she wasn't.

Across the table from me, Charlie was vigorously erasing something in her sketch book. "Sure you don't want to come with us?" I asked.

"Hey, I know you two go over there to drink instead of doing it in front of me. I'll stay out of your way tonight." She put down her drawing and pushed back her thick shag. It had returned to being black now. From what I had learned of Charlie, that could change to any shade, at any time. "Anyway, Jan has a date tonight so I can't hang with her."

I only nodded. No need to comment on that. "Hey, John says the surf shop downtown is closing," she told me. "You expected that, didn't you?"

I shrugged. "It's happened to every other competitor over the past ten years. People jump in without realizing what's involved."

Charlie snickered. "I think you just did that with Mom."

I couldn't help but agree.

A few minutes later Michelle and I were cutting across the back-yard of the vacant house next door, on our way to the Bells. It was good to see that it was being kept mowed now, not that a lot of that was needed this time of year.

"I really am thinking of trying to buy this place," I said.

Michelle turned her gaze toward the house for a moment. "If I get a decent job, maybe we could swing it."

I knew that was true. "I wouldn't make an offer right now. Best to wait until the season winds down." We stepped into the Bells' back yard. A bark — there was Kay, with both their dogs on leashes.

"If the Bells can always have a dog or two around, maybe Charlie could too," I mused.

SHAPER

"We know you don't really want one, Ted Carrol. Just having the two of *us* around is asking a lot of you. Hi, Kay!"

"Go on in," came the response. "We still have unfinished business out here."

Jan opened the back door, the door into the kitchen, to us. I think she was expecting someone else.

"A dress?" asked Michelle. "This must be a serious date!"

"Even surfer girls dress up sometimes," I told her. "You look good, young lady."

"Thanks, Shaper." She looked out into the dark and then shut the door behind us.

The Richard Bells, senior and junior, were clearing the table. Dinner was apparently just over. "Hey, guys," I greeted them.

"Help yourself from the fridge," said Rick. "Some of the stuff in there is yours, isn't it?"

It was, indeed. If I couldn't have wine in my own house the next best thing was to stash it at the neighbors' place.

"We'll wait for Kay," stated Michelle. Well, okay. But not too long.

More barking outside, much louder this time. That was likely to mean a stranger. A stranger to the dogs, that is; I knew full well who was out there.

I pushed the door open to see Dave Blake crouching to pet both of the Bells' pooches. That would be a good recommendation to Rick. "Hey, Dave," I called, "good to see you! What brings you here?"

18

Darned if that didn't stump him momentarily. "He's here to see me, Shaper," said Jan, pushing by me. "Come on in, Dave."

Rick did give the young fellow at his door a thorough inspection. I don't think Dave's age mattered a bit to him but Bell tended to be mistrustful of policemen. And pretty much anyone else in authority positions.

As for age, Dave was basically a kid, at least beside the two of us.

"Good evening, Mister Bell," he said. "Hi, Richie."

"Hi, Officer Blake," replied the boy, apparently not surprised at all to see him. I do think the coat and tie provided him a certain amount of amusement.

"Hello, Blake. How are you?" asked Rick. He turned and continued rinsing dishes in the sink.

"Doing well, sir." He glanced at Jan, maybe hoping that she was ready to go.

"Let me get my purse," said she, and headed upstairs.

Kay had not come in yet. Either the dogs had a lot of business to transact out there or she was just avoiding us. So it was up to Michelle to interrogate our prisoner. "How do you happen to know Janice, Officer Blake?" she asked.

"We used to run into each other when I was on bike patrol, ma'am. And, ah, we said hello at times during the — events, last month." Meaning the whole affair with Ray Manuel and his drug smuggling operation. "But mostly, it's because of your daughter and John Brody." He relaxed a tad and gave us a smile. "We cops do drink a lot of coffee, you know."

So Charlie was the link here. I could see that. Down the stairs came Jan and in a few seconds the couple was out the door and off to wherever.

We would undoubtedly learn the location of 'wherever' tomorrow.

Chapter 5

"He's kind of old, Shaper."

"What, four or five years older that you? That's not a big deal. My dad was five years older than my mom." I could have added that I was ten years older than Charlie's mom.

"I do like him." Janice Bell sipped her tea. "But I will be going off to the university soon."

"Nine months isn't soon, Jan. An awful lot can happen in nine months." I thought maybe a change of topic would be good. "Speaking of the university, have you decided on a major yet?"

"Yes, I have. Finally!" She seemed suddenly a bit shy about the whole thing. "Promise you won't laugh, Shaper?" I nodded.

"Journalism." Jan was the one who laughed. "I know, that's not at all the sort of thing I've always said I wanted to do." Pretty much everyone had assumed she was headed for a career in education or social work.

"My eyes were opened up by all the stuff that happened last year. There's a world I didn't know existed out there. I mean, I had read about it but it wasn't real to me."

"Janice Bell, intrepid reporter. I like it."

She giggled. "Are you making fun of me, Shaper?"

"A little. I think you would make a great journalist, kid." I looked around the empty shop. "Slower than slow this morning." It was cold and windy out. Maybe customers would show up later.

"Charlie told me she can't work at the coffee shop," said Jan.

"Yeah. They won't hire her until she has her GED. I guess you need that to make coffee."

"She'll find something. And she'll pass the test in May."

"We'll make sure of that."

She nodded resolutely. Neither of us was going to allow Charlie to slack off.

A kid came in, a middle school-aged boy. One of the surf rats that hung around. He wouldn't buy anything but I didn't mind him and his friends being here. Give them a couple years and they would be customers.

But someone did have to keep an eye on them. "You need to stay up front with that drink," I warned him. "Don't get near the clothes."

"Okay, Shaper." He noisily sucked some reddish slush through his straw. Probably purchased at the convenience store on the other side of the Bells' place.

Jan smiled at the boy, a tad wistfully. "Not long ago, going out and meeting someone for a couple of those drinks and hanging at the beach would have been about all I expected from a date. I'm not used to dressing up like last night."

"Dave wanted to make a good impression."

"He'd already done that." She looked up at the clock. Almost noon. "He's kind of an impressive guy."

Was he? I'll admit that he seemed a bit, well, bland to me. But a good man and a competent one. Give him a few years and he could be a candidate for Chief Cotton's job. I turned the conversation back to her education. "You settled on University of Florida, didn't you? That's not so far away."

"Yeah, Shaper, I'm gonna be a Gator." She got up from her seat behind the counter and began straightening a stack of tee-shirts.

22

"What were the teams called where you went to college? Florida Atlantic, right?"

"Owls. There were burrowing owl colonies on the campus so it was a natural."

The rat had wandered over and listened to this. "I don't think I'd want to be an owl," was his opinion.

"They're cute. Certainly cuter than a gator or a pelican. I did meet a rather nice looking Seminole once, though."

"Best not tell Michelle about that," warned Janice.

"My dad was a Seminole," interjected the rat, apparently considering himself part of the conversation.

"I meant a real Seminole, kid," I informed him. Just what was his name? "I used to live near the Everglades."

"Cool. Real gators there too, huh?"

"Yep. And lots of snakes and lots and lots of mosquitoes. I like it better here." My eyes went to the front windows, to the highway and the dunes beyond it that prevented me from seeing the ocean. "I believe this is about the best place I know."

I don't think either of those young people believed me. That was okay.

Chapter 6

I was 'mowing foam,' that is, running a power planer along a polyurethane surfboard blank, when Charlie came back to my workroom.

"That going to be the anniversary board?" she asked, when I powered down. The girl had waited patiently for me to finish.

"It is." I surveyed the still-rough board. "Pretty much one of my generic shapes. That seemed best for a giveaway."

She held up her sketchbook, open to a drawing, for me to see. "Would this be okay?"

I took it from her and gave it a closer look. Probably should have had my reading glasses but they were somewhere inside. "That's not the same script I use on my logo," I noted.

"Maybe you could switch from that hippie look. It's awful dated, Shaper."

"So am I. Pat Edwards designed it for me, long before I ever opened the shop." I handed Charlie's book back to her. "I suppose it was kind of old-fashioned even then."

"You don't like it, do you?"

I wasn't going to lie to the girl. "It's kind of busy. Do you think you could simplify it some?" Oh, what the heck. I might as well show her. "Have a pencil on you?"

She handed one over without comment, and I squatted and roughed out a simplified version of her idea. Charlie watched over my shoulder. "Why aren't you an artist, Shaper? You're really good with a pencil."

"Because I realized I didn't have anything to say as an artist. So what's the point?" I handed the sketchbook back to her. "That's just an idea, Charlie. I know you can come up with something better."

"I'll try." She disappeared into the other side of my workshop, the glassing room, which had been doubling as her 'art studio.' Or at least that was where she stored her stuff.

Back to the board. It would be a typical 'thruster,' a three-finned board, the sort most riders wanted. Not the sort of surfboard I liked to ride myself, but I knew how they worked and how to make them. I should put up some sort of announcements about the giveaway and the anniversary in the next week or so. February was getting closer.

Another visitor wandered in, Rick this time. Either done with work or he had none this afternoon. He stood and watched for a while, nursing a beer, until I finished all the rough shaping and put aside the power tool. It would be hand work from here, smoothing things out.

"I see you bought the fridge," he remarked, looking toward a shoulder-high unit against the back wall.

"Yeah, thank Kay for telling me about it." She had told me a used refrigerator was available, maybe hoping to get my wine out of her own. I'd slapped on a coat of paint and added a hasp and padlock. I didn't mistrust Charlie but there was no point in tempting her, nor any of the other kids that hung around the place.

"Jan is going out with the cop again tonight," he suddenly said. Rick seemed slightly perplexed by that fact. "She's never seemed this serious about a guy before. Shoot, she's never seemed serious about a guy at all."

I was aware of that. "Her first steady boyfriend. She could do far worse, Rick."

"Oh, I know that. And it probably won't last."

Probably not. Even if they managed to stay together until she went off to college, that would be likely to put an end to it. Too much distance, too many new guys around her.

But what did I know? "This is the board I'm giving away," I told him, as I repositioned it in my shaping stands.

"One of your regulars, huh? Would barely float me."

"I could build you a longboard. I've been thinking of doing more of those."

"Hmm, maybe." Probably didn't have the cash for one. He looked toward his house. "I'd better get back. Maybe I should be sitting on the back porch cleaning my shotgun when Blake shows up." He chuckled and headed across the back yards.

A few seconds later, Charlie poked her head around the corner. Of course, she could hear everything going on in the other side of the workshop. "Jan likes Dave," she informed me. "A lot."

"As much as you like John?" I asked.

"Oh, Shaper, no one has ever liked anyone that much!" I knew not to take that seriously. "Hey, there's Mom."

Her Dodge minivan was pulling into the drive. That was all right; it was near closing time and I would be sending today's young part-time employee home shortly.

And welcoming my older part-time employee. But today, Michelle had been someone else's employee. Yes, she had found a job, cashiering at the new-ish *Winn-Dixie* out west of town. I didn't really like the idea, I'll admit.

Don't go thinking that's some male thing about women-folk working. I just didn't like that big supermarket and never shopped there.

"Take off the padlock," she demanded, as she slipped out of the van. "I need wine!"

Chapter 7

"You are all alone again, Ted?" asked Sara Trejo, as we exited *Our Lady of the Sea.*

"That I am. Too early for the girls, I think."

"Early for us, too!" she said. I was not accustomed to seeing them at this mass. Maybe they had plans for later. Maybe Jim had a shift today. Maybe lots of things.

"They might feel uncomfortable coming to church with you," Jim said, not very loudly. "You are living in sin, after all. Not that Father Paul would ever say anything." He shifted the squirming toddler he held.

I shrugged. "I'm working on making it official. It may take some time."

"Keep after her," advised Sara. "She needs to know."

"But without scaring her off," added Jim, with a chuckle.

"Yeah. I'm planning to formally propose on Valentine's Day."

"Ooh, that's wonderful." Sara said something in Spanish to her husband. As ever, I couldn't follow her Cuban accent. I wondered if Jim ever had that problem. He nodded, but I don't know what he was assenting to.

When he addressed me then, it was about another matter altogether. "Dave told me about the chief. Have you talked to Cotton since?"

"Nope. Whatever he had on his mind has stayed there."

"He is really thinking about retiring?" asked Mrs. Trejo. "But he has done such a good job!"

I could only agree. "His handling of events last month demonstrated that." Even if he kind of muddled through while the feds did most of the work.

"The prestige of the drug bust won the chief some approval, that's for sure," said Jim. "It reflected well on the department as a whole. But I've heard there are those who felt it hurt the image of the town."

"As if he could do anything about that!" objected his wife.

"I guess we need to post signs on the beach," I said. "Drug smugglers not welcome!"

"Yeah, we should've thought of that, Ted, and saved ourselves a lot of trouble. Ready to go?" Jim sniffed. "I think Stevie needs a diaper change."

Sara laughed. "You were wise to find an already grown daughter, Ted!" The two headed off toward their surprisingly plain and practical subcompact.

A minute later, my old Toyota truck was pulling out of the parking lot and headed over a block to A-1-A. South past the pier I drove. It was a rather nice day for the time of year and quite a crowd was already at the beach this Sunday morning.

I should probably open up the shop as soon as I got home. Good enough weather I could leave the front door open to invite folks in.

Ah, someone knew how I thought. The door was already hanging open when I pulled in. I was predictable, wasn't I? Old Ted, set in his ways.

Maybe it was time to change those ways. There was no future in owning a little surf shop for me and this family I had acquired, was there? That was the sort of thing a kid did, not a guy my age. I had taken on responsibilities.

Charlie waylaid me before I reached the backdoor. She said not a word, only held out her open sketchbook.

As expected, she had come up with something better than what I had sketched. "The board is sitting on the glassing stands, ready for your artwork," I told her. "I'll get it into the window as soon as we both finish with it."

She practically sprinted to the workshop. I was more leisurely about going inside. Michelle was up front, where a couple of potential customers browsed.

She gave me a peck. I might have gone for something a little more had we been alone. "How was church?"

Exactly how does one answer that? "You could come with me, you know, and find out for yourself."

"But I'm not Catholic."

"Everyone belongs to the Catholic Church," I told her. "That's what the name means. I see you decided to open early."

"Oh, I came up to answer the phone and figured I might as well let in the fresh air."

"Anyone important? On the phone, I mean."

"It was Pat. He would have known you were at church or surfing, so I think he wanted to talk to me and see how we were doing." Michelle gave me a knowing look. "You wouldn't be likely to open up about any problems."

Yeah, Pat knew me. More shoppers wandered in. Looked like we might have a good day of it.

"I thanked him again for coming over during the Christmas break. Betty, too. It was good of them to help us settle in here." A soft laugh. "Even though we didn't have much to move and it was only half a block."

"They're still on for next month?"

"Sure. I told them we could throw Charlie out and let them have the spare room."

"I suspect they would prefer a motel. Though we actually do have a lot of space up here." I waved an arm toward the showroom. "All we need are some cots!"

"No thank you, Mister Carrol. I had quite enough of the motel business."

I had wondered how Michelle got into that business. One couldn't just walk in off the street and say they wanted to lease a motel. But I had not pried.

"Will that be all today, ma'am?" I asked the woman who brought a puka shell necklace to the counter.

Chapter 8

Kay stood on her front steps, watching the sign go up. Having nothing better to do, I ambled down the sidewalk to join her.

It was a big sign, right out on the corner, angled. "So that's what's going to happen to the *Easy Breezes*," she remarked.

"A condo. We shouldn't be surprised." But we were, sort of.

And upset. Neither of us wanted to see our neighborhood change. "Coming Soon!" it read, "SAND CASTLES of Cully Beach," and then contact information for sales, and the name of the developer. I didn't recognize that.

When the crew finished their work and drove off in a couple of rather large trucks, we both crossed the highway to examine it more closely. I looked at the rendering of the coming condominium. "Five stories? Zoning doesn't allow that here. Or it shouldn't."

"They must expect a variance."

"I haven't seen anything about that. There would have to be public hearings."

She nodded. "We need to know more about this." Kay stared at the sign for a moment. "I don't like that 'castles' bit. Are there going to be more of them?" Then she chuckled at a sudden thought. "If they build this, you might finally get those street lights you wanted, Ted."

I regularly complained that they did not extend this far south. "Too high a price," I replied.

Who could I talk to about this? I wasn't particularly friendly with anyone currently on the city council. That shouldn't matter, I know, but it does. Yes, it does. Well, I did know people and I would talk to someone. And I wouldn't be the only one to notice those five stories, would I?

Doris Boone, maybe. Doris had been a councilwoman at one time but had lost her seat a couple cycles back. That didn't keep her from remaining active in the community. I could go by her bank. The venerable *Bank of Cully Beach*, that is, where she was a vice-president.

That was close but I didn't have anyone to watch the shop just then, Michelle being off at her part-time cashier job, Charlie being — well, I wasn't quite sure where Charlie was, other than in close proximity to John Brody. She had finished her work on the commemorative board and I had glassed it; I only needed to give that a final buffing before putting it on display.

Dick Warner might know something about all this. Wouldn't hurt to ask about the house next door while I was at it. Maybe I needed to buy it before someone put a condo there, too.

Hmm. I'm making decisions on my own. I shouldn't do that. Before anyone else, I needed to talk to Michelle. Her shift ended at Two today. I could wait.

The mailman came by a bit before noon, as usual. "I have one here you need to sign for. For Ms. Jackson but your signature will do." Michelle's mail was forwarded to the shop now. That meant a certain amount of it was intended for the shut-down motel and of no concern to anyone. This one had a law firm's name on it; I wondered about that but wasn't about to open her mail.

Michelle apparently hurried home and pulled up out front shortly after her shift ended. I'd want to get away from that job as quickly as possible too.

As I gave her my news, she looked through the mail on the counter, and then tore open the mystery envelope from the attorney. "Hmm." She looked over what appeared to be a cover letter. "They are making me an offer to sign off on any questions concerning the lease. Pretty much returning anything I paid on it, plus some." Michelle raised her eyes to me. "Why would they do that?"

"If the developer wants to move ahead quickly over there, he won't want the chance of a law suit or a lien," was my thought. "He'd want a clear title."

"Oh. Yeah, that makes sense." She stared at the letter a while longer and then at the form that had accompanied it. "We could slow them down over there if I didn't sign and sued them instead."

"I'd say, take the money and run."

Michelle nodded. "It could help us buy that house."

Us. Yes, we should buy the place in both our names. That was another instance where having a legal marriage might help. "In fact," she said, "I am going right over to the Bell's and have Kay notarize my signature."

"Sure you don't want to let someone see it first?" I meant an attorney, of course, but she handed it to me.

"Go right ahead."

"My legal opinion isn't worth much," I informed her, as I read both pages. She wasn't likely to get a better deal than this, was she? And she hadn't expected anything. It was a fair amount of money.

"It looks good enough but I'd still check with Liz or Sammy." That would be Elizabeth and Samuel Inez, of *Inez and Inez*. A copy had probably been sent to them anyway.

"Who would charge me for their time and slow everything down. No, Ted, I'm going to do this." Off she went, out the door and toward *Kay's Korner*.

A half an hour later I wondered what was taking her so long. Gossiping with the Bells? A half an hour after that, my afternoon employee came in and I decided to go check on her.

Both women were up front, in Kay's shop. "You haven't heard about Chief Cotton, have you?" was Kay's greeting.

"No. What happened?"

"He was suspended. And they say there may be criminal charges."

Chapter 9

"There haven't been any formal charges against the chief. All that's been announced is that he was suspended during an ongoing investigation."

"So who's in charge? Millie?" I asked.

Dave nodded. "Yep. But she sure doesn't want to be."

Millie ranked as Number Two at the department, but had been counting her days to retirement lately. In fact, I was pretty sure she was the longest-serving member of the force.

Jan sighed. "I can't believe Chief Cotton would do anything wrong."

"I don't think any of us do," I told her.

"Rumors are there were funds misappropriated," continued Dave. "Exactly what that entails, I have no idea." He glanced toward his car and then toward Jan. Probably wanted to be on his way.

But we weren't ready to let them make their escape. "We should do something," stated Charlie.

"We're not the police, Charlotte," said her mother. "Leave it up to them."

"I think maybe I'd like to be a cop," came the girl's reply. "I've been looking at the courses I could take next semester."

Dave nodded. "That's the way to do it. I went for my degree and I'm glad I did."

"Criminology?" she asked.

"Pre-law, along with the courses required for certification. But criminology is a good way to go too." Dave seemed slightly hesitant to say more. When he did continue, his voice was decidedly serious. "You know your background might disqualify you. But all the trouble was while you were a minor, wasn't it?" Charlie slowly nodded.

"That might not hurt then. Not by the time you would be ready to be certified. The loss of your driver's license might be a bigger problem."

"I should be able to get that back this year." Charlie suddenly brightened. "Maybe I need to look for a car!"

"You'd better look for a job, first," came Michelle's comment. "Ted can't pay for everything."

"That's okay. It's good to have Charlie available to work in the shop." I turned to the girl. "You know, all the teen-aged boys like to come in when you're there."

"So that's why you have us around the place!"

"You're just figuring that out now?" asked Jan. "Let's go, Dave. See you later, guys."

"'Evening, folks," said Dave and followed her to his sedan. Almost as practical and sedate as the Trejo's vehicle. I knew that wasn't a cop thing. They just weren't flashy guys — could take some lessons from Bill Cotton and his aloha shirts.

"Want to say hi to Kay?" I asked. We had waylaid the young couple in the Bells' backyard, when Michelle spotted Dave arriving, wanting to get any news we could of Cotton's situation.

Michelle shook her head. "I talked to her earlier." We headed back toward my place. Our place? I wasn't sure how to think of it anymore.

"So when did you get this cop idea?" I asked Charlie, who trailed behind us. "Oh, I know, from Agent Albritton." She had been one of the DEA agents here in December. I didn't know her first name, did I?

"Maybe," she admitted.

"More likely from hanging around with Dave," was her mother's opinion. "Does your John have an opinion on this?"

"I haven't said anything about it to him." She was silent almost until we reached the back door. "I still might go for art instead. But," Charlie added, with a bit of a giggle, "his dad has been teaching me how to shoot. I don't think John likes that very much."

"Neither do I," stated Michelle.

"I'm going to go paint a while," said Charlie, making her escape to the workshop before her mother said anything more.

But Michelle did not speak of firearms when we got inside. "It would be good for Charlie to get a job of some sort."

"And I don't mind having her help out around here," I replied. "Honestly. She does a lot."

"Yeah, Ted, I know. She's way more use to you than I would be."

"Oh, I have other uses for you, Miss!" I took Michelle in my arms and we kissed for a while. No, I couldn't tell you how long.

She whispered, "I fear if I hung around here neither of us would ever get anything done."

"And we wouldn't care," I whispered back. "You don't have to work at that grocery, you know. I wouldn't mind if you sat around here eating chocolates all day and got fat." Not likely — Michelle was naturally on the scrawny side.

She gave me another kiss and then pulled away. "They've only been willing to take me on part-time. I think maybe I prefer that, anyway. It's temporary, while I look for something better."

"Such as?" I had been reluctant to ask that before. But, hey, she brought it up, didn't she? Maybe I would hear of something that might interest her.

"Anything other than checking out people's groceries!" she laughed. "I've done lots of things over the years and some were even worse than that. Like waitressing. Most recently, I was at a property management company. That's how I was able to talk my way into leasing that damned motel."

"Ah, I learn more about the mystery woman. That was in Orlando?" I opened the fridge. "Like anything to drink?"

"Only if it comes from the other refrigerator," she answered. "Yes, Orlando. Officially, I had the title of Administrative Assistant. That sounds like a better job than it is."

I knew what title I wanted to bestow on Miss Michelle Jackson. Maybe soon. "I'll go out and get a bottle," I told her.

"Make it white." I nodded as I stepped out into the cool night air. I wouldn't have drank this late before Michelle moved in; I typically had allowed myself a small wineglass before supper, and no more. Certainly nothing this close to my bedtime.

I could see the light on in the other side of the workshop, over in the glassing room. "Isn't it getting too cold out here?" I called to Charlie. Maybe I should get a heater for her. Though all the volatile chemicals stored over there made me a bit leery of that.

"Yeah, Shaper, I think I'm gonna go in. I'll ignore whatever it is you're clinking over there." The light went out a few seconds later.

SHAPER

"Charlie's gone to her room," reported Michelle when I came back into the kitchen, chardonnay in hand. "We can sit and sip a while." I could faintly hear the television. We had put their set in the spare room, now Charlie's room, when they moved in. I hadn't had one.

But Michelle turned on my radio, and Mozart filled the room. One of the symphonies. I couldn't tell you the number. I uncorked and poured.

She took a sip and then asked, "Are you serious about buying another place?"

"I was thinking about this long before you moved in," I said. "Now we need the space even more." I leaned forward, elbows on the table. "I really could expand my sales area into the extra bedroom. I think I'd make it into a dedicated board room, instead of having the surfboards all around the main room." They were mounted high on the walls right now, not the most convenient location if someone wanted to look one over.

"And," I added, "we would have an indoor shower, even if we did have to go next door to use it. I did promise one, after all!"

"And I gave you ten years to do it." Her eyes went toward the hallway and Charlie's room. "The girl won't be here forever, you know. She'll want a place of her own. Or a place with a guy."

"She and John seem pretty serious." I kept my voice low.

"He's terribly straitlaced. I can't see them moving in together."

"Not now, anyway. Things could change when he goes off to college next Fall, and gets away from his family." I suspected the Brodys were considerably more conservative than their son.

"Gainesville, like Jan?" asked Michelle.

"Jacksonville. University of North Florida." I was surprised she didn't know. Charlie had mentioned it to me more than once.

"Oh. Is that closer?"

"Not by much. Both are a pretty easy drive from here." I smiled at a thought. "That may be why Charlie is eager to have a car."

"She'll need her license first. Or are you willing to let her drive your baby, Ted?"

"Not a chance. Shoot, I haven't even let you behind the wheel."

"I know better than to ask. Gosh, I've kept you up way past your bedtime, haven't I? I'm afraid we're both going to fall right asleep tonight."

I turned so I could see the clock on the stove. Didn't have a wall clock in here. After ten. "I'll be back in a moment." I said, getting up and shoving the cork back into the wine bottle. "Just need to put this back under lock and key."

"I'll be waiting."

I was closing and locking the door to the shaping room when I saw headlights over at the Bells, someone pulling in. Dave's car. Must have been a short evening.

A week night, a work day coming for Dave, classes for Jan. They were doing well to set aside a couple hours to have dinner.

Standing there in the dark, I watched them kiss at her back door before Jan went inside. Janice Bell, the little surfer girl I had watched grow up. Damn, I felt old.

Chapter 10

"I don't want to see that eyesore go up any more than you do, Ted. It's not the right kind of growth for Cully Beach."

"A weed in the garden," I quipped.

"Some might say that about your place." Dick Warner looked up the street. "This whole area, in fact."

"It would help if they go ahead with the plans for the park." I nodded toward the other side of A-1-A. Nothing was over there but a vacant lot and a long-closed filling station.

"I know that would be great for you and your shop, Ted, but it looks iffy for passage. Mayor Parish doesn't seem to support it."

"Remind me not to vote for her. Not that I ever did."

Dick and I had just walked through the house next door. The listed price was way too high, but I had expected that. "You know the house on your south is on the market too," he said. "I suspect it would go for a lot less."

"I have it on good authority that the place has termites." That authority being the DEA agents who had camped there during their investigation.

"And I know it has been inspected. Let me find the listing on it —" He leafed through his binder. "Says it's sound. Mostly cypress, and that should hold up." He looked up at me. "Has for nearly seventy years." Dick read some more. "The shed behind it is falling down, though."

I had figured that wooden bungalow was at least a decade older than my place. Dick's info would make it two decades. "I had the opportunity to see the front room in there a few weeks ago," I told him. "Might not hurt to look at the rest of it sometime. No hurry, though, Dick."

"I know you have enough else going on in your life right now. And a celebration coming up?" He gazed at the sign in my front window. "Ten years." He sounded like it was hard to believe. I had trouble believing it sometimes, too.

But it was. Ten years ago I had closed the deal on this little house and moved in. Back then I built the boards in the open air, out behind the place, and didn't sell much else. "You wouldn't believe how little I paid for this house back then," I told him.

"You could sell for a lot more now. Let me know if you ever want to list it." He went around his Caddy and opened the door. "And let me know if you want to look at that place down there," Dick added, turning his eyes in the general direction of the house south of mine. One couldn't actually see it from here with all the bushes grown up around it. In he got and off he went, making a quite illegal u-turn in A-1-A.

So, a Friday afternoon. Michelle would be home soon; this was one of the days she worked until Two. Management kept moving her shifts around but wouldn't let her have more than twenty hours a week.

I was at the counter, trying to make sense of the receipts — the kids I hired were pretty good about getting the money right but it was sometimes hard to tell exactly what they had sold — when she pulled up, parking her minivan out front.

"How about celebrating tonight?" I asked as she came in the door.

She raised her eyebrows at me. "Groundhog Day?"

"No, the true anniversary of opening the *Cully Beach Surf Shop*. Or at least the date I moved in."

"Oh. I hope you're giving something away." She came over and put her arms around me.

"Of course. Let me give you a sample now." Our lips met. "But the main prize is for later."

She sleepily whispered, "Sure you don't want to give it to me now?"

"You look more like you need a nap." I had to be honest.

"Yeah, I guess I do, Ted. I really do." She gave me a weary little smile. "I think I'll go lie down an hour or two and be refreshed. You're taking me out, right?"

"That was the idea." Though maybe it wasn't a great idea on a Friday night in the peak of the tourist season. What the heck, we'd do it anyway.

The Keaton girl would be coming in soon to take care of the shop until closing time. Since I had taken her on last year she had proven one of my most dependable employees. And she wasn't even a surfer, just the former girlfriend of one who had talked her into applying.

"Hi, Mr. Shaper," she called as she came in. That was a bit of a joke between us. She had been reluctant to call me 'Shaper' at first.

"Hi, Joan. I'm going to ask you to close and lock up this evening." She nodded her head. That was a common enough occurrence. "As always, close up when you feel proper." The sign on the door said

Six but at this time of the year it was pretty dark by that time and the shop was usually empty.

"Yes, sir." I couldn't break her of saying 'sir' either. "Are you going to need me on the holiday weekend, Shaper? Your anniversary?"

"Not necessarily. If you have plans, it's no problem. After all," I told her, "I should be in the shop myself on those days."

"Okay." She sounded guilty about abandoning poor old Shaper. "Are you going out, Shaper?"

"Later. Right now I'm going out back to work a while," I said. "You may or may not see me before I go."

Work consisted of surfboard repair, one of the least attractive parts of running a surf shop. I didn't make much off it, either, but it helped with customer satisfaction. A boring hour and a half and then into my shower. It wasn't too bad this afternoon, even outdoors, as I rinsed the grit of foam and fiberglass from myself in the outdoor stall, screened partly by solar block and a strategically placed tarp.

Wrap in a towel and in the back door. "Aw, now you're cleaned up and I shouldn't get you sweaty again," said Michelle, giving me an up-and-down. "Where are we going?"

"I have no idea," I told her as I disappeared into our bedroom. No idea about tonight, no idea about all the days and nights to come. I was winging things these days and didn't completely like the feeling. What the heck was I doing, anyway?

It was pretty crowded downtown, and everything was lit up. Traffic crawled along A-1-A, pedestrians crowded the sidewalks. I drove the truck around a couple blocks before I found a space to park. "You haven't been out on the pier yet," I said. "You can't call yourself a true Cullian until you walk to the end of it."

"Someone once told me to take a long walk on a short pier," she replied.

"That sounds like a great friend."

"Ex-sister-in-law. Is there food on the pier? I'm hungry."

"There *is* a snack bar but that wasn't exactly what I had in mind." We crossed the highway to the pier entrance. It was a couple bucks to walk out, if I remembered right. Or it had been years ago when I had last been on it.

Okay, it still was. I handed over the bills to a young lady at the entry.

"Hey, there is Jim," said Michelle, nudging me in the ribs. He was slowly coasting our direction across the weathered boards. I did know that the pier was part of the regular bike patrol route. "I don't see his partner."

"I'm surprised he's still on duty this late," I whispered as he drew near.

"Hi folks," he greeted us, putting a foot down onto the boards. "Nice night to be out."

"Is that why you're out so late, Officer Trejo?" asked Michelle, keeping a straight face.

"Ha, not hardly, ma'am. It's Millie, er, Chief Stuart's idea. Acting Chief, I mean." He shook his head. "She thinks we should have later patrols on these weekend nights."

"That doesn't seem like a bad idea, Jim. And call me Michelle, okay?"

"I've heard the kids around here refer to you as 'Mrs. Shaper,'" he replied.

I kind of liked the sound of that. "It beats 'Motel Lady,'" I said. Which was the usual name when she was still running the *Easy Breezes*.

"And Charlie is 'Shaperette,'" he added, with a chuckle.

Michelle shook her head. "Oh God, this is the future I dreamed of?"

"You can thank me for it later," I told her. "Have a great evening, Jim. Hope you get off soon!" We resumed our stroll onto the pier, as he pedaled toward solid land.

Below us, small waves collapsed onto the sand. "I've seen days when waves broke over the top of this pier," I remarked.

"Like the day you almost drowned last year?" She was not going to let me forget that. Not that I was likely to.

"It wasn't quite that big. Even I wouldn't go out if the waves were higher than the pier." It almost certainly wouldn't be possible to paddle out on such a day.

"I don't understand why you would go out at all when the surf is big. It isn't fun, is it?" She was asking seriously.

"No. Not fun at all. It is — forgetfulness. Everything else disappears, all the world that sometimes seems to be too much." I turned to her. "In a way, I am like Bradley." Her late, junkie ex-husband. "The other side of the coin, maybe. Being out there, alone, is my equivalent to shooting up."

"I've never understood that. But Charlie does, doesn't she?"

"Yes, she does."

Michelle wrapped her arms around me, tightly. "I lost Bradley to an overdose. Don't you ever kill yourself out in those waves."

"I won't. I promise." I wasn't sure if I would ever paddle out on a really big day again. But one never knows.

We stood a while at the end of the pier, watching the stars over the Atlantic, the distant lights of passing boats. A few fishermen, well-bundled, dangled lines, drank coffee, smoked. "This beats a restaurant," said Michelle. "But I'm still hungry."

"There's a little place in easy walking distance, up that way." I pointed north. The wait didn't prove too long when we reached it and it was no more than nine or so when we pulled back into my drive.

"Is that John's truck?" asked Michelle. It was parked a short way up the street.

I stopped before driving all the way in and looked. "Yep." His beat-up ride was even older than mine. "Must be inside."

Undoubtedly inside, but not to be seen when we came quietly in the back. Charlie's door was shut. "Well, I think we both expected this to happen sooner or later," I whispered to Michelle.

"I was just wondering why it took so long. Come along."

"I hope they lock up properly when he leaves," I mumbled, and followed Michelle into the bedroom.

Chapter 11

When I had moved to Cully Beach, the public library had been within easy walking distance, in the same area as the police station and post office. A couple years ago it had moved to a larger building up north of the pier — I kind of located everything in my mind by its relationship to the pier — and the police had annexed the old building. The chief's desk was near where the card catalog once had been placed.

Or, as Jim had made sure to point out, acting chief. That would be J. Miller Stuart, better known as 'Millie.' I knew that the J. stood for Jean, but she had decided to use the initial early on, feeling it seemed more professional. It had been tough for a woman cop when she started out. Maybe it still was.

Anyway, her maiden name had quickly been turned into Millie and that was what she had been stuck with since. She used it herself, now, but I still felt more comfortable calling her Jean.

I hadn't had any plans to see the acting chief today. Then I had received a phone call —

I rapped on her open office door. It was Bill Cotton's door not long ago. "Got a moment, Jean?"

She looked up, a narrow face surrounded by curling gray hair, reading glasses perched on her nose. "Sure, Ted. Come in." Then the inevitable, "Tripped over any dead bodies lately?" That was sort of a running joke down here.

"I'm more concerned about a living one, Jean," I said, settling into a metal and vinyl chair. "Bill."

She sighed. "We're not supposed to talk about it."

I shifted my weight. This chair was not only ugly but rather uncomfortable. "So I have heard. Let's talk about it anyway."

"I really don't know much. The word is that money was misappropriated. But, Ted," Jean confided, "I'm the one who handled the money here. I would have noticed if something was wrong." She gave me an appraising look. "Have you been talking to Bill? I know you two are pretty close."

Close? Well, maybe not that but friendly enough. "Yeah. He gave me a call last night and asked if I would sort of, um, check things out for him. Since he's not supposed to." Not only because of his suspension — his lawyer had warned him to stay clear of the department, too. Or so he told me.

"Oh." She paused a second or two, then went on, her Mid-Western twang becoming more evident than usual. "Well, it's all in the hands of the county DA. Maybe the Feds, too. If this is considered a case of public corruption, they might look into it. Ted, you know I'm nothing but a glorified meter-maid. I don't have any call to be running this place."

That was a considerable exaggeration. It was true that Jean had been behind a desk for as long as I had known her. I had never seen her with a gun. But she had kept things operating smoothly in the department for a long time as Deputy Chief, Bill's second in command.

"No desire to run it, either. I just want to retire and spend time with my grandchildren." Those grandchildren, surfer kids, were the primary reason I was friendly with Stuart. Otherwise, our worlds might never have intersected.

"Let's hope it's not for long, then," I told her, rising. "This will get sorted out."

"I pray that it will." Jean sighed. "I will say this — if money is missing, someone in the department will have to be in on it. Or someone at City Hall. Someone who could change the books." I nodded. It made sense. Why someone would do it made much less sense. "Ted," she continued, "thanks for helping the chief. He may need you in the upcoming weeks."

"Yeah, sure." Upcoming weeks? Had I volunteered for some-thing?

Officer Bob Redding was standing by the front desk as I headed for the doors. The big man regarded me with decided suspicion. Maybe I would too, in his position.

Okay, where to? I had been in the area anyway, running various errands. Not grocery shopping; I was near the Pig where I was accustomed to buying my food but now Michelle was getting a discount where she worked. Not much sense in me picking up anything.

Not much sense in hanging around at all. But not much sense in going back to the shop yet, either. I parked by the pier and watched the Atlantic for a few minutes. It was rough and windy today, not surfable. Not many people out on the beach.

Just a week till Valentine's Day. Saint Valentine's Day, I should say. To me, that date had always signaled that the 'season' was winding down, that we would be moving quickly into Spring now. The snowbirds would be spreading their wings and flying north over the next couple months. Easter usually sent the last of them home; that would be a bit late this year.

However, the Fourteenth of February meant something else to me this year. In one week I intended to propose to Michelle. And I was not going to back out, however tempting that might be!

Chapter 12

"Not everyone on the force has an, um, high opinion of her leader-ship."

Officer Jay Johnson, back on bike patrol, agreed with his partner. "They've been calling her Millie Vanilli," he reported. "Just faking it all."

These guys would have been teens when the whole *Milli Vanilli* scandal struck. They would remember it.

Jim nodded. "Yeah, I've heard that too. It's unfair."

"But she doesn't really want to run the department," I said. "That's pretty obvious."

It was rare for Jim and Jay to extend their patrol as far south as my shop. Not unheard of, but rare. I suspected that they were allowed a certain leeway in that.

Officer Trejo's radio crackled. "Bad reception in here," he said, and stepped outside, the unit held to his ear. Half-heard police jargon came through the open front door.

Charlie, who had listened quietly until now, asked Jay Johnson, "Do you like riding with Officer Trejo?"

"He's a good guy," came Jay's somewhat cautious answer.

"Meaning he can be a pain," I explained. I knew that well.

"Yeah, he can," admitted Officer Johnson. "But he is a good cop. There are other towns trying to recruit him." A pause. "I don't think Cully Beach is going to hold Jim. He's too ambitious."

That made sense. Trejo was a veteran, a minority, and a pretty darn competent policeman. Any force in need of Spanish-speaking officers would be interested in him. But then, Johnson was a veteran and a minority, too, although very much a rookie here. Maybe he'd be looking to move on in a couple years.

"Anything important?" asked Jay, as his partner stepped back inside.

"Just a complaint about kids loitering. We can send them down here to do that."

"Okay with me," I told them. "Need to be on your way?"

"No hurry. I wanted to talk with you, Ted." He glanced at his partner. "You don't mind, do you, Jay?"

"Hey, I'll just ride on up there myself," replied Johnson. "Where did the call come from?"

"*Seven-Eleven* north of the pier." Trejo chuckled. "Of course." It must be something that happened regularly.

"Ha, of course." We watched Jay head north on his bike, long legs pumping.

Then Jim got right to it. "Are you going to be our connection to the chief?"

And I answered honestly. "I have no idea. He only phoned me once since all this began."

Trejo cursed. It was in Spanish but I recognized it for what is was. Uncharacteristic, it was, too. "Everyone wants to help him but we don't know what we can do. We're not supposed to contact him."

"I'll let you know if I talk to him again." I reconsidered. "If he says it's okay."

Jim slowly nodded. "Right. Blake noticed there was something going on before the rest of us knew about it. He says the chief was being secretive."

Charlie put in her two cents. Or maybe it was a whole nickel. "We see a lot of Dave these days."

"That's true," I said. "I could probably get in touch with him pretty quickly if something came up."

"That's the way to do it then," decided Jim, "but let me give you my home phone, just in case." He wrote it out on the back of one of his department-issued cards. Then he was on his way, peddling north at a somewhat more leisurely rate than his partner.

"Poor Shaper, roped into fixing other people's messes again," Charlie commiserated.

"I'm not fixing anything," I declared. "Well, maybe the occasional broken surfboard."

"But you would rather make new ones. John is going to order a custom from you soon. He's been saving for it."

"He could have had it by now if he didn't spend money on you, young lady."

"Not very much. We mostly just go to his folks' house to eat." She snickered. "Or raid your refrigerator."

"Oh, so that's the real reason he is here at night."

"Shaper!" Then, a bit wistfully, she said, "I wish he would stay overnight."

"His parents?"

Charlie nodded. "Exactly. They wouldn't approve."

"As long as he's living with them, it's best not to upset things," was my opinion. I thought it a pretty good opinion, as opinions go. "I reckon John will want one of your pictures on his new board."

"Yeah. I already drew one he likes. I'll show it to you sometime." She surveyed the boards displayed around the perimeter of the room. "He'll want one of those boards with three fins. What do you call them? A thruster?"

"That's as good a name as any. It's the one that's stuck."

"More fins make it easier to turn, right?"

"Um, sort of. And sort of not. It's way more complicated than that. It's not as if they were rudders or something." I liked to expound on surfboard theory, I will admit. "In fact, they have exactly the opposite function — they help to stabilize the board and hold it in the wave. Without fins, the board would tend to slide sideways instead of turning."

"Like my boogie-board!"

"Exactly. Unless it were a hundred-pound-plus log like Duke Kahanamoku might have ridden. Those could be pretty stable on their own."

"I think I need a whole lot of fins, Shaper. I tend to slide all over the place!"

Chapter 13

I had known better than to ask Michelle to marry me at Christmastime, when she had given up on the *Easy Breezes* and on making a life on her own in this town. It might have seemed like pity or like I was trying to take control. That would not have set well with her right then. I recognized that. I had instead offered her a job with room and board included, which was a face-saving way of asking her to move in with me.

And she had taken it. Otherwise, she would have driven away from Cully Beach that day and I would have again been alone. I'll admit, a part of me would have been okay with that. I'd always managed on my own, owing nothing to anyone.

Most of me, though, was glad that did not happen.

Anyway, the day was here, Valentine's Day, the day I was going to propose. But not the evening — I had a few hours yet and quite a lot of jitters. Why, I couldn't say. After all, Michelle and I had been together for a good while now and under the same roof for almost two months.

Would *The Fiddler Crab* be a good place to take her? Michelle would have both good and bad memories of that seafood restaurant, a pleasurable meal with Charlie and me, the intrusion of the hoodlum Ray Manuel. Maybe I'd better think of a different spot for a romantic dinner.

If I had ever eaten out over the past few years, instead of making those bland vegetarian meals for myself, I might have had a better idea of what places were good. And I might have even made a reservation somewhere.

I pulled the truck into a parking space along the beach, and looked out at the gray-green Atlantic. The surf was just as unrideable as when I had checked it at dawn, a tiny swell, and now a stiff onshore breeze was chopping it up. But I hadn't come for waves.

Cold. Good thing I wore a windbreaker. Traffic was lighter on the highway here, north of the pier and the Scott City Road intersection. It would be a couple blocks back — two blocks to the west — to the offices of *Inez and Inez, P.A.* I angled across A-1-A toward Second Street — Second North, of course.

Sammy had rung me up a couple days ago, asking me to come in. As with a number of folks with whom I occasionally did business, I knew the Inezes from church. And, as with many of those folks, they were Hispanic. That's probably true of Catholic parishes almost anywhere in the U.S. and certainly true in Florida.

Or Sam was Hispanic, I should say. Liz was a transplanted northerner, out of Boston or someplace like that. I had no idea what her maiden name might have been. Anyway, not needing the services of lawyers or accountants or any professionals of that sort very often, I tended to just go with my acquaintances. Probably a terrible way to do business.

It was Liz who was ready to see me, in their cramped storefront offices. She got right to the main event. "Your Ms. Jackson took the deal she was offered, I see." She held up a copy of a document. It appeared to be the acknowledgment Michelle had received a few days ago. "It was probably a good decision, but it wouldn't have hurt to run it by us first." She smiled but I knew Liz was serious about it.

"So I told Michelle. She doesn't listen to me much." I leaned forward on the book-strewn table and told her, "I am glad that I could just talk her into letting you send that letter. She would have let the entire thing go."

Liz nodded. I had explained Michelle's desire to distance herself from the whole affair when I had first talked to her and Sammy. She pushed the full ashtray at her elbow a little further away. The woman would probably light up as soon as I left — the room reeked. "It all seems to have turned out well, Ted. I doubt Ms. Jackson will have to wait very long for a check to arrive."

"And then," I said, rising, "we may need your services in a real estate transaction."

"More our line, really," Liz replied. She got up and took my hand. "Call anytime. We're always ready to help."

And send a bill, of course, I added, only to myself. But it would definitely be worth it this time. "Thanks," I said, and found my way out onto the cracked sidewalks of Second Avenue and headed south, toward the Scott City Road.

That was about a block and a half. Strictly speaking, the road was named Main Street inside the city limits but hardly anyone called it that. It was rarely referred to by its number as a state road, either, until beyond Scott City. This was the oldest part of Cully Beach, even older than that frame house south of my place, buildings that were put up in the Twenties.

There was bound to be a centennial celebration in a decade or so. Would I still be around here for it?

SHAPER

Turn left and there is the *Bank of Cully Beach*, the original, founded by Sebastian Cully himself in the boom days of development here, before the Great Depression. Not much of the tycoon's legacy remained in the town that bore his name. There was once an hotel, I had heard, over where the post office and police buildings stood now. Long since fallen into ruin and demolished before I ever came to this coast.

Doris said she would be expecting my visit. We had things to talk about, Doris Boone and I. Darkly tinted double doors opened into the bank, set in gray-veined white stone. Some folks thought it was marble but I knew that the building was of granite, shipped here all the way from New England. There was a placard inside the lobby with just that information but I suppose not everyone is the obsessive reader I am.

That stone would have come by railroad, back then. The tracks had been abandoned years ago, the station on the other side of the 'river' closed, though freight trains still rolled through Scott City.

"Mrs. Boone is expecting me," I told the woman at the front desk, just in case she was wondering, and went on to Doris's office. Down the hall to the right, first office — yeah, Senior Vice-President Doris Boone was seated behind a small, dark desk that might have been nearly as old as the bank itself.

The woman wasn't that old, however. Despite her silver hair, I suspected Doris had less than a decade on me. "Close the door, will you, Ted?" she asked, glancing up at me. She signed some paper she had been perusing and put it aside.

"So," Doris began, as I slipped into a green leather chair, "development rears its ugly head in your neighborhood."

"My neighborhood today, yours tomorrow," I countered. That was why she was concerned, right?

"Yeppers. And there goes everyone's neighborhood. I don't want Cully Beach to lose the things that set it apart." I nodded in agreement, and she continued.

"There are those around this town who like the idea of wall-to-wall high-rises along the beach. They think it means prosperity."

"I've seen that kind of prosperity in other places," I remarked. "It was a big part of why I left my hometown." Where was Doris's neighborhood, anyway? I didn't really know where she lived. Look it up when you get home, Ted.

"Everything ties together, Ted. You know that. We allow five stories to go up now and there will be more to come. That can be counted on."

"I'd rather not have a condo over there at all," I admitted. "It is a condo, right?" I realized it could be an hotel. I hadn't really checked any of this.

"It is. And I think it is inevitable that it will go up. We'll just have to make sure it doesn't go up too far!" I gave that as much of a smile as it deserved.

"How soon, do you reckon?"

The sound of someone passing in the hallway — Doris glanced up and then turned her attention back to me. "I know that the sale of the land is closing shortly. We can expect an immediate request for a variance," she informed me. "They can't do that until they actually have title."

No wonder they decided to pay Michelle off.

"The owners are required to schedule a meeting with city staff to discuss it before making their application but I have it on good authority that their lawyers have already done this." Doris had her sources. Having been on the city council herself not long ago, that was not unexpected. "These people are being accommodated," she stated flatly.

"So they have friends in City Hall, I would assume." I could see that. I'm not as dopey as I look. "Friends who will make exceptions for them."

"Right-o. I would expect them to file on March First if they close in time. Applications are supposed to be made on the first working day of the month."

"Some time, then." But enough time? Heck, what could we do, anyway?

"Some," Doris agreed, then hesitated. "There is something more, Ted. I have heard that they want to close the Eighth Street beach access."

That was *my* beach access, the street by the motel, and the first place south of the public beach where one could get at the Atlantic waters. This was not good at all.

"That would be inconvenient," I allowed.

"And bad for your business."

That was certainly true. "Bad for my whole neighborhood. Unless the city goes ahead and develops the park over there."

Doris sighed. "I'm not hopeful about that. You know I supported the idea when I was on the council."

"Well, then we need to reelect you," I decided. "Get ready to campaign, Mrs. Boone!"

"I've been considering it, but we're a long way from election time, Ted." She cocked her head and gave me a curious look. "I take it you are being drafted into representing your neighbors on all of this. Or maybe you just volunteered?"

I had to laugh at that. "I just took the job when no one else stepped forward, Doris. That's the way it usually goes for me."

"Things just fall into your lap, don't they, Mr. Carrol, whether you want them or not?" She rose, an apparent end to our conversation, so I stood as well. "Are you planning a romantic evening with your Miss Jackson?"

"That I am, Doris. How about you and Don?" If she could tease me, I could return it.

"Oh, I'll try to get him out of the house. That's not easy!" We made our goodbyes and I stepped out of the *Bank of Cully Beach*, briefly looking across the road to the diminutive city park. That was as old as the bank, part of the original city planning. No one there on a cold breezy day like this — no one except the lonely statue of old Sebastian Cully. I ambled east on the sidewalk, toward the ocean.

And as I walked toward my truck, I couldn't help think of Bill Cotton's statement that there was something shady going on in City Hall. Could he tie into all of this somehow?

Chapter 14

"This is a terrible cliché, you know," Michelle informed me. "And it is not your sort of thing, at all."

I couldn't deny that. It really wasn't my sort of thing.

None the less, I was taking my Valentine out to dinner. As was everyone else in the world, apparently. I drove by *Dee's* — the place we had dined two weeks earlier — and saw there wasn't a chance of getting in.

Circling the block took us by *Our Lady of the Seas.* "I think they have bingo and pot-luck on Wednesday nights," I told my date. Fortunately, she did not take me seriously.

So where? *The Fiddler Crab* didn't take reservations so we could always head down that way. Nah, too many fresh memories there for Michelle. I turned right when we got back to the Scott City Road and headed west. Wasn't there a sea food place next to the bridge? Ooh, very crowded. I traveled on across the span.

Michelle looked out over the dark waters of the Intercoastal Waterway, what locals referred to as the River, and then asked, "Do you know where Betty and Pat are staying?"

"Just down the street from us. At the, um —" What the heck was it called? "Oh, yeah, *Tres Palmas.*" That was a little motel a couple blocks south of the shop, on the inland side of the highway. "Coming in Friday night, but I don't know if we'll see them then."

"Hmm. Okay." She stared out the window some more. "Do you know where we are going?"

"West," I answered. I couldn't help myself. And I was surprised to get nothing back from her. Michelle seemed introspective this evening. Did she have suspicions about what I intended?

"Do you know if that little place by the *Winn-Dixie* is any good?" I asked her. After all, she worked there and we would be passing by in a minute or so.

"Never tried it," was the only answer I thought I would get. Then she added, with a light laugh, "But I know they don't serve anything alcoholic. I think I need a glass of wine tonight."

"Ah! Good thing I didn't take you to *The Fiddler Crab* then."

"Yeah, they don't serve alcohol either, do they? That's why you took Charlie and me there." She shook her head. "That seems so long ago now, but it's only, what, three months? No, two."

"And change," I said. We passed the Greenwood Road intersection, the only place with a traffic light between Cully Beach and Scott City. Michelle's place of employment and other stores were lit up in the small shopping center to our left. Didn't Doris's husband have his office somewhere around here? Insurance and bail-bonds, if I remembered right. I hoped he was taking her out somewhere tonight. Somewhere not too crowded.

"Isn't that the road to the Brody's place if we turn right? I should meet them someday." She looked at me. "You too."

I nodded absently. She probably couldn't see it in the dark of the truck cab. "I think Brody is an old friend of Bill Cotton."

When I added no more, Michelle asked, "Are we going all the way to Scott City?"

"Maybe. And if I can't find a place there I'll drive on to Palatka or Ocala or somewhere." We passed under the Interstate, I-95. There was a fast-food place there but I didn't bother to suggest it.

"We could always show up at Pat's house."

"I *will* have to take you over to Ruby one of these days. Maybe in the scalloping season." Darn, I shouldn't have said that. It brought up memories of going after scallops with another woman, another time. Was I going to end up disappointed again? Was I crazy to think of proposing to Michelle?

None of that, Ted. There was the place, and not too crowded. I pulled into the gravel parking lot. The flood-lit wooden sign told us it was *Mama Toni's.*

"Pizza?"

"If you want it. And wine."

Michelle slipped out of the truck and stood looking at the unim-posing little concrete-block building. "How the heck did you know of this place, Mr. Carrol?"

"Jan told me about it. But I'm hoping she and Dave intend to dine someplace else tonight."

"Dave's apartment. Charlie says he's cooking dinner." She leaned in to confide. "Yesterday was his birthday, by the way, so they have an extra event to celebrate."

That was the first I'd heard of that — any of it. I didn't know if the girl had even been to his place before. Not the best of neighbor-hoods — I did know that. "That's a step toward something," I decided. "No idea what."

"Charlie also tells me Jan's been keeping the cop at arm's length so far." Michelle giggled. "I probably shouldn't share that with you!"

"It's up to me to keep tabs on both of 'em," I informed her. "Jan is like the daughter I never had. And now Charlie is like the other daughter I never had."

"Well, we know where Charlie is right now. Wednesdays mean GED class."

"But John is driving her. And he will most certainly stick around after driving her home."

"True." She headed toward the red-painted door. "Let's go on in."

It certainly *smelled* Italian in there. And something else, too, something a bit more *Southern*. Not crowded at all. "Probably doesn't attract much of a Valentine's crowd," I whispered to Michelle. A skinny boy in a black vest led us to a table. Darned if it didn't have the stereotypical checkered table cloth.

"Best Redneck-Italian cuisine in town," said the menu. One side was devoted to Italian dishes; the facing page featured barbecue.

"I wonder if they ever mix them?" asked Michelle.

"Only at home," spoke the tall, graying woman who brought water to our table. "My husband does the barbecue. I'm Toni, the Italian half."

"Are those your paintings?" I asked her. The walls were lined with colorful primitives and I had noticed the 'Toni' signature on them. "They are rather good."

"He would know," confided Michelle. "He is forever telling me he has a degree in Art History."

Hey, it was only a couple times. Or maybe three.

Our hostess laughed aloud. "You sound like that girl who came in here the other night. She wanted to put some of my pictures in her mom's shop!"

"A little tan round-faced girl?" asked Michelle, giving me a wink.

"With a policeman in tow, no doubt," I added.

"Is that what that boy is?" asked Toni. "He looks too young. Are you two ready to order or need some more time?"

"We could get one plate of spaghetti and do a 'Lady and the Tramp' bit," suggested Michelle.

"Give us a minute or two," I said to Toni. "But do bring some Chianti. A whole bottle, you think?" I asked my date.

She considered this. "We'd better go by the glass. Even though I'm hoping to get you drunk and take advantage of you later."

"Okay with me. Just remember who has to drive home. So a couple glasses, please, Toni."

"I know you aren't going to order any barbecue, my fine vegetarian fellow." Michelle peered at me over the top of her menu. "Don't you miss meat sometimes?"

"Surprisingly, no. I don't think I ever really liked it that much," I told her. "But I would have a hard time giving up cheese. I hope there is something on here that I can eat. Other than bread."

"Let's just split a pizza," she suggested. "We'll leave the meat off your side."

That sounded okay to me. "Give it a few minutes," said Toni when she took our order. "We do our pizzas fresh. Spinach on yours?" she asked me.

"Yes, please." I gave Michelle a plaintive look. "I guess no onions though. I do love onions, you know."

"Not unless you plan to sleep in your workshop tonight. I'll have sausage on my side," she told Toni.

"Good enough. I'll get it started and come back to refill your glasses." We probably should have just ordered the bottle.

I looked across the table toward Michelle Jackson. "You called this evening a cliché, and now I intend to add one more cliché to it." I reached out and took her hand; I had no intention however, of going down on a knee. "Michelle, will you marry me?"

I saw doubt in her face. I saw uncertainty. It *was* too soon.

"Ted, I — I don't know. It's been so little time since Bradley passed. What would people think? What would Charlie think?"

"Charlie would cheer an announcement. You know that." Michelle was just seeking an excuse. She didn't really care what anyone might think. "But don't give an answer, if you don't know. Just give me one when you are ready.

"But know that I do love you and do want to marry you."

"Can't we just go on the way we are? Aren't you happy with that?"

"The happiest I've ever been," I admitted.

Chapter 15

The rest of the evening might have been awkward for some couples. But I had told the truth — I *was* happy, and so was Michelle. No wonder she was leery of the possibility of that changing.

So we drank our wine and ate our pizza and laughed at each others jokes and went home and made love. As anticipated, Charlie and John were shut in her room when we arrived. I heard him slip out around One.

For, as often before and no doubt often to come, I had a fitful night. Sleeplessness is no stranger to me, even when I don't have a lot on my mind.

Anyway, it was out there and that was that. I was up at my usual hour and followed my likewise usual routine, crossing the highway to go check the surf. There was some warmth in the air this morning. A taste of Spring?

But no waves. I stood and watched the dark ocean for a while longer than I normally might, before turning and heading back home. If I took too long, Charlie was likely to drink up all the coffee before I got there.

"Ted." Who was that? Oh, over on the front steps of the Bells' place. Rick. I wasn't used to seeing him at this hour.

I walked on over and sat down beside him. "Hi, Rick. Something up?"

He sighed deeply. "Jan never came home last night. Yeah, yeah, I know, she's a grown woman and I had to expect it someday." He sat and looked out at the glimmer of dawn on the horizon. "But it hits you when it finally happens."

I think it kind of hit me, too. Change sucks, but change must come. "How does Kay feel about it?"

"A hell of a lot better than me."

That was to be expected. "I asked Michelle to marry me last night," I suddenly blurted.

"Congratulations."

"She didn't say yes."

"Oh. Damn."

"Yeah."

"Too bad it's too early to get drunk."

"I just got over getting drunk. Want to come over and have some coffee instead?"

"Nah, thanks, Ted. I'll sit here a little longer, I think."

"Okay, man." I got up and headed on down the sidewalk. When I got home, Charlie had, indeed, drank up most of the coffee.

"I'm starting a new pot," she told me. "How did it go?"

I gave her a blank expression. What was the girl talking about?

"The *proposal*, Shaper. Everyone knew you were going to ask my mom last night."

"Oh." I glanced toward the hallway before speaking. Our bedroom door, on the right, was still shut. "Well — we're not engaged."

Charlie seemed surprised. She slipped into the seat opposite me and whispered, "She turned you down? Why would she do that?"

"I think she's afraid of upsetting what we have now."

"But everything would be the same, really." Charlie sat for a moment before she smiled and added, "And I thought you were the one who didn't like change!"

That was true enough. Did I propose because I wanted to make sure Michelle stayed, to prevent anything changing between us? Maybe.

But I didn't say that to Charlie. "I need to show her all the legal advantages of marrying me. There are plenty of them."

"Now that is romantic," was her dry response. "Coffee is ready." She brought the freshly-brewed pot over and filled both our cups. I should probably fix myself some breakfast, but I felt rather disinterested in the idea.

"What's with the box?" I asked. I recognized the cardboard container sitting on the table.

"I want to make sure no one is cheating," Charlie replied, dumping out its contents — slips of paper, chances for winning the commemorative surfboard on Saturday. "I've seen kids sneak in a second slip." She started sorting through them, laying them out alphabetically. "Here's a duplicate," she proclaimed. "Should I throw out the extra chance?"

"Throw them both out. He has disqualified himself. Or she has — don't tell me who it is. Best I don't know!"

"Ooh, you're a real hard-nose, Mr. Shaper." She looked at the next paper. "I can't read this one."

I held out my hand and puzzled for a few seconds over the slip she handed me. "It says Jeff. He should have put more information but that's okay. I know the kid."

Charlie nodded. "Robby's bud. I'll have to go over these again before the drawing." She put a rubber band around the slips she had sorted. "These ones I'll just put aside and return them to the box on Saturday."

"Dang, you're organized, girl."

She smiled shyly. "I know. Like you are, Shaper. People who didn't know otherwise would probably think you were my dad."

And maybe I would be, sort of, in time. We would just have to wait on that. "Do you know anything about your dad, Charlie?" I asked her. "Your birth father." So she wouldn't think I meant Bradley Jackson, the deceased step-father.

Charlie shook her head and stared into her coffee cup for a time. "Only his name. Douglas Furr. Doug, I guess they called him. Mom says I have an aunt somewhere that used to keep in touch. Hasn't heard from her since I was little."

That might have been the sister-in-law Michelle mentioned during our walk on the pier. "If Daddy — Bradley — hadn't adopted me, I guess I would be Charlotte Furr," she continued, and then giggled. "Who knows, maybe I'll change it to Charlotte Brody one of these days."

That, I suspected, was one proposal that would have more chance of success than mine.

Chapter 16

I was standing at the doorway of the narrow utility room when Michelle came up behind me. "Get lost in your own house, Ted?"

"I was wondering if I could fit a shower stall in there." My outdoor shower was on the other side of the wall. All the water pipes in this old house were pretty much in line.

"We would have to move the washer," she observed.

It had been a considerable hassle getting it into that space, some years back. The machine hadn't seen that much use with just me here, going around in board shorts most of the time. "Yeah. And then we'd need another place for it." Which might not be a bad idea.

"You sure there is no way to put one back into the bathroom?"

I shook my head. "No way at all." I had deleted the bathtub and shower early on in my remodeling here, and divided the space into two restrooms, one for the shop, one for my private use. That was handy now that I had to share with Michelle and Charlie — I had taken to using the one up front in the mornings and leaving the other to them. "The trouble here," I went on, waving an arm toward the utility room, "is that this is narrower than most bathrooms. I could fit in a shower stall but not much else. Not a tub."

Michelle shrugged. "So we use the leftover space for linens. I say go for it, Ted." She did want her indoor shower.

I nodded in as thoughtful a manner as I could manage. "Have to build some sort of shed for the washer first." Maybe right next to the outdoor shower. Yeah, that would work.

"We'll have money soon," Michelle reminded me, softly. "We could use it for remodeling."

"*You* will have money, Michelle. I have no claim on any of it."

"Then maybe you should start charging me rent," she replied, obviously a bit miffed. Michelle was smart. She knew I was pointing out that we had no legal relationship.

And I knew that I had probably pushed the point a little too hard. I'm not so stupid, either. Not most of the time.

"There are better ways to spend the money," I said. "Your money. If we put yours and mine together, it would go a long way toward buying a house with room for everyone. Even John Brody."

"Or I could just get a new car, Ted."

Well, yeah. She could do that. Wasn't exactly a bad idea, either.

"But right now I need to get into my old car and get to work," she told me, and gave me a peck before heading for the back door. "You keep thinking up projects to keep yourself busy till I get back. Then I'll keep you busy."

A minute later, her elderly Dodge minivan was backing out the drive. It was early yet but I could expect business to start picking up on this Friday morning, the prelude to a holiday weekend.

And to my anniversary celebration. I wandered back to the utility room doorway. Yeah, I could make it work. First step would be to put in a concrete slab out back where I intended to move the washing machine. I guess I should be environmentally responsible and have a drain pipe, too, though I just let the water from my shower go into the ground.

After the weekend. Was that a car I heard outside? Walking up front to the shop, I could see Jan Bell's old gray Malibu pulled into the drive. The vee-eight's throaty exhaust was clearly audible, unlike the polite tones of newer vehicles.

"You're early," I called from the front door. It wasn't time for her to come to work yet, not for another couple hours.

"Yeah, I know, Shaper. I'm taking Charlie to her meeting." She added, a tad apologetically, "I should pick her up later, too."

"Not a problem. At the Catholic church, right?"

"No, Shaper," said Charlie, slipping past me. "This one is at the old fire station."

"Shoot, girl," I told her, "you could walk that far."

She paused before pulling open the Chevy's long heavy door. "I have, sometimes. It's not very far from *Coastal Coffee*, you know." She turned, smiling, to Jan. "You can pick me up there. Whenever."

The old firehouse, huh? It must be a different AA group than the one that met at *Our Lady of the Seas*. I watched Jan back out and the two head north on A-1-A. Not bad out — I might as well leave the door open.

What, someone else stopping? That's what comes of opening the door at Eight-thirty. Well, no. A woman in a business suit stepped out of the dark sedan that had parked at the curb, and, stopping only once to give the surf shop a looking over, strode up the driveway.

Can one actually stride in high heels? Maybe not, but she came close to it, anyway.

"Sir," she asked me, "does a Michelle Jackson reside here?" The woman sounded a bit doubtful of the idea.

"She does. Michelle is at work right now," I told her. "Won't be back until after Two."

"Ah. Very well." She pulled out a business card and handed it to me. "Could you ask her to contact us, please?"

It was a law firm's card. I looked up from it. "Pertaining to?" I needed more info than that, lady.

She smiled, perhaps at my suspicious attitude. "We have a sizable check waiting for Miss Jackson. She needs to come up and sign for it in person."

Carver, Carver, and McGee, the card read. That was a Daytona law firm, wasn't it? But the address was local, up the highway a bit. Must be a branch. "She doesn't need to call," my visitor added. "If she would come by before we close at four, we'll have it ready."

I nodded. "Al lright. Thank you, Miss."

The woman snickered. Softly, but it was a snicker, none the less. "You don't remember me, do you, Ted?" I peered at her. Was she familiar?

"We went out a few years back when friends set us up," she continued.

Oh. That was completely possible, not that I remembered it. "I take it we didn't hit it off." Sally is her name. Sally Something-or-other. I think.

"Neither of us was at all what the other was looking for, I am sure," she responded. "And I am also sure we both went on that date only to keep our friends from nagging us."

Now I recalled. "You were Dick's secretary, weren't you?"

"Yes. But now I'm a paralegal." She certainly looked like one, or like the cliché of one my mind conjured up.

"Moved up in the world, eh? I'm the same impoverished surf shop owner as always."

"But apparently you found someone. Someone who is shortly to come into money!" Sally laughed at that, and I joined her.

"So did you find the sort of guy you were looking for?" I asked.

"I wasn't looking for a guy at all," she admitted. "But I did eventually find a pretty good girl."

"Both of us then." I heard the note of Jan's exhaust again, as she pulled in just ahead of Sally's sedan. I guess it made sense to park here if she intended to go back for Charlie in an hour or two. Though it was only slightly farther if she left it at her own home.

"I'll be on my way," said Sally, heading for her car. "It was nice seeing you again. Really!"

I waved a good bye and turned my attention to a curious Jan walking up the drive. "An old girlfriend," I told her. Which could almost be considered true, if one stretched the meaning of girlfriend a bit.

"Yeah, sure, Shaper. I know Sally Stuart. Her lover teaches at the college."

I shook my head. "I'm always the last one to learn of these things. It's early yet. Want some tea?"

"Okay." She followed me in.

"I really did date her once," I told Jan, as I put on water to boil. "I guess she was keeping things private then." Something came to me, something I had forgotten. "Sally is related to our acting police chief, isn't she? A niece, maybe."

"I think so. Yeah." Jan regarded my tea-making process. "Do you make sure everything stays really hot and boiling? Someone told me that's the right way, like the British make it."

"That makes it too strong for my taste. Too bitter," I said. That should be hot enough. I poured into the teapot. "It's no wonder the Brits have to put milk into their tea to make it drinkable."

"Oh. That sounds convincing, Shaper. You always sound convincing but I don't know if you really know what you're talking about."

"Neither do I," I admitted. "We'll let that steep a while. How are things with you, kid?"

"Hmm, okay, I guess." Apparently she didn't want to talk about herself, so she said, "You convinced Toni Charles to bring some paintings by."

"Charles? I thought there was a different name on the pictures."

"Tomaso. Toni's maiden name was Tomaso."

"So she really is Italian."

"Uh-huh." She glanced toward the teapot, maybe hoping I'd get up and pour instead of continuing our conversation. "Pat's paintings will have competition."

"Very different stuff. But both good."

Jan nodded. She wanted to talk about Dave and their relationship, didn't she? But didn't know where to start.

I did. As I poured us each a cup, I asked, "Any news on the Chief Cotton front from Dave?"

She sipped before answering. "Nothing at all. Dave says he's investigating some things on his own."

"Good. Dave is a competent guy. And a good guy."

"He is. He's interested in things. Important things." Then Jan sighed very deeply and went on. "I like him so much, Shaper, but I don't know where we are going."

Had Jan even had a sexual relationship before? Certainly not a serious, long term one. "A secret, Jan. No one knows where they are going."

"Ha, maybe so, Shaper. I do know I am not going to move in with Dave. It would be temporary with me going off to the university in the Fall, and what good is that?"

"Considering the neighborhood Dave lives in, I wouldn't want to move there, either."

"Good point. You lived over there when you first came to Cully, didn't you?"

"Yep. Not for long."

Jan suddenly burst into laughter at some thought. "I should tell him to move in with me! Imagine what the parental units would think of that!"

Chapter 17

"So you're wealthy now, huh?" asked Pat Edwards, glancing up from his linguine.

"She is," I told him. "She'll probably dump me now she doesn't need me anymore." I turned to Michelle. "Of course, you are paying tonight."

"You'll be paying for that later on, Mr. Carrol," she told me. "It's not really all that much," Michelle told Betty and Pat. "But it would go a long way toward buying another house."

"Only if you truly want to," I told her.

"The vacant house next to yours?" asked Betty.

"The one where Ted found the body. That should bring the price down a little bit," said Pat. "Be sure everyone knows about it!"

"Or the house on our south side," I said, and turned to Michelle. "We should look at it."

"You really want it to be adjacent to the shop, don't you?

"It wouldn't have to be," I told her, "but it would be convenient."

"So we only have two choices." Michelle sounded resigned but I doubted she actually was.

"Unless the Willets want to sell." That was the house directly behind mine. A tall but decidedly dilapidated fence, overgrown with Virginia Creeper, separated us. No one found it a deterrent when they needed a shortcut.

I added, "I used to daydream about that old gas station across the road but that's way out of our range."

Pat leaned back and looked around. "This is a nice little place. Even the paintings."

Betty gave him an indulgent smile. "Pat isn't fond of primitives."

"I know," I replied. "Can't say I am either, but these are pretty good."

Betty nudged her husband. "Tell him about the artist who phoned you. The old friend."

Pat looked like he would rather have waited, but he started in. "Guess who got in touch with me last week." He didn't wait for me to guess but went right on. "Patty Singer."

That name brought up memories and I guess it showed. Michelle arched an eyebrow and gave me an exaggeratedly suspicious look. "An old girlfriend?"

Pat chuckled at that. "She wasn't ever Ted's girlfriend. She hung around with a bunch of us guys who surfed."

No, we hadn't dated or anything. But my first sexual experience had been with Patty when we were both alone and lonely in the dormitories one weekend. One remembers that sort of thing. Well, if one is me they do; I can't speak for Patty.

No one needed to know about that. "She is still Singer?" I asked. "I assume she didn't marry Rob then. Have you heard from him lately?"

Pat gave me a bit of an odd look. "Rob passed a couple years ago. I thought you knew that." I shook my head. "Oh. No reason you should have, I suppose. You don't keep up with any of our old friends, do you?"

"Never did, Pat. I did see Mike a few times when I lived over his way."

"It's probably even longer since I saw him. Anyway, Rob went down from a sudden heart attack. Most of his kids were grown, at least. He had a mess of kids — took his 'be fruitful and multiply' seriously." We both chuckled. Rob had gotten religion in his college years. That was the first wedge in our tight-knit little group of friends.

"After reminiscing a while, I told Patty about this place and she intends to, um, come and visit. She's looking to slow down her life and thought Cully Beach sounded like a good spot for that."

"So when is she coming? Easter?"

"Um, tomorrow."

Great. "You couldn't talk her into Ruby instead?" I asked.

"She thinks our little village is a terrible backwater," said Betty. "And she is right."

"She liked that you have waves here, too," added Pat. "She is still a surfer girl at heart."

I shrugged. "I guess we'll be seeing her, then. If Patty gets here early enough, she can even get in on the drawing for the free surf-board."

"When?" asked Pat.

"One in the afternoon." To Michelle, I said, "I think you should pick the winner."

"Are you sure I won't cheat?"

"Charlie is keeping an eye out for that sort of thing."

"Hmm, yeah, she would." For some reason, we both decided that was funny and laughed.

"You two ready to head out?" asked Pat. "And even if you did come into money, Michelle, I'm paying tonight." He looked at his wife and winked. "Or Betty is. She's the one with the job."

I was aware that Pat pulled in decent money between his paint-ings and occasional teaching, but it looked like Betty was the bread-winner if one didn't know this. "We'll let you get away with it this time," I told him.

Pat went over to the counter to pay and probably jaw about art with Toni, while we slipped out into the parking lot. Definitely warmish for a mid-February night. I knew that was prelude to another cold front, maybe not that powerful but bound to bring up some waves.

Also bring rain tomorrow, most likely. Michelle and I found the back seat of the Edwards's Subaru wagon. "Good place to make out," she whispered in my ear.

"Too cramped for action," I replied. "Wait till we get home."

"You'll be asleep. I know you, Ted Carrol. We've kept you up past your bedtime again." I chuckled at that but I was almost out when we reached the Atlantic Ocean and turned south onto A-1-A.

"Okay if I just let you two out here?" asked Pat, as he pulled up in front of the dark shop. I didn't see John Brody's truck. Charlie and he must still be out somewhere.

"Sure," said Michelle, opening the door. "We'll see you in the morning?"

"You will. Make sure you get out the good coffee!"

Chapter 18

The thing was, I *did* think about Patty from time to time. She wasn't one of those memories that just faded into meaningless images. Patty had been too real for that.

I saw her in the girls who had passed through my shop in the past decade, the surfer girls I knew for a season or two before they moved on to adult life. Jan Bell sometimes reminded me of her, physically, though they were very different otherwise.

It was raining this morning, a light misty rain borne by a west wind. A warm rain, so far. I was getting damp as I stood and watched the surf in the early morning dark. Or not quite so dark; it was definitely getting light a little earlier now.

The waves were coming up, but not surfable yet. Maybe by afternoon. I turned back toward the shop, crossing the highway and going south along the sidewalk. I'd better change to dry clothes when I got inside.

Someone coming up the walk from the opposite way. That was rare at this time of morning. Oh, Pat. Well, it was only two blocks down to the motel where he was staying and he did know I would be up and about at this time. "Come on in, man. Coffee should be ready. And I'll get us both towels!"

A few minutes later we were settled at the kitchen table, mugs in hand.

Pat went right for it. "Did I miss something or are you two still not engaged?"

"We're not, though I've asked." He gave me a questioning look but said nothing. "Yeah, I did. I think Michelle still doesn't feel quite right about depending on me for support, and she may be a bit gun-shy when it comes to marriage."

"Both her previous husbands are dead, right? I could see that making her a bit cautious about taking another one."

"Ah, but I would die a happy man. More coffee?"

"Sure. Ted, how much does she know of, um, your past?" I knew what he was referring to.

"Almost nothing. I know about the same of her past and I'm okay with that."

"She should know about your — your struggles."

"The depression, you mean." He was right. "You know that's not the problem it was when I was younger."

"But it's still there, isn't it?"

"Yeah. I'm not hiding it. Michelle knows I've had problems." The Bells would certainly have filled her in on some things, too. "And I'm not telling anyone else to hide it."

"Okay, my man. With both Patty and me here this weekend, there is bound to be old stuff dredged up."

"So be it. There may be waves later. You said Patty is still a surfer?"

"A surfer girl, I said. I doubt she's actually been on a board in a long time." He looked at me over the rim of his coffee mug. "You are the only one of us who really stayed with it, Ted."

I heard a door squeak and a moment later Charlie's head poked out of her bedroom at the end of the hall. "Oh," she said, and disappeared.

"I think I scared her away," was Pat's comment.

"She'll be back. Especially if I start another pot of coffee." I got up to do just that.

Pat got up too. "I should go. Betty might be wanting me to take her to breakfast by now." He opened the back door and peered out. Rain blew into the kitchen. "It's coming down harder," he stated, and plunged into the mess of a morning. Shoot, if he'd waited a moment more I would have offered him a ride. Really.

Or at least an umbrella.

Charlie's door opened again and she slipped into the bathroom. Maybe I should put a door at the end of the kitchen so visitors couldn't see into the hall, huh? Another project I had thought about once or twice but never tackled. No need when I was the only one here.

A moment later, our master bedroom door also opened and Michelle, a pink and somewhat ratty quilted robe pulled tight about her, took a look at the occupied bathroom and came on into the kitchen. "I'll pee up front," she mumbled and went into the shop.

I poured a cup of coffee for her when she returned. Sugar, no milk, for Michelle. A barbaric way to treat coffee, if you ask me. But, of course, you didn't.

She sat and sipped for a few seconds before setting her mug on the table and saying, "When I took that check into the bank yesterday to deposit it, your friend Doris asked me if I might like to work there."

"A teller? That's as bad as checking folks out at the *Winn-Dixie*. Plus you can't bring food home."

"No, silly nincompoop of a boyfriend. I have a background in property management, remember?"

I did. "Do you want to do it?"

She picked up her cup and took a deeper drink this time. Cooled down some, I reckon. "I think so. But I would be working regular full-time hours, Ted. I won't be able to spend so much time with you."

"Some folks would say that's a good thing," I jibed.

"And now Shaper and I can get into all sorts of trouble without adult supervision," added Charlie, shuffling into the kitchen. She pulled open the refrigerator. "There should be some cake in here," the girl said. "I remember bringing home cake."

She pulled out a paper plate, plastic-wrapped, and set it on the table before turning to pour herself coffee. "Wedding cake?" asked Michelle. "Is that where you and John went last night?"

"Yeah, Mom. Some cousin of his got married. It seemed like an awful lot of fuss." Charlie sat down with her mug and began to unwrap the slab of yellow cake.

"Can I fix you anything this morning?" I asked Michelle, rising. "I'm going to have some cream of rice myself, I think. The stomach doesn't feel like anything heavier."

"I'll get something later. Time to claim the bathroom."

She did just that while I poured water into a pan, set it on a burner, and retrieved the box of cereal from the fridge. It was in there to keep the bugs out of it.

"That's even more bland than your usual breakfast," remarked Charlie, between forkfuls of cake.

88

"Tummy is a little queasy this morning," I told her. "There are still some blueberries in the freezer, aren't there?" I was rummaging but didn't see them.

"Should be." Oh, there they were, one plastic bag and only about half-full. I added a handful to the water, which had almost been ready to boil. Would take longer now. I got those berries from Susan and Joy, who had some bushes at their nursery, over by the river. Almost all of them were used up by this time of year.

I added the rice to the now-boiling water, stirred it, covered it and took it off the heat. The contents of the pan had taken on a lovely purple shade. Eggplant, maybe, or fuchsia or something like that. "You are going to be here for the drawing, aren't you?" I asked Charlie, leaning back against the counter.

"Abso-tively, Shaper. You know," she went on, "if Mom had a better job, it would help you two buy a place. Don't you think she has that on her mind?"

I nodded. "Sure. She wants to be my equal partner. I get that, Charlie."

"Better than she does, I think." That might be true. "Is Mom gonna do the drawing?"

"For first prize, yeah."

"The surfboard."

"Right. Maybe you would like to pull a slip for second or third."

Charlie shrugged. "Okay with me. Or get Betty to do one of them."

"Good idea," I agreed. "My cereal is ready."

Chapter 19

The *Cully Beach Surf Shop* was crowded. That was expected, or at least hoped for. Slips kept slipping into the box for our drawing. Charlie would need to check them over again first, to make sure there were no shenanigans.

A commemorative surfboard, with Charlie's art — I hoped it would be cared for. Too many boards were trashed within half a year of use.

The Bells stopped in early, pretty much as soon as I had opened the door. "It's clearing off, isn't it?" I asked.

"Still windy. I think the swell is coming up," said Rick.

"For once, I wish it wouldn't. If there is surf I will have fewer customers in here."

"You're just pissed, man, 'cause you're going to be too busy here to go surfing."

"Shoot, I could just leave Charlie in charge and play hooky." I looked up as a knot of surf rats came in. Someone needed to keep an eye on them. "Oh, I think we're going to have another for tomorrow night," I told them. "An old college friend is coming into town."

There were plans for a backyard get-together at their place. Or in their place, if the weather didn't clear.

"We can manage," replied Kay. "I'd better get home and open my own shop." She looked at Rick expectantly. He probably wanted to hang a little while but he followed her out the door.

"Be sure to come back for the drawing!" I called after them. "One this afternoon."

There would be no Jan Bell to help out today, nor any of my

other young part-time employees. That was okay; the Jackson girls and I could handle things. We were kept busy.

Betty and Pat popped in and back out almost as quickly. Nothing for them here this morning. "We'll swing back by later," said Pat. He scribbled his name on a slip and put it into the box. "You want to take a chance, Betty?"

She shook her head and they went their way. Even on a dreary morning like this, there were things to do in Cully Beach, places to shop, parks to visit. Tourist stuff.

And the day was getting nicer. By noon, the thick overcast was changing to scuttling high clouds and the sun was breaking through. The surf shop was also filling up. "Last chance to win," called Charlie, holding up the box. "Get your names in now!" A few minutes later, she carried it into the back, no doubt to sort out the slips again and add the ones she had put aside earlier.

In came the Bell men, Richard Senior and Junior, and Betty and Pat with them. I glanced at the clock — they were just in time for the drawing.

No time to say 'hi.' I waved to them as Charlie brought the box back into the shop.

"My lovely assistant will pick our third prize winner." More than one surf-rat cheered that announcement. I think one of them whistled, too. Charlie reached in, stirring all the slips of paper around before pulling one out and handing it to me.

"For third prize, our winner of an anniversary tee-shirt, is Jill Metz," I told the crowd. A little blond-haired girl, no more than a third or fourth grader I would think, stepped forward.

"What size tee do you take?" I looked at her. "The smallest I have, I would think, and that is size small!" I had made sure to have a number printed for the occasion, with the *Secret Surfboards* logo on them. It was the anniversary for my brand, too, as I had chosen that name when I opened the shop.

I had used a variety of other labels before then, when I wasn't shaping for some other surfboard company.

She would float even in a small, but I found one that size and handed it to the girl. "Thank you, Shaper," Jill said, clutching the blue shirt to her chest as she returned to her friends.

I walked over to the Edwardses. "Betty, would you like to draw our second place winner?" I held the box out to her. "That would be a leash," I announced to my audience. "A surf leash, of course, though some of you kids could use the other kind." Good-natured boos rose from the assembled rats. Betty withdrew the first slip she touched and passed it to me.

I recognized the scrawl. "Jeff." I looked around the shop. "Not here? That's okay, he'll be in sometime." The kid was a regular.

Who was that woman who had just slipped in? Someone's mom, maybe. I was pretty certain I had seen her before. Dressed like a tourist, though, in shorts. Locals bundled up on breezy February days.

"Okay, time for the main event." I waved an arm toward the commemorative surfboard, hanging just above the sales counter. Maybe I should have gotten it down first. Won't worry about that now.

"Now let me find someone completely impartial to draw the first prize." I turned to Michelle. "I have never met you before, have I, madame?"

"This man is a complete stranger," she informed the gathering. One or two tourists who had wandered in might have believed her; the rest of the crowd laughed. Michelle plunged her arm into the box and retrieved the winning slip.

I didn't know the name. "Marty Guzman!" I looked around, expecting a boy to step forward or raise a hand.

"That would be me, sir," came a soft voice at my elbow. I turned to see a dark-haired girl, sixteen, maybe. "I'm Martina Guzman."

"She's new in town," Richie informed me. "Marty's a really hot surfer!" Knowing Richie, he probably thought she was hot, period. He and some other boy — darned if I could remember his name — hopped up onto the counter to lower the board to Marty.

The girl gave it a very discerning looking-over once she had it in her hands. I guess it met her approval. "Thank you, sir," she said.

"Call him Shaper," Richie told her. "We should go try it out. The waves are getting good." The shop did clear out pretty quickly after that, most of the youngsters heading elsewhere. The woman I had noted earlier, who had watched unobtrusively from the back during all this, came forward now.

"You would never have stood up in front of a crowd and performed like that in the old days," she told me.

"Patty!" How could I have not recognized her? And I don't think Pat did, either. In our defense, it had been an awfully long time. A little longer for me, but still decades for both of us.

93

Betty, being an observant sort — probably necessary for a teacher of fourth graders — immediately came over and took her hand. "Patty?" said Betty. "We didn't expect you until this evening."

Pat followed his wife's lead. But, being Pat, he gave our guest a hug. "Great to see you, Patty!"

"You too, Pat. And Betty." Patty turned to me. "And they still call you Shaper, do they?"

"There are worse things one may be called," I told her.

"That's for sure!" She smiled broadly. "I have become accustomed to being called Susan or Sue. Or Ms. Singer. I think I would like going back to Patty."

I remembered Patty's smiles well. Those hadn't changed. But Patty herself? She had put on weight, for sure. Patty had never been slender, but always athletic. Still was, I would guess. The white visor she wore had some golf club logo on it; her whole look sort of said 'golfer.'

Inwardly, I shuddered at the idea of being on a golf course instead of in the water. But outwardly, I realized introductions should be made. "This is Michelle," I said, "and Charlie."

Chapter 20

Inevitably, we all went out to dinner. Except Charlie, of course; she had something better to do on a Saturday night than spend time with old folks. That something better was named John.

Patty's treat this time. Once again we dodged the bullet there. Yes, I'm cheap. Surely you have learned that by now. We headed down to *The Fiddler Crab* this time, about two miles south of my shop. Michelle and I hadn't been there since our encounter with Ray Manuel, drug smuggler and generally bad guy. That was in the past and Ray was behind bars. Still awaiting trial the last we had heard.

We had to spin that tale for Patty. There was a lot of catching up to do, lots to tell each other, but that was a little more exciting than most of it. In truth, my life had been more exciting all along than those of my companions, despite my protestations of only wanting to live quietly and build surfboards, to be nothing more than the guy the kids called 'Shaper.' Somehow, things tended to get in the way of that.

Maybe no more. That's what I hoped.

"So I sold my share in the design firm, sold my furniture, sold my condo," Patty was telling us. "I'd had it with Atlanta." She gave her head a resolute nod. "I'm gone for good."

"Will you be looking for a new job here?" asked Betty.

"Nope. I'm gonna do like Pat and paint all day!" We all had to laugh at that one. But I thought it was a pretty good idea, if one could afford it.

"Kay would take on another artist, I believe," I told her. "If you wanted. She has dreams of owning an actual gallery instead of a what-not shop. Ah, here's the grub."

Michelle added, "Our neighborhood is getting more upscale. A real gallery might be a possibility."

Five orders of seafood were passed out to the appropriate diners. I would never be able to get that straight.

"I don't think so, not yet. Maybe a few blocks further north would work." I nibbled a shrimp. Not bad and not forbidden on my vegetarian diet. I'm pretty sure I mentioned that earlier.

"That's the shop on the corner, right?" asked Patty. She had been briefly introduced to Rick Bell but had yet to meet Kay. "Where we are going tomorrow?"

"That's right," Pat told her. "You'll like Kay." Betty nodded agreement.

"Hmm, I noticed the house between them and Ted's shop is for sale. I may be looking for a place like that." Michelle and I exchanged slightly panic-stricken looks. Maybe not for quite the same reasons.

"So you are actually considering moving here?" asked Betty. "It is a nice town."

"That it is, what I have seen of it. But I need to see more before making that sort of decision." Patty took a bite of a hush-puppy and wrinkled up her nose at it. "I'll head down to Miami in a few days, to stay with relatives, but I am certain I shall be back."

"I can lend you a surfboard if you want to get into the water," I volunteered. "You too, Pat."

"Oh, Ted, it has been ages since I surfed." She paused, maybe thinking of those ages. "The water is still cold, isn't it? Not like where we used to ride, down in Boca."

"You would want a wetsuit," Michelle told her.

"We have those, too." I looked at Pat. "You would be harder to fit."

"I have one with me," he responded. "I sometimes dive around the Ruby area. No board, though."

"His old one is pretty much rotted away," said Betty.

I hadn't seen that old board in a couple years or so. It wasn't in the best of condition then. "Well, you know where you can buy a new one." No sense in saying more than that.

"Only if Charlie does a graphic on it," said Pat. "You saw her artwork on the board they gave away," he told Patty.

Patty nodded. "Do you paint anymore, Ted?" she asked me.

I only shook my head. I didn't want to go into that.

"Would you like some dessert, folks?" asked our waitress. I normally wouldn't, and neither would Michelle, but we were to be outvoted here. Patty slipped on her reading glasses, which dangled from a fine chain around her neck, and looked over the menu.

"Key lime pie? I haven't had that in ages but now I'm back in Florida, I should, shouldn't I?"

Most likely it wasn't made from real key limes at all, but that didn't matter much. "Sounds good to me, too," I said.

"Sunshine cake?" Betty asked the waitress. "With an orange filling?"

"Yes, ma'am. Our specialty."

"I'll have that. And so will he." She nodded toward her husband, who raised no objection.

"Peanut Butter Pie," ordered Michelle. After the waitress left with our orders, she added, "Never had it before."

"Ah, you're the adventurous one in the couple, then," said Patty.

"Absolutely," I agreed.

We all split up at the Edwards's motel, having crammed the five of us into their Subaru. Patty got into some sort of little sporty thing, silver I think, but it was dark so don't hold me to that. She sped off north on A-1-A, toward a more upscale motel, while Michelle and I followed in a more leisurely fashion, on foot. It was only two blocks home, after all.

No one was there and I hoped to be asleep by the time Charlie and John-boy slipped in. When John left, too. That was tending to get later and later; if the boy didn't watch it, he'd end up spending the whole night here sometime.

Michelle was already under the covers by the time I had finished checking all the locks. I do tend to be obsessive about that.

"There is more to your past with Patty than your friends know about, isn't there?" she asked, as I slipped into bed.

"Yeah. There is." Michelle should probably know about that — she seemed to have sensed it, hadn't she? But not Pat. Never Pat. Let his memories of those times be as they were.

"You didn't have sex with her, did you?" She practically gasped this, quite theatrically. I understood her not wanting the question to sound serious. But it might have been.

"Well, stuff happened. I don't think either of us would have called that stuff 'sex.' But it was sexual."

Michelle considered this. "Sort of like our former President, huh, Ted?"

"Pretty much. She may not even remember it." We were both kind of drunk, after all.

Nothing more for a few moments. I could just make out Michelle's shape in the dark, sitting up in bed. "Charlie would say that doesn't count. I'm not so sure, myself. But it was long ago, Ted. *Really* long ago." She sort of snickered when she said that.

Thirty years, almost. More than half my lifetime. "You were only ten at the time," I told her. "A little young for me."

"That's as good an excuse as any, Ted Carrol."

Chapter 21

The south side of Jumento Inlet was the place to be this morning, as the jetty tamed the side wind and allowed the northerly swell to wrap in to a decent beach break. On big days, in better conditions, some surfers would paddle out to the bar at the mouth of the inlet itself.

Not me. There were far too many sharks in the water at Jumento. Maybe it wasn't as bad as Ponce or even Sebastian, but it was bad enough.

I paused to look at the surf from atop the bridge, where A-1-A crossed the inlet. No traffic this morning so I could sit there a moment or two. Jumento was not a large pass, and it curved southward at its mouth, with a more prominent point on the north side. It was obviously not to be ridden over there today, the long wind-blown walls closing out in thunderous collapses. I drove on and turned right onto the sand road that curved back beneath the bridge, where a few concrete picnic tables and a spray-painted restroom stood.

The handful of cars would be those of fishermen, mostly. The jetties were popular with them, especially overnight.

It wasn't really that far, fifteen minutes or so from my shop, but I rarely came down to this spot. There was a different crowd here, not the kids who surfed at the pier, the ones who all knew 'Shaper.' The ones who, despite their smart-mouthing, respected the old guy.

Pat was probably at church. He rarely missed Sunday mass and I didn't ask him to come along. For me, surf would always come first — I would worship in the green cathedral this morning, to use a very hoary surfing cliché. I guess he would find out where I was sooner or later, when he stopped by the shop.

I was quite alone, in fact, and had pretty much decided to come on the spur of the moment, after my morning surf check, telling the girls where I was headed and hitting the highway before the sun was fully above the horizon.

Alone. I needed some time to be alone this day. That's why I took off. I knew that. I stood on the beach, checking out the set-up before paddling out.

The waves were wrapping in to form a nice peak for take-off, allowing a short, well-formed right hand ride toward the jetty, or a longer left that pretty much closed out at the end. A couple guys were paddling out already, apparently arrived just before me. I joined them.

Well, not guys, I could see when I got outside. The wet-suits made it hard to tell from a distance. One was my prize-winner from yesterday, Marty. The other — I knew her by reputation but not personally. Kim Timble was a former top pro, a champion back in the Eighties, who had grown up and learned her skills not far from Cully Beach. 'Kim-Tim' they used to call her.

She was also competition for me, of a sort, as she and her husband operated a surf shop a little further down the coast.

"Hi, Shaper," called young Miss Guzman, waving to me as I paddled into the lineup. She wasn't on the board she had won, but one of Timble's offerings. I could see that from the big 'KT' logo on it. Yeah, Kim shaped surf boards, and pretty good ones. The husband ran the shop and left that side of things to her.

SHAPER

So was Marty a protege or something? As soon as the girl took off on a wave, I realized I was going to have to share this break with two extremely talented surfers. They would ride circles around stodgy old Ted, on 'Big Red,' my trusty pintail single-fin, this morning.

At least, this morning wouldn't see much of a crowd. I wouldn't hang very long, either, what with having guests and needing to open the shop. I grabbed one of the lefts, speeding down the steep, chest-high wall until it threatened to close out, then pulling over the top to paddle back out.

It might have been easier to let the broken wave carry me to the beach, walk back up and paddle out closer to the jetty. I would remember that on the next wave, unless I went right.

Kim paddled over to me when I got back to the lineup. "So you're Ted Carrol? I hear you have an anniversary this weekend."

"That I do. It amazes me that I've lasted this long!"

She laughed at that. "You don't need to tell me. We're lucky to eat some months, much less keep the shop going."

I looked toward Marty, paddling into another wave. A steep vertical drop, a hard turn, and then she was hidden from our view as she rode on toward the beach. "She's pretty good, isn't she?"

"More than just pretty good. Don't think of stealing her from our team, Mr. Carrol!" She said this with a smile but I was quite sure she was serious about it.

I shrugged. "I don't do the team thing." To be honest, I loathed competitive surfing. But Ms. Timble would not be where she was now without it. Then, I had to smile, myself, and add, "Of course, if she likes my boards better —"

Kim didn't have time to answer that, as she dropped into a peak, herself, and carved left. Like me, Kim-Tim surfed goofy-foot, left-handed, facing a left-breaking wave. She turned only once before pulling out and paddling back.

"Not much room for maneuvers that direction," she reported, rather loudly, to her young friend. "I'll leave the lefts to the old guy."

Marty wasn't sure what to make of that until I laughed, and Kim joined me. "You'll be old someday too!" I warned her. She was already in her mid-thirties, right?

A couple young guys joined us in a while and that was it for our early Sunday morning crowd at Jumento Inlet. I got my share of the lefts — as everyone else pretty much ignored them — until I decided it was time to head back. Must be around Nine but I never wore a watch so I was guessing.

I could spy a few people on the beach, fishermen maybe. I paddled into what would be my last wave of the session. Straight down and a hard bottom turn right. I'd go backhand on this one. Off the lip and back down. Not much power this direction. I coasted out onto the shoulder, cut back into the curl, and then straightened out and rode what was left of the wave almost to the beach.

"Damn, Ted, you *do* still surf don't you? And pretty good, too." Patty was standing there, bundled up a little better this cool morning. She looked past me. "Not as good as her!"

I turned to see Kim showing us why she had been a champion.

She, too, came all the way in, hopping off her board in barely ankle-deep water. Wanted to talk to me, maybe?

She undid her ankle leash, letting it drag behind her as she walked up the beach to us. "Is this the girlfriend? Michelle, right?"

"No, I'm his woman on the side," announced Patty.

Fortunately, the wind was making my face red already. "This is my old friend, Patty Singer," I told Kim. "Kim Timble," I said to Patty. The name meant nothing to her.

Kim turned to look out at the waves. "I wanted to talk to you about Marty," she told me. "She just moved up to Cully Beach so she's sort of in your, um —" Kim searched for a word. "Sphere, now. I'm hoping you can help her get settled in there."

"Sure. Nothing new to me."

"Me, neither. Part of our job description, I think. Her dad is Air Force, just retired, after being stationed down in Cocoa."

"You were sponsoring someone that far away?"

"She's worth it," responded Kim. "And I'll keep sponsoring her." She grinned and added, "But she can ride the board she won now and again."

"It's not a great board," I admitted. "Pretty generic."

"But nicely built. You do good work, Shaper." She headed back out into the water.

"Is she somebody?" asked Patty.

"Former champion surfer." I chuckled. "Yeah, somebody."

"You're somebody these days, too, aren't you? And not who we all expected you to be."

Too many people expected too many things. I wouldn't say that to her. "Let me guess. College professor?"

"Yeah, that was the consensus." Patty sighed. "I ended up different than expected too." She looked out at the surfers, at the surf, at the blue Atlantic. "I think I want you to build me a surfboard, Ted. I hear you do good work."

Chapter 22

"She didn't just ditch a career in Atlanta," Pat told me. "There was a breakup, too, a relationship gone bad." He took a pull of his Heineken. "She confided that to Betty, but it wasn't a secret or anything. I hope."

"Too late if it was."

"That's true. Shouldn't go beyond her friends, anyway." Pat Edwards looked toward my girlfriend. "That would include Michelle."

That remained to be seen, in my opinion. But they were *friendly* and that was good enough.

"I understand she drove down to watch you surf this morning," he continued. "What's that place called?"

"Jumento. Jumento Inlet."

"Never heard you mention it before. Anyway, I had stopped by early to see if you were headed to church —" He gave me a look of mock disapproval. "And learned you were playing hooky. Seems Patty came by a little later and heard the same."

I nodded, absently. "It wasn't bad this morning. Wind's onshore now, so this swell is shot."

"And you can spend some time with your friends." The disapproval wasn't mock this time. "Are you having problems, Ted?"

"None that a couple hours in the surf didn't fix." That was more or less true. I had recharged. "This party is kind of dead. Even by my standards."

"When are the young folks showing up? They'll improve things."

"If they stay. Jan and Charlie are sitting in the surf shop until closing time. When that comes is up to them. And their boyfriends," I added.

"Maybe we should send a chaperon over there. Richie would do." He looked around. "The boy has deserted us."

"I don't blame him." So it was only the couples — the Bells, the Edwardses, Michelle and me — and Patty on this afternoon. It had turned into a rather nice day, sunny, not too cool to be standing around in a back yard. Rick was at the grill, while Kay bustled in and out of the kitchen, sparing an occasional moment to sit with the other women at the picnic table. Rick had built that with lumber liberated from one of his carpentry jobs.

"We're being antisocial," opined Pat. "We should go stand closer to Rick."

"You're just saying that because the cooler is over there."

He laughed but didn't deny it. We ambled over and Pat retrieved another 'greenie.' He'd brought them so he was entitled to as many as he wanted.

"I'm trying out something just for you, Ted," our chef informed me, as he flipped patties over the fire. "Veggie burgers. They stick a lot."

"I sometimes make my own. Lentils work better than anything else I've tried."

"These are store-bought. Michelle brought them." Rick turned to us. "She's quitting that grocery gig, isn't she?"

"I think so. She hasn't said so to me, yet."

"She told Kay she was going to. The job opening won't be there for long."

"Job?" asked Pat.

"At the bank," I told him. "It sounds like a good deal." But I know I didn't sound overly enthusiastic about it. I would rather have Michelle around the shop, wouldn't I?

A small sedan, a sedan that was notable only for not being notable, u-turned in Eighth Street and pulled in behind Rick's truck. "That would be Dave," I informed Pat. Dave hadn't been in the picture the last time Betty and he visited.

The young policeman exited his vehicle and stood looking at the other parked cars for a moment before coming over to us. "Who drives the Miata?" were the first words from his mouth. Not a hello, not a 'where is Jan?'

As David Blake was still in uniform, I would have been reluctant to admit to anything.

"That's mine, officer," responded Patty. "Is anything wrong?"

"He's just Jan's boyfriend," Kay told her. "Ignore him."

"It's a very nice car," said Dave, almost wistfully. "Very nice. Is Jan around, Mrs. Bell?" I think he might have preferred to spend time with the sports car at that moment, instead of his girlfriend.

"Over at the shop, Dave," I informed him.

He gave the silver Miata one last lingering look and started in that direction. No need — here came everyone. Everyone being Jan and Charlie, John, Richie, and, yes, that was Richie's girlfriend, Cathy, wasn't it? They might have been keeping watch for Dave's arrival. No need to spend any more time with the old folks than necessary, after all.

Of course, they were cutting across the rear lawn of the empty house. Everyone did that. Maybe not if someone else bought that place.

"You must have hurried right over here," I remarked to Dave.

"I did. I have civvies in the car." Probably always kept a change of clothing. Dave was the organized sort.

"Well, go get them and change inside," Kay told him. "Then we can all eat!"

"I don't think we are going to stay," Jan informed her mom. Dave looked sort of apologetic but held his tongue.

Patty broke in. "Ridiculous, young lady. We all want to get to know this handsome gentleman better."

"Just for a few minutes," Dave told his girlfriend, and went to retrieve his clothes.

Pat came up behind me and whispered, "They do look alike, don't they?" Jan and Patty — yes, now they were side-by-side I could see that I hadn't imagined the similarity, built it out of inaccurate reminiscences. Patty didn't have Jan's tan, though; she had always been more inclined to freckle.

But different, too. Of course. Still, a younger Patty could have been sister to Jan.

"You know, my guy isn't ugly either," spoke Charlie.

"It's the uniform," the guy said. "Gets the girls every time."

"His taste in cars didn't hurt, either." Patty gazed toward the Miata. "I bought that just before I left Atlanta. It would be nothing but me and the road and a couple suitcases!" She chuckled. "Although I do have a storage unit packed with stuff."

"Waiting for a place to put it?" asked Betty.

Patty nodded. "Not in a hurry on that."

It was getting dark, and cooler, but I don't think any of us wanted to go inside. We had enough lanterns and there was wine and plenty of burgers, veggie or otherwise. I was willing to sit there on a wood bench indefinitely. No need to even speak.

I think Patty was feeling about the same. "Do you remember Spanish River Park, Ted?" she asked. "We had picnics like this there. You and Pat and Rob and me. And Mike with his girlfriend of the week." She laughed softly. "You still ate meat back then!"

"If I had to live on these slabs of 'textured protein,' I might go back to it," I answered, holding up a veggie-burger.

"It is a nice evening," said Michelle.

"It is," agreed Rick, "and there aren't any bugs to bother us at this time of year. The no-see-ums can be pretty bad."

"Give it a month," I told him. "We called them sand flies down where I grew up. They were thick at night."

Pat nodded. "I remember that." He had visited Genoa a couple times while I still lived there. "We have a slightly larger version around Ruby and call them sand gnats. Just as aggravating."

"So even paradise isn't perfect," mused Patty.

"Maybe so," I allowed, "but you would never get me to leave."

Michelle put an arm around me. "We all know that, Shaper."

Chapter 23

To my surprise, the swell was not 'shot' as I had predicted. It was small, to be sure, but the wind had become light and fitful, shifting around a bit.

"If any of our visitors want to try surfing, this is the morning," I told Charlie, on returning from my daybreak walk.

"Are you going out?" she asked.

"Don't think so. It's still the anniversary weekend and I should man the shop."

The aroma of freshly-brewed coffee filled the kitchen. I was continuing to use the good Colombian stuff I had gotten out for guests. "What do you think of Patty?" I asked, pouring myself a cup.

"She's — disappointing, Shaper. A bit. If that's what being a successful artist is like, I don't think I want it."

"Commercial art is a job like any other."

"Yeah. I would rather just paint and do something else for a living. I *am* going to take those criminology courses." Charlie wrinkled up her nose. "Was that you, Shaper?"

"Sorry. It's those darned burgers Rick fed me. I don't get along well with soy."

"I'll bet Mom had a great night stuck in the same room with you." She changed course, suddenly. "I don't think she likes Patty."

"Maybe not." I sat down across the table from her. "Patty never had many female friends. She just seemed to get along better with the guys."

"She's not, um, you know —"

I had to laugh. "Definitely not."

That brought a slightly suspicious look but no comment. "I like her okay," she said. "She's independent."

She likes to give that impression, I said to myself. "I'm sure she will want to spend time with Pat and Betty today. They go home this evening."

"But Patty is staying a couple more days, right?"

Charlie had fallen right into calling her Patty. To John and Dave and even Jan, she remained Ms. Singer. "Through Wednesday. We'll see more of her."

She nodded and then backed away in disgust. "Aw, Shaper, not again!"

My guts had settled down by the time my three old friends showed at my door. That was around Eight. "This is your last chance to get into the surf," I informed them. "Surfboards or body-boards are at your disposal."

"Will you come?" asked Pat.

Why not? "For a while. I'll have to come back and man the barri-cades here. Charlie wants to go." Actually, I was sort of drafting her but knew she would not object. She didn't right then, anyway.

Pat eyed his wife. "Betty and I should —"

"Michelle and I are shopping this morning," announced Betty, cutting him off. "She needs new clothes for a new job."

Michelle nodded and added, in a low voice. "I'm giving my two-week notice when I go in tomorrow." They apparently hadn't even thought to invite Patty along. Or thought of it and dismissed the idea.

"Shaper will have to drive us, anyway," said Charlie. "I don't think Pat wants to get his car all wet and sandy inside."

This was true. Charlie needed to get her license reinstated, and soon!

"And there is no room for a board," Pat observed.

"And we'll want it," Betty told them.

Patty had stood there with a bemused expression through all this. "I thought the last time we three would surf together happened thirty years ago," she said.

"Welcome to the Twilight Zone," said Charlie. "We need to fit you with a wetsuit." She looked the older woman up and down, maybe trying to decide what size to try. "Do you think she would wear the same size as Jan, Shaper?"

"Just about," I figured.

"I've gotten fat," Patty declared. "It's no wonder. All I do is work and play golf."

"Neoprene stretches," was Charlie's reply, and both giggled.

"Come out back, Pat," I said, "and we'll get some boards."

"And we'll be on our way," said Betty, as she and Michelle headed out the door ahead of us.

I grabbed the longboard from my shed — well, actually, it was leaning on the outside, due to its length — and then chose the 'Michelle' board, the one Charlie had decorated with a portrait of her mother. That was what is often called a 'fun shape,' not too long, not too short.

"Two boards should be enough," I told Pat. "We can switch off or even let Patty try one if she's up to it." We stowed them in the

113

back of the truck. "Charlie will have to be back here, too. I don't think all four of us would fit in the cab."

"Make Patty ride back there. She would enjoy the adventure."

I knew he was joking but there was some truth to it. "Another time! That your wetsuit?"

"Yeah, had it in the car."

"Better get it on now. Mine is in my workroom." I would probably go double suits again today. The water was still pretty frigid.

A few minutes later, two rubber-clad figures entered the surf shop, to be greeted by a similar pair. Patty had squeezed herself into a short-sleeved one-piece. That should work.

I had a slightly dinged repo body-board, one I used as a rental now, Patty could use. That was no concern. She would need swim-fins, too. Hard to catch a wave without flippers. I grabbed a pair of the cheapest I carried. "Try these on." They fit. "Okay, Cinderella, it's off to the ball. You ready, Charlie?"

"Waiting on you, Shaper!"

We all bundled into the truck and did manage to wedge Charlie in with the rest of us in the cab. She wasn't very wide. Neither was I, for that matter, but Pat the bodybuilder took up a lot of space.

"Going to the pier?" asked Patty, who was pushed up against me. That wasn't going to make shifting easy — and maybe even a tad embarrassing — as I had a manual on the floor in there.

"Yep. I doubt anywhere else is rideable today."

Six blocks north, and into a parking space. A bit of a circus out there, lots of kids in the tiny waves. That was why I rarely surfed the pier on weekends.

But it was surf and it could be ridden. Might get better if the tide went down a little. The swell still angled some from the north, but not the long, lined-up walls of yesterday. Today, one would paddle around in pursuit of the shifting peaks.

Not surprisingly, the short, quicker waves wedging off the north side of the pier attracted the bulk of the kids. "South side for me," I stated and got out. "Get your boards and come on!"

"Damn! That's *cold*, Ted!" exclaimed Patty as she waded in. "Hey, isn't that the girl from yesterday?"

I followed her eyes. Yes, it was Marty, scooting backside across a left. And it was my board, wasn't it? "My advertising dollars are paying off!"

Charlie was already kicking her way into her first wave. I could let her keep Patty company for now. I paddled on out, on my funboard, as Pat lumbered behind me on the longboard. With his muscles, he shouldn't have any trouble paddling into a wave or two. Riding them would be another matter.

Over there. I angled toward a rising peak to my left, hoping to reach the steepest part in time to take off. Yes, just behind the peak. I slid in and under the falling crest. Barreled. I hadn't felt that partic-ular rush in a while. Out onto the shoulder, cut back and then turn again and the wave pretty much petered out.

It was just a little wave, little more than waist high, but that didn't matter. A ride like that reminded me why I rode at all.

I turned back out to the break, to see Pat botch his first takeoff. He would get his rhythm back, even on an unfamiliar board. Even

Patty, I suspected, would be back in form in no time if she gave it a try.

Where was Patty? She and Charlie would be up closer to the sand, most likely, catching the quick, short shore-break waves. I couldn't see them from here.

Ah, Pat had one now. He pretty much just coasted right, staying in trim. No need for anything more, if one is enjoying it.

But thirty years ago? Pat would have been tearing it up. He was definitely the better surfer back then, a master of hard bottom-turns and power cutbacks. He should be the one on the 'Michelle' board today. It would suit him, if he had any of those old moves left in him.

Later maybe. I paddled into another wave.

Chapter 24

I left them all there, about an hour later. It was near opening time and someone needed to be in the shop. If Michelle got back in time, she could keep an eye on the place when I went to pick the trio up. If not, I would just close up for a few minutes.

It wasn't like I never did that. People knew I kept irregular hours. Not on weekends so much, though — I might need to shoo customers out of the place first!

I managed to open at Ten, as advertised. It didn't matter as there weren't any shoppers waiting at the door. A few minutes later, I did have someone walk in. Bill Cotton.

That was something I had been expecting for a while, that sooner or later the suspended Chief would come over to talk. And we did talk, over coffee in my kitchen, with the door to the shop propped open. I only had to go up front once for a customer.

"I'm not supposed to talk to anyone from the department," he told me. "I would ignore that but I don't want to get Millie in trouble, or anyone else. And my lawyer tells me the same thing."

"Your lawyer? Anyone I know?"

"I doubt it. Tony Milton from up in Augustine. Know him from way back." I was aware that Bill had been with the Saint Augustine police before coming to Cully Beach.

"So why me?" There had to be loads of people he could turn to. People who had clout in our community.

"I know you're friendly with some of the guys and I know you don't have an agenda."

I couldn't help laughing at that. "Everyone has an agenda, Bill."

"Maybe so." He drank coffee for a while without speaking. "You know someone set me up, right?"

"That's what your friends think. It's what Jean Stuart is pretty sure of." I remained reluctant to call her Millie.

"Yeah, she knows where the money goes. I had a lead about corruption at city hall and was looking into it, privately, y'know?" I nodded. "Didn't want to tip anyone off before I could figure out what was going on.

"And I didn't know if anyone on the force is involved but I couldn't take that chance. Seems like someone figured out what I was doing anyway. Now I'm shut out and can't investigate anything. Maybe I should just take the offer of retirement. I'm told the charges will be dropped if I leave quietly."

"How soon do you need to decide?"

"Very soon. Darn it, Ted, I want to fight this but don't think I can."

"You have friends on the force, Bill. They are willing to look into things where you can't." Dave Blake, in particular, but others too.

"I know. That's why I brought this." He picked up the folder he had carried in with him. It was not particularly thick. "This has copies of pretty much everything I learned," Bill said. "I want you to pass it on. If you are willing, Ted, only if you are willing. You can turn your back on all of this if you want."

"Would you retire if I did?" Consequences. Before all else, those needed to be considered.

"I think so. This is the only chance I've got to prove anything."

Part of me thought maybe it would be best if he did retire and let it go. I would be enabling him, so to speak, if I took that folder and gave it to Dave or Jim or whomever, giving him hope where there might be none.

I took it from him. "I'll give it to someone, Bill. I might even look it over myself."

He rose. "You're welcome to do just that, Ted. You have more brains than anyone on the force, anyway. Yeah, and you know it." He reached over and shook my hand. "And you have smart friends." Bill chuckled. "I spent enough time standing around and watching the feds last year. Now I guess I'll have to let others run the show again."

A car door slammed outside. "Sounds like customers."

I peered out. "No, Michelle getting back from shopping. I need to hit the road myself." We exited the back door together, Bill stepping across the low hedge to his LTD, parked in the drive next door. He waved to the women as he backed out and turned onto the highway.

Michelle and Betty were at the curb, unloading shopping bags from the back of the wagon. "Watch the place!" I called, as I backed down our own drive. I had come to depend on Michelle for things like that, even in the short time we had been together. That would change some when she started working at the bank.

Heck, I'd gotten along before and I would get along again. And Charlie was a help. Sometimes.

There was Charlie, sitting at the top of the beach stairs, when I pulled in by the pier. Marty Guzman was seated beside her. Who was that on the steps just below them? Oh, Richie and Cathy Collins.

"Hey, Shaper," called Richie. "We're watching the old folks try to surf."

"Those old folks are my age, kid."

Charlie kept a straight face while informing me, "You shouldn't admit to that."

"I wouldn't have guessed it," added Marty. "Honestly."

There was Patty, on the longboard, and Pat right next to her, waiting for waves. "Gotten smaller, hasn't it?"

"But breaking better since the tide went down," said Richie. "Still good for the longboard, huh?"

"Yeah, I would think so."

"I like the board," spoke Marty. "The board I won." Then she sort of screwed up her forehead, before adding. "Kim's boards have more rocker."

"Yeah." I had noticed that. I always look at the boards. "I'd shape in more curve for someone like you, too. I aimed for the average surfer with that board."

"It *is* easier to catch these mushy little waves with it."

Richie turned his head to look up at me. "Maybe you should have a surf team, Shaper," he said.

"Well, maybe so, if I knew any kids who surfed well enough."

Charlie snickered. "Ooh, that was mean, Shaper."

"He's just hoping to get a free board, anyway," was Cathy's comment.

Patty was paddling, rather raggedly. Wave-catching technique was what went first, wasn't it? Not the ability to ride. "She's in," said Richie. A moment later, the board's nose went under the water and Ms. Singer joined it.

"She's been doing that a lot," said Marty. "Oh, there's my dad." She grabbed her board and slid it into the back of a big old station wagon that had pulled up, parallel to the road instead of into a parking space. A wave to all and she was gone.

Pat was on a wave now. He attempted one of his old power turns and managed to catch a rail. A face-plant in the water ensued. He retrieved the board — attached to his ankle by a leash — and followed Patty who was already paddling in to the beach.

I shook my head when they reached the bottom of the stairs. "What a pair of kuks!"

"We know it, Ted," admitted Patty. "I embarrassed myself almost as much as Pat out there." As she came up the steps, she added, "And I haven't enjoyed myself so much in ages!"

Chapter 25

"I was married, for a very short time, right after college," Patty told me. "It was a disaster. I went back to my maiden name and went north to seek my fortune."

My own life was pretty much of a disaster in that period, too. She knew that. "Atlanta isn't very far north."

"Far enough. How much to build me a board?" She was watching me work in the shaping bay. Not shaping, just cleaning up and organizing. New blanks and chemicals and such had been delivered on Friday and this had been my first opportunity to get at them.

"If you have to ask you can't afford it." I had to laugh at my own stupid joke. "I've always wanted to say that. Minimum is around three-hundred. They go up from there. Charlie's art is extra." The generic production boards sitting in my showroom mostly carried two-ninety-five price stickers. I would not deal on those.

"If she ever quits you, I can do your graphics. I'll be needing a job eventually," Patty informed me, "so I can afford one of your boards."

"Charlie thinks I need an up-to-date logo. That's the kind of thing you did, isn't it?"

"Yes, and I was extraordinarily sick of doing it! As soon as I get my easel out of storage I will be sticking to pictures of palm trees and sunsets."

"I remember you being rather abstract in your college days."

"Now I want real things," she replied, softly. "Like you have."

"This is a pretty good place to find them."

"It has been for you. You have your shop, you have friends." Patty paused oh-so-slightly before adding, "You have Michelle."

"Six months ago, I didn't think anyone like her would ever happen to me."

"I get that, Ted. I really do. I never married again but I managed to mess up more relationships, anyway." That was not a subject I was going to question her about.

"There's Pat," I announced. The Subaru was pulling up out front. "All we need now is Mike to get the old gang back together," I said. "Most of it." Rob, obviously, would never be rejoining us.

"He doesn't surf anymore, either."

"Yeah, I know. I saw him now and again in the Seventies and he'd already lost interest."

"I saw him just a couple weeks ago, right after I quit Atlanta and drove straight through to Miami. Skinny, long-haired Mike is balding and pot-bellied now, and on his third wife."

"He was working on his Master's degree the last time I ran into him. Social work."

"He never struck me as that bright."

"Me neither."

"But a charmer. He could always recognize what someone needed."

"And provide it."

"Mostly to young women," she finished, and we both laughed.

"Let me lock up," I said. Patty went to greet the arrivals. It would be our last get-together while Betty and Pat remained in town — they would drive home tonight.

So, once more on the town. "We have decided to go over to

Mama Toni's again," announced Pat when I entered the shop. "Patty needs to check out her artistic competition."

"Okay with me. I doubt any place is very crowded tonight. And things will wind down pretty quickly between now and Easter," I told them. "After that, Cully Beach will be just plain dead."

"That actually sounds good to me," replied Patty.

"You could probably get an off-season rental cheap." I was surprised to hear Michelle make such a suggestion. "Everyone ready to go?" She turned to me. "You don't mind closing the shop a half-hour early, do you?"

"Can't Charlie lock up?"

"Nope, Shaper," said the girl. "I'm coming with you!"

"Okay then. Which vehicle?" I looked at the group. "Vehicles, I think."

"We're already packed and will continue homeward after dinner," said Betty. "Someone could ride to Scott City with us. Charlie and Patty, maybe."

"Should we take the van?" I asked Michelle. "I don't want to crowd four of us into the truck cab on the way back."

"No need," spoke Charlie. "John is meeting us there. I'll ride home with him."

It was actually Michelle and Patty that rode with the Edwardses, and Charlie and I in the Toyota. I think the women wanted to talk. And Pat was trapped with them.

John-boy and his old truck were waiting in the parking lot when we arrived. "You again!" I greeted him. "Why don't we just simplify matters and let you move in with us?"

He laughed good-naturedly. John was notably good-natured. "My folks do like Charlie, you understand." He turned to his girl-friend. "My folks really like her. But they would not exactly approve of us living together."

I think you kind of like her too, John. We filed through the doorway and into the small dining room. Toni herself showed us to a table.

"Wine for everyone," I ordered, "except Charlie." I looked at John. "Oh, you're not quite old enough, right?"

"I wouldn't drink when I am with Charlie, anyway," he answered, giving her a look with just a little too much adoration in it.

"His parents aren't drinkers," said Charlie. "It's a Baptist thing, isn't it?"

"Sort of," replied her boyfriend.

It was simplest just to order pizzas for everyone. As we waited, Pat and Patty made a circuit of the paintings hung around the room. "I've seen worse," was one artist's appraisal, on their return to our table.

"Me too," was the other's. "Ted is more qualified to critique them. He's the one with the Art History degree." They both looked at me.

"You two know I hate everything," was all I would give them.

"But he's too nice to say so," was Charlie's opinion.

There were nods of agreement. Was that how they saw me?

"And if he *is* pressured, he's inclined to hide in his workshop or go surfing," declared Michelle.

"That sounds like Ted," agreed Patty. "Hasn't changed all that much since college."

"That was a long time ago, huh?" Charlie asked me. "I know you guys are old. Probably have memories of being at Woodstock or something."

They all knew Charlie well enough by now to laugh at that but it was Pat who gave a serious reply. "None of us." He turned to me. "Wasn't what's his name there, Ted? Your first roommate at college."

"So he claimed." It took me a few seconds to dredge up the name, though I could picture him well enough. "Carl. Carl Some-thing-another."

"Yeah. He went by Chip, didn't he?" I nodded. He had indeed. "You made quite a pair, the Jewish boy from New York and the surfer kid."

"But both kind of nerdy. I didn't have anyone to talk with about science fiction when I switched to rooming with a bunch of surf rats."

"That didn't keep you from talking *to* us about it. I wonder what became of Chip."

"On track to becoming a teacher the last time I saw him. Didn't he share some classes with you, Betty?"

"He was still plugging away when we graduated. When Pat and I graduated." There was a bit of an awkward silence. No need to mention that it was a graduation I had not had a part in.

No need to mention that I had dropped out and lost contact with all of them for a while. No need to revisit any of that.

Chapter 26

I sat up in bed, reading through Bill Cotton's folder. "No real evidence in here," I said. "Mostly notes about stuff he observed." I turned over another paper. "He doesn't say who tipped him off in the first place."

Michelle looked up from her novel. "Any suspects?"

"Some. There were meetings that raised some flags. At least in his mind." They did seem a tad suspicious, at least all laid out together like this. "And requests for, um, preferential treatment, I guess you would call it, by certain officials.

"He needed to look at some people's bank accounts but didn't have enough to call for a formal investigation. Hmm, he mentions *Carver, Carver, and McGee* here."

That got Michelle's attention. "The lawyers who gave me my check?"

"Yeah. I wonder how they're involved."

I closed the folder and reached over to place it on the dresser. "I'll hand this along to Dave. Ready for lights-out?"

She wasn't. "Pat talked to me some about your past," she said. "Patty and Betty, too. You went through some rough patches, didn't you?"

"I've had my ups and downs," I admitted. "Sometimes the downs got pretty deep back then."

"But you survived."

"Yeah." Barely. I might never tell Michelle how close I came to throwing it all away. I might never tell anyone.

"So, if you dropped out of college, when did you actually get that degree?"

"In the Eighties. I went back and finished up." I rolled over and propped myself on an elbow to look at her. "Even took some post-grad courses but decided I didn't want to pursue that."

"Oh, you could have been Doctor Carrol? I would like that."

"But if I were Dr. Carrol, we would never have met."

"I don't know. Maybe it was destiny."

"I don't believe in destiny. Only in free will."

"Hmm, I can believe that. Maybe not agree with it, but believe it. You're big on taking responsibility, aren't you Ted Carrol? You may moan about it but you will always step up and get things done when necessary."

It was pretty much true. Maybe I even took too much pride in having pulled myself up.

Michelle did not pursue that. Instead, she asked, "Do you think Patty will really move here?"

"She might change her mind about this little town when she gets back to the big city," was how I felt about it. How could Cully Beach hold someone like Susan Patricia Singer very long? "Patty might not admit it, but she's kind of ambitious. Once she recharges, she'll be back at it."

Michelle agreed. "I think she gets what she wants." She gave me a long look. "I hope she doesn't want you."

Me? No way. Okay, maybe. "I hope so too. She would be quite disappointed. But," I continued, with a wink, "it's not like I'm engaged or anything."

She gave me a dirty look.

"Okay, sorry. I said I wouldn't push that, didn't I?"

I went on, not giving her time to respond. "I was surprised you gave her advice about moving here." Not that Michelle wasn't knowledgeable about rentals and that sort of thing, but I didn't think she wanted Patty anywhere near us.

"Why not? She's our friend." Michelle reached over and turned out the light.

Chapter 27

I heard it before they actually started working. A backhoe. A really big backhoe, being unloaded from a long trailer, pulled up on Eighth Street beside the *Easy Breezes*.

A dump truck was in the parking lot. No, two dump trucks. So demolition was to begin.

"Michelle!" I called. "You might want to take a last look at your motel. It won't be there when you get back from work."

She came up to the front door of the shop and stood beside me for a moment. "Good," she said. "I really hated that place. I'd better get going. I'll be giving my notice as soon as I get there." Her goodbye kiss was surprisingly passionate this morning, not that I'm complaining.

I would kind of miss that old place myself. It had been standing there ten years ago when I moved in. I shut the door — nowhere near opening time — and returned to the kitchen.

Charlie had her books spread on the table already. Her GED class would normally have been last night but the holiday got in the way of that. She looked up as I entered. "Back to classes tomorrow night," she announced. "Gotta get busy learning stuff!"

"It's still, what, eight, ten weeks till the exam?"

"It's a while. May Fourth." She snickered. "I may have to banish John during April."

"You'll just have him on your mind all the time if you do. There's an Easter break, isn't there?"

"Yeah, the college will shut down for a couple weeks but we're only gonna lose one class. Pat and Betty said they might come back then." They hadn't mentioned it to me.

"They're always welcome," I mumbled. "I think I'll make, mmm — tea. Yes, tea. I had too much coffee this past weekend."

"Patty likes tea."

I had to stop and stare at the girl for a second or two. "She *does*, doesn't she? How could I have forgotten that?" We had shared more than a few pots of tea in the dormitories. She was about the only one of my friends who cared for it.

Of course, we had also shared bottles of *Boone's Farm* and pipes of pot, but it was a little early in the morning for those. Nor did I have either on hand.

"That's what she ordered when she came into the coffee shop," said Charlie. "Whichever morning that was." She screwed up her forehead, trying to figure it out. "Doesn't matter. Back to studying."

I made tea and Charlie did math problems. What should I do with that folder? Carry it over to the Bells and leave it with Jan or Kay? It would find its way to Dave if I did that.

Maybe I should make copies of this stuff for myself, first. Not that I intended to investigate anything, just to have a backup, if needed. A lot of pages. It would cost to run them through a copier.

And take up a lot of time. Leave it to Officer David Blake.

I sat down with my tea, pushing a few of Charlie's papers aside to make a space for the mug. "Want any?" I asked her.

She only shook her head, absorbed in whatever problem she was puzzling over. In half a minute, I was on my feet again, carrying my mug up into the shop.

The heavy machinery had not started in yet. I doubted that there was anything left inside the motel to salvage. Loads of furniture and washing machines and even some of the windows had been carted away over the last couple weeks. Even Michelle's ice maker that the Feds had shot, that cold December night when Ray Manuel's men had tried to move a shipment of heroin through the place.

Oh, they were going to take down the sign first. I would never again see 'no vacancy' flashing over there. The backhoe pretty much pulled it out by its roots — those being concrete footings — crumpled it and dropped it unceremoniously into one of the waiting trucks.

I stepped out and parked myself on the front steps. Might as well watch a while. There was Kay, doing the same in front of her place. Rick, too.

I would go over there later. Let them enjoy the show right now — we would all get bored with it in a while.

Cars slowed down to get a look as they passed the demolition. It was still early enough for people to be heading to work, not yet Nine. I saw a little silver machine, a convertible with its top down despite the cool morning air, pause and then speed back up as it traveled south. It slowed again as it approached and then pulled into my driveway.

For a moment, I saw only a plump, graying woman getting out of that Miata, rather than the Patty I had known. Weren't we really just strangers now, pretending to know each other?

"Hi, Patty. Want to come in? I've made tea."

"Only stopping for a minute or two," she responded, joining me on the steps. "I am going to look at some rentals." She gazed toward the work at the motel. "Maybe that place over there would be nice when they get it built."

"We're going to fight to keep it from going up five stories."

"Oh, then I should support you. Strike the *Sand Castles* from my list!"

"At least the top two floors," I replied.

"I still have my eye on the place next door. But you are interested in it too, aren't you? Betty told me that." She turned and surveyed the empty house for a few seconds. "There would be room for a studio there."

"A lot of old houses around this neighborhood would work for that. A lot of them actually *do*."

"Um-huh. I think maybe I would like a house in a neighborhood like this."

"I'm afraid it won't last," I told her. "Development may sweep us all away."

"You're as gloomy as ever, Ted!" She suddenly thought better of the remark. "Oh, I shouldn't say stuff like that about you."

I laughed. "I say it about myself. Don't worry about any of that. I haven't come near self-destructing in ages."

"That's good to hear." That could have been no more than a polite remark from some, but I was pretty sure Patty meant it.

"I'll hit the road tomorrow afternoon," Patty said. "I took my time driving up here. It's going to be a quick trip down I-95 on the way back."

About three-hundred miles, wasn't it? She could be back in

Miami by her bedtime. Which, chances were, was somewhat later than mine.

She continued. "I intend to come back by Easter. Sooner, maybe."

"You are always welcome."

"If I move here, you may change your tune, Shaper!" She rose. "I'll be on my way but I'll stop back by later. I promised to visit Toni and look at her studio." There might have been a touch of embarrassment in her laugh. "Already networking."

I suspected that came natural to her.

Chapter 28

"I remember what you said once about waiting for the perfect surfer girl. Don't fool yourself into thinking Patty is that woman."

"She's not just a surfer girl," I informed Kay. "She has money, too!"

She gave me the look. I was used to the look from Kay Bell.

"Come on, Kay, you know I love Michelle."

"Just remember that. She's the best thing I've seen happen to you."

"I know." Maybe a better thing than I deserved. "I don't even know what Michelle sees in me. I'm kind of boring."

"No, Ted. You *want* to be boring but it doesn't work very well. People like Rick and me are boring." A small smile came with that thought but Kay quickly became serious again. I think she was serious. "But you *are* self-absorbed and self-doubtful and a bunch of other 'self' things. That's why she's been so good for you."

"But you have to admit we don't seem to have much in common."

"I think Michelle is a lot like you."

I probably had a stupid look on my face, so she tried to to make it simple for the simpleminded. "You both are terribly independent, take-charge-of-your-life types. Willful, even. Maybe your pasts made you that way. Anyway," she finished, "you seem able to draw each other out of the worlds you created for yourselves."

Then, in a complete change of subject, she asked, "What do you think of my additions?" She waved an arm toward the paintings hanging on the south wall of her shop. Well, south-east I should say, as *Kay's Korner* sat at an angle to the street.

"Toni's work? And did Pat bring you some new stuff?" Not that I hadn't noticed them when I came in. There were four by each artist — quite a contrast they presented, too, Toni's shiny naives, Pat Edwards's painterly landscapes. "You will have that honest-to-goodness art gallery if you keep this up."

"You used to paint, I hear."

"All lies," I claimed.

Kay shook her head, but didn't press me. "I don't think your friend Patty is interested in showing in this little shop. She kind of ignored my mention of it."

There was a reason for that. "Like me, she only used to paint. I doubt she has any recent artwork to hang." And probably didn't like to be reminded of it.

"Oh. I didn't realize that." Kay sighed. "I think I jumped to judgment there. She's going to be as complicated as you, isn't she, Ted? Difficult artists!"

"Let's hope she doesn't buy the house between us."

"We could find worse neighbors. But it would be better if you and Michelle grabbed it." Kay stopped to straighten a rack of tie-dye shirts. "You do still hope to, don't you?"

"Yeah. It would be — convenient. More space." I probably should have left it at that. "And it could be convenient for Michelle and I to have different addresses. Once we're legally married it wouldn't matter, but for now." We were going to be legally married. That was not open to question.

Kay tilted her head at me. "So it doesn't look like you're living together? Do you think anyone cares?"

"The Catholic Church kind of frowns on it," I replied. "I am hoping for a marriage in the church."

"Oh. Again, something I didn't see! Michelle can always list her residence here if it would help."

"Thanks. Until I can convince her to say 'yes' it doesn't matter much."

A thunderous crash sounded outside. "There goes another wall," commented Kay. She walked over to the door, hanging open on this mild day. "No, they just knocked down the roof on the arcade."

"I'd best get back," I told her. "Charlie will think I deserted her."

"You may need to depend more on her now."

"I expect so. I'll hate losing Jan as an employee next year."

"I'll hate losing her, period," replied Kay. She held up the folder. "I'll make sure to give this to her when she gets home. I think she is going to see Dave this evening."

"Good enough." I headed down the sidewalk toward the surf shop, mission accomplished.

Chapter 29

"I met your new boss," Patty informed Michelle. "Doris Boone. We have a standing invitation to dinner when I get back."

"Doris?" I asked. "How did this happen?"

"I went in and opened an account." That ended any doubts about Patty moving here. Patty caught the expression on my face. It was possibly on Michelle's face, as well. "Yes, that's a decisive move, isn't it?"

"Welcome to the neighborhood," was all I had to say.

"Do you think he means it?" she asked Michelle.

"Who can tell? You've known him longer than me."

"Does anyone really know the mysterious Shaper?"

Michelle had to laugh. "I can see why you two were friends. You have the same goofy sense of humor."

"Maybe," was all I would admit. "But we needed someone solid like Pat to hold us all together, we and our friends."

"Yeah, Pat was our lynch-pin, wasn't he? Our little gang sort of fell apart after he started spending time with Betty, and Rob and I broke up." Patty turned her sky-blue eyes on me. "And you just disappeared."

"Yeah, I did." I wasn't intending to volunteer anything more.

"What happened to you, Ted? I've wondered all these years. I know you signed up for another semester and dropped out again. Did the draft get you?"

Ah, I might as well fill her in. Michelle, too. "Medical deferment. While I was trying to, uh, find myself —" I had to chuckle. "That's quite the cliché, isn't it? While I was trying to find myself, I went and worked with kids in a migrant labor camp and, in the process, contracted Hep-B. That kept me out of circulation and the army for a while. Till the draft was ended, anyway."

"Damn, Ted, hepatitis? No good deed goes unpunished, does it?"

"But it worked out well for me, in a way. I know Mike did the military."

"Yep, and Rob was a conscientious objector. That was a part of the Evangelical thing he joined."

"What about Pat?" asked Michelle. "I've never heard him mention being in the service."

"The boy simply lucked into a good lottery number," I told her. "Plus he got married."

"He lives a charmed life, doesn't he?" asked Patty. "Just sailing along while the rest of us weather our storms."

"I think I hate him," I told her.

"Me too!"

Michelle shook her head disapprovingly. "It's a good thing you waited until he took his muscles home to say that, Mr. Carrol."

"Did he order a surfboard?" asked Patty.

"Nope. He always threatens to but never follows through."

"Well, I will. I want a board, Shaper. Will you make me one?"

"Of course. I never turn away a paying customer! Come on back to the workshop and we'll discuss it." That would give Michelle a chance to unwind. She had arrived from her job at the *Winn-Dixie* barely seconds before Patty pulled up out front.

"What length are we thinking?" I asked her, as we strolled up the drive to the shaping bay. "Maybe mid-length like the one I was on yesterday?" A fun-board would be a good idea.

The door was hanging open. I had been working in there off and on today. "If that is what you recommend. You know it's been decades for me." Hmm, maybe a little more length than my 'Michelle' board, then. I reached up into the racks and pulled down a longboard blank.

"No," I said, looking down it. "I was thinking I could trim this into something that would work, but — no." I would have to shape in too much rocker and probably end up weakening it. I set it down. "This one. Yeah." It was intended for a gun, a big wave board, but I could definitely work with it. "Let's say somewhere around eight foot."

"We would have thought that was way too long in the old days."

"But we're both old enough to have started out on longboards," I reminded her. I might use my 'Big Red' template for the outline. But square off the tail? Possibly. "Want any special graphics?"

She pondered for a moment. "Not on this one. No offense intended to Charlie."

"She needs to concentrate on her studies anyway."

"GED, right?" I only nodded in response. She could ask the kid if she wanted to know more.

"I'll start in on it in tomorrow," I told Patty. "This is not a busy time of year for me."

Michelle stuck her head out the back door. "Bring something from the fridge, will you? I need it this afternoon!"

"The fridge?"

I undid the padlock, retrieved a bottle of merlot, and turned to my guest. "Yeah. And it is not for me to explain why we lock this up." I held up the cool green glass. "But you can come in and have some."

"Great idea." Patty followed me into the kitchen.

"We could eat right here," suggested Michelle. "Unless you two are set on going out somewhere." She turned to Patty. "Ted's a good cook, you know. Though his meals tend to be bland and boring." That was an old joke between the two of us but I smiled anyway.

"And vegetarian, too, right?"

"'Fraid so," I told her.

"Lots of time to decide," Michelle added. "It's not even Three yet.

"Is Charlie coming back?" she asked me.

"She decided to go to a meeting this evening. The group up at the church."

Patty's interest was piqued. "Charlie is religious? I wouldn't have guessed."

I wasn't going to try to explain. Again, this was Charlie's business. That didn't stop her mother.

"AA meetings. Charlie has a problem."

"Oh." Patty looked at me, suddenly understanding the locked refrigerator. "Well, that shouldn't stop us from staying here and drinking wine. I vote for letting Ted cook."

"It's unanimous, then," stated Michelle.

"Hey, I didn't vote," I objected.

"No need. I voted for you."

Chapter 30

I felt ambitious the next morning and cut the outline for Patty's board before opening the shop. I had chosen the 'gun' blank for the generous upward curve in its front-end profile. No nose-dives on this board! I would start carving the polyurethane foam with my power planer later on.

Soft, forgiving rails, of course. Three fins, but a larger one in the middle, what is called a two-plus-one setup. Those extra side-fins would give back control I took away by giving the board thicker rails.

It would ride well enough. I knew this from experience.

Patty herself stopped by around noon to say goodbye to both of us. Charlie and me, that is; Michelle had another morning shift at the grocery store. Then her silver sports car sped south on A-1-A. She would jog over to meet the Interstate somewhere further down, and head back to the part of Florida where she grew up.

Back home. As with me, I don't think that home felt like home anymore. This was home for me now, Cully Beach, the place I fitted. It had taken me a long time to find it.

I hoped that Michelle considered it home now, too. For once, she did not hurry back to that home after work, showing up well after Three.

"No more shifts this week," she announced, after giving me a somewhat perfunctory kiss. "I think management intends to cut my hours back before I leave." She looked around the shop. "Is Charlie in the back?"

"Already gone," I told her. "We won't be seeing her until after her class tonight."

"If then. Let me go get cleaned up. I don't suppose you built that shower while I was gone."

"No, but I thought about it once."

"Great." Michelle disappeared into our living quarters.

I should probably figure out how to run the pipes out there, first, both water and drainage. There was already a hot water supply in the utility room, hooked up to the washing machine, so I might as well extend it out the back. If I did that, I suppose I could add hot water to my outdoor shower stall. That would be kind of nice.

And maybe long overdue. In fact, that would be my first step. Then the girls could at least have hot showers, even if they were still outdoors. I should get Rick to help me. I could even pay him if he insisted.

There came my after-school employee of the day. Josh. He was graduating this year and I would lose him. To be honest, I was surprised he had stuck with my low-paying employment.

"It's slow this afternoon, Josh," I said. "I'm going to work out back. Oh, and Ms. Jackson is in the back so don't be startled if she wanders in."

"Um, the younger Ms. Jackson or —?"

"We'll let it be a surprise," I answered, and headed out the back door, through the kitchen, and out to my workrooms. Might as well work some more on that board.

It was still sitting on my shaping stands. I'd made those myself — they allowed me to work with the board flat or tipped up on its side. I got down the trusty Skil 100 planer, old but still as good as or better than anything else, and went to work, cutting long bands along the top, then flipping the board to run more shallow cuts lengthwise on the bottom.

Sometimes I did that in opposite order. It didn't matter. I didn't hear Michelle come in, between the whine of the power tool and Beethoven in my headphones. She may have watched for some time.

As the spinning blades on the plane came to a stop, she spoke. "Patty's board?"

"Yeah." I looked it over. Good enough. "Hand tools from here."

Michelle had seen enough of my boards now to know a bit about them. "Looks different from your others," she said.

"She needs different. Patty's not exactly an athletic teenager."

Michelle couldn't help but smile at that. "But she was, wasn't she?" I nodded. "Hey, open up the fridge, will you. That's really why I came out here!"

I handed her a bottle of chardonnay and relocked. "I'll be in to help you with that. Give me a minute to wash off."

"Another cold shower."

"That may change soon," I told her.

Chapter 31

"It looks like a war zone."

"The war has just begun," stated Doris Boone. We surveyed the lot where the *Easy Breezes* had once stood. Only rubble remained. Even the swimming pool had been broken up and removed.

The young man — young compared to the two of us — who accompanied her nodded absently. I knew he was an attorney, Howard Deland, but only because his teenage daughter, Lisa, had worked at the shop last year. A couple of months and then she said she couldn't anymore, right after Christmas. I didn't pry.

Doris continued. "It's only five days until they will file and then they will try to push it through quickly."

"They?" I asked.

She waved an arm toward the billboard. "Burkhardt Development, like it says." I had no idea who *Burkhardt Development Group, Inc.* was.

"And their lawyers," added Deland.

"As well as certain allies in city government. They'll be cooperating."

"Undoubtedly," came his dry reply. "If everything is in order with the request for a variance — and we can be pretty sure it will be — a hearing will be set. All the nearby property owners will need to be informed at least fifteen days prior. I think that would include you, Mr. Carrol."

"They'll need to post a notice here, too."

"Right, Doris, and one in the newspaper."

"Which one?" I asked.

"*The Courier*," he replied. "It is the largest circulation local paper.

We can expect them to push for a public hearing as soon as possible after those requirements are met."

"So, about three weeks."

"If they can arrange it. Usually, the Board of Adjustment holds these hearings on the fourth Wednesday of the month."

Doris remarked, "We can bet there will be pressure to alter that."

"I would expect them to try to move it forward a week," said Deland. "They will try for any edge they can get."

"How can you stop that?" asked Charlie, who had not interrupted her elders to that point, nor even seemed to pay much attention.

"Raise a stink!" answered Doris. "Make sure everyone knows about it. Not just those who live within three-hundred feet."

The girl nodded. She was getting ideas.

"What about that other thing?" I asked. I nodded toward Eighth Street. "Closing the beach access."

"Closing down the street would be a city council decision," said Deland. "They may order a temporary closing for 'safety issues' and we will have to make sure that doesn't become permanent.

"Word is there may be a request to put a high fence up around the property too. Again, a temporary safety issue, but possibly with the street inside its bounds."

"That would suck," said Charlie.

"But the vacant lot is still there," I pointed out. "Beach-goers will just walk across it." That vacant lot belonged to the city, the piece of land that might or might not become a park one day. There had been talk of buying the abandoned gas station beyond to add to it.

Beyond the station lay some older apartments and private homes on the beach. They were too far away to even receive notices, weren't they? But I was sure folks there would be interested.

"I'm glad you invited me to this little, uh, conference," I told Doris and Howard. "By the way, I would be happy to have Lisa back as an employee anytime."

The man may have allowed his mouth to tighten, just for a moment, but his voice remained level. "Her mother decided to leave town and took Lisa with her. She'll be back with me for the Summer."

Divorced. That pretty much explained it. Not a great thing for any kid to go through but maybe worse for shy, unsure Lisa.

"We'll look forward to seeing her on the beach."

The pair got into a nondescript sedan, his I assumed, and headed off, north up the highway, as Charlie and I crossed over and strolled back toward the surf shop. "Man, it is dead," she said. "And it's a Saturday morning!"

"There are still plenty of snowbirds and tourists in town," I told her. "We'll see them out and about. It's not a bad day."

"Should I go ahead and open the shop?"

"Might as well. I think I'll work out back a little while."

"On a board?"

"On plumbing."

Rick was going to bring over a heavy concrete drill so I could run a hot water pipe out the back wall. Once I had that in place, I could hook things up out there as and when I felt like it.

Once he arrived, it didn't take long to put a hole through the

concrete blocks. Connecting to the old metal pipes took a bit longer
— I was mating them to newer plastic ones for this extension.

"You could replace all those pipes," said Rick. "Well, except for
the ones embedded in your concrete floor! And that old water
heater. It won't last forever."

"I know. It's small, too." The heater sat in a little closet-like space
at the end of the kitchen cabinets, accessed from just behind the
utility room door.

"You could put it here outside."

"That's a project for another day. Maybe for another year."

"Yeah. But as long as I'm here today it wouldn't be a bad idea to
drill for a drain pipe, too," he suggested. "Your washer drain is up
too high for a shower stall." So we did that too. Didn't actually hook
anything up but I could get to that later.

"That's good enough," I said. "I owe you, Rick."

"Let's count it toward a new board," my friend replied. "Say
maybe a, um, small discount?"

"I'll just do you one for cost," I told him. "Materials only, not my
time."

"That would be great, man." He reached out and shook my hand.
"And I'm holding you to it!"

Chapter 32

Michelle hung up the phone. "That was the grocery. They would like me to do an afternoon shift tomorrow."

"Ten till Six?" She usually had one of those every week.

"Uh-huh. And then six hours on Wednesday morning and that, it seems, will be that."

That was kind of short notice, calling her on a Sunday afternoon, but I doubt anyone there cared. "You'll have a long weekend before starting the new job."

"True. I may spend it sleeping."

"Good luck with that. I saw the Guzman girl at church this morning."

"Marty?"

"Yep. Her father, too. He wants to help with the zoning thing. The man is a bit peeved that they want to mess up Cully Beach right after he retired here." I would suspect that his daughter had something to do with it, too. She and Charlie had suddenly become as thick as thieves. Or as conspirators.

"Is there a Mrs. Guzman?" Michelle asked, somewhat offhand, while watching a couple browsing through the tee-shirt section.

"No, Al is a widower."

She turned to me, with an expression definitely akin to a smirk. "Ah. Maybe we should introduce him to Patty."

"I would be hard pressed to think of a worse mismatch." Maybe I smirked a bit myself. "Even worse than us."

"Impossible."

"But they are about the same age —" No, no, don't even think it.

"Oh, he's old like you and Patty. You need younger spouses to look after you."

"I expect you to spoon-feed me my gruel every morning, young lady." I decided to get away from that subject while I had a chance. "Did you use your new hot water shower this morning?"

"I did. It's a bit tricky getting the balance right but it definitely beats a cold shower. I don't know how you lived with that so long."

"Real men just take hardships of that sort in stride and don't snivel."

She came over and leaned on the counter. "Okay, seriously, what is Mr. Guzman like? Al, you called him?"

"Alvaro Guzman. High-ranking non-com in the Air Force, retired after something like thirty years. He was stationed at Patrick, down by Cocoa, the last of those years." I brought up a picture of him in my head, a picture that was part verbal description. Combining the two was a more effective way for me to remember. "Graying hair, short, of course, and a neat mustache, even grayer. Not a big guy; I might have an inch on him." And I was barely average. "Fairly dark. Trace of an accent. Puerto Rican, I would guess, but don't hold me to it." The hands. "Small, square hands. He was bundled up some but I would guess him fairly large boned."

"But you said he was small."

"Large bones means thick bones, not long ones. I'm pretty small boned myself."

"Yeah, you have wrists like a girl."

"Thanks for noticing. Hmm, the nose was a bit misshapen. I would wager he boxed when he was young."

"Or he is accident-prone," laughed Michelle. "Enough. Marty looks almost, um, oriental. Or do we say Asian these days?"

"Her mom was from the Philippines. That I got from Charlie."

"Oh! Marty has sort of latched onto Charlie, hasn't she?"

"She could do worse."

"I suppose." The couple wandered out of the shop without buying anything. Nothing unusual there but disappointing, none the less. "You don't have any kid coming in to work this afternoon, do you?"

"Nope. It will be you and me and the surf rat who just walked in." I didn't even attempt to think of the boy's name. He picked up a flier from the stack by the door.

After puzzling over it, maybe half a minute, he raised his head and asked, "Hey, Shaper, can I take some of these?"

"That's what they're for. Spread 'em around." They were Charlie's work. As suggested by Doris, she was raising a stink about the variance.

The phone rang again. I answered this time. "*Cully Beach Surf Shop.*"

I listened a moment. "Is he going to be okay?" More. "All right, Kay, thanks for calling. I'll go right over."

I turned to Michelle. "Dave Blake is in the hospital. Someone beat him up outside his apartment this morning."

Chapter 33

"The Bell girl went over there around Ten and found him hurt in his apartment. He'd been attacked in the parking lot but managed to get inside before passing out."

Bob Redding filled me in, outside Dave's hospital room. "It must have happened real early or maybe even last night."

There was any number of reasons why someone might want to hurt Dave. He was a cop, after all, and cops do make enemies. Well, I guess we all make enemies but their enemies are more likely to be violent criminals.

I couldn't help thinking, though, that it had something to do with his unofficial investigation.

"Is it okay to go in?"

"Yes, sir. The girl is with him." He ran his thick fingers over his blond buzz-cut. "Sir, uh, Mr. Carrol. I may not be the smartest guy on the force but I know something is going on here. Things are *wrong*, sir, first the chief and now this." He glanced toward the hospital room door. "And if I can help, I want to."

I nodded, not sure how to take all of it. Best I pass Bob's offer on to Dave or Jim. I went on in, quietly.

Jan looked up from a bucket chair, upholstered in battleship-gray vinyl. Not the most cheerful color choice. "They have him sedated, Shaper," she whispered. "He'll be okay. Some broken ribs, the doctor says, and a lot of bruises." No concussion, then, or internal injuries. That was good.

But Dave didn't look very good, swollen and bandaged. "You found him, I understand."

She only nodded. I knew where Dave lived, over on the west side of the river, south of the Scott City Road, where rentals varied from reasonable to downright cheap. I also knew it wasn't the best of neighborhoods.

"There had been threats," Jan said. "Dave didn't take them seriously."

I turned my eyes to the injured policeman. "He's learned the hard way that he should."

A weak smile. "That's just what I've been sitting here telling him. But he's asleep so he can't hear me."

"What sort of threats?" I asked.

"Oh, they were, well, almost cartoonish, you know. Like gangster clichés. Keep your nose out of where it doesn't belong and that sort of thing." She shook her head. "There would be notes under his door or on his car."

I wondered if he had told Jim Trejo, or anyone else, about this.

"Thanks for coming over, Shaper. I know it's a bit of a drive." The hospital was on the outskirts of Scott City. Not exactly a new facility, going by its looks.

"Do you need a ride back home? You came in the ambulance, right?"

"I am going to stay with Dave overnight. Maybe you and Dad could go over and get my car, though, and take it home."

"Better yet, we'll bring it here. Take care, Jan." I slipped out of the room. Redding still sat impassively in a chair outside the door. Did someone think there would be another attack on Blake?

And was Redding's offer legitimate? For a moment I felt mistrust of the man. I had never gotten along with him. But no, everyone knew Bob was as honest as they came, and as loyal. And he was too dumb to try to deceive anyone.

It was dark by the time I got home, outside and inside, and everything was locked up. I stood there for a few seconds in the drive. This was the way it always had been, year after year, until the past few months. Me, alone in this place. Sometimes I missed being able to hide away like that.

But I pretty much knew where everybody would be. I hiked across the backyards to the Bells' house. They must have seen my truck's lights because the back door opened to me. One or the other of their dogs barked.

It was Rick who let me in. He had been away all day, something job-related, I think, which was why Kay asked me to go check on Jan. Michelle and Kay sat facing each other across a corner of the bare Formica-topped table. No one else? I had kind of expected more of a crowd in their kitchen. "Thanks for going over, Ted," said Kay, and came and gave me a hug.

Over her shoulder, I told Rick, "We need to collect the Malibu and take it to Jan."

He nodded. "Okay. I'll be right with you."

"You probably passed Charlie and John on their way to the hospital," said Michelle. "Maybe you will see them there."

"Maybe." Rick came back into the room.

"I had to find the spare key," he explained. "Let's take my truck."

No problem. And I would get to drive Jan's muscle car. I would wager even Dave wasn't allowed to do that.

Chapter 34

I almost didn't make it out of bed at my usual time in the morning. My internal clock is what tells me to do that; I never set an alarm clock.

But that internal clock needed winding this morning. I had been up way too late into the night. A different cop sat outside Dave's door when we got back to the hospital. He seemed to know who we were and passed us on in without comment.

Dave was awake. Groggy but awake. We exchanged a few words, told Jan where we parked the Chevy — she had her own keys with her, of course — and took off again, leaving her with Charlie and John for company. It was past midnight when I finally climbed into bed, next to a sleeping Michelle.

New security lights were shining at the site of the former motel this morning. But there could be no beginning to construction until Burkhardt got their variance. I wondered if they had an alternate three-story design ready if it was turned down.

Well, of course they did. I could live with three stories rising over here. And continued beach access, naturally. I took that beach access to the end of the road and gazed out at the Atlantic, where just a touch of peach color showed in the sky above the horizon.

No waves. I would have been surprised if there were — not that I wouldn't like such a surprise.

There was something of a surprise in the kitchen when I got back. Both Charlie and John sat there, drinking my coffee. "His parents think we spent all night at the hospital," explained the girl. "We almost did."

"Dave was okay when you left?" The coffee carafe was near empty. I'd best start another.

"He seemed to be," responded John. "He was even kind of talkative by the time we took off."

"But we were all too tired to talk back," added Charlie.

Someone official would be taking his statement this morning, no doubt. Eventually, we would hear all the details.

"I'm too tired to talk much right now," I admitted.

"Not that you are ever that talkative, Shaper," commented Charlie. Then she asked, "Do you know when Patty is coming back?"

I shook my head. "Her wetsuit and fins are waiting when she does." Actually, they were in the rental section of the shop now. No reason not to be making money off them. If Patty didn't want the equipment, they would be offered for sale as 'used.' "And her new board is almost ready."

"She told me definitely by Easter."

"I'm pretty sure it will be sooner than that. I can't see Patty sitting in Miami, doing nothing, for two months."

"She could always meet a guy," Charlie offered.

"That is true. Your mom thinks we should introduce her to Marty's father."

The girl thought that was hilarious. Perhaps it was.

John glanced toward the clock on the stove. "I'm opening the coffee shop this morning," he said. "I should probably shove off." He rose, a bit slowly. Tired from last night, like all of us. "I'll pick you up for your class tonight," he told Charlie, and was out the door.

156

"He has to count the muffins or something," she told me. "Jan said she would come home after her morning classes, so we can get the news out of her then."

"You're hanging here today?"

She nodded, and turned her head suddenly toward the hallway. "Mom's up," she announced. Must have slipped across the hall into the bath, because I saw nothing when I looked.

"Has to work today," I said. With all the rest happening yesterday, she probably wouldn't have thought to tell that to Charlie. "Later shift."

"It's going to seem strange when she has a Nine-to-Five."

"Yeah." It would. I was too used to seeing Michelle pretty much anytime I wanted. "It sucks," I proclaimed.

"For you," was her answer.

"Yeah," I had to admit. "For me."

Chapter 35

Dick Warner's gold Cadillac pulled into the drive next door. Showing the place?

Michelle came and stood by me at the window. We were up front in the shop, looking out over a rack of aloha shirts. "Showing it bright and early," she noted. "I need to get going."

I recognized the man with the real estate agent. "That's Al Guzman," I told her.

"Oh." She peered out at the gentleman. "I don't know if I would recognize him from your description." She gave me a peck. "Bye now." Michelle hurried out to her van, waved toward Dick, and backed out.

I went into the kitchen, where Charlie once again had her books spread out, doing some sort of homework. "I should have caught this up yesterday," she mumbled, in lieu of a greeting.

"Did you know Mr. Guzman was interested in the house next door?" I asked.

"Nope." She leaned back and stretched. "Marty has seen the place, of course. She must have told him about it."

That seemed likely. "They're in an apartment now," she went on. "Up north, right near Officer Trejo's place."

Okay, I knew where that was, several blocks north and west of the downtown area. "I suppose the best way to snoop is to go out and say 'hello,'" I told her. "Coming?"

"Sure."

They took their time going through the place, so I busied myself in the shaping bay. "I promised Rick a new board," I said, as much to myself as Charlie. "I guess I should have asked him what sort."

"Couldn't you just do your regular thruster thing but make it bigger?"

"Sort of. There would have to be compromises and changes." I though about it for a second. "As in anything. It's not a bad idea." I think Rick saw my fun-boards as being for older riders. He was not willing to admit he fit into that group.

"I'll ask him about it next time I see him," I said. "They're coming out."

Al and Dick slid open the glass doors and stepped out onto the patio. Guzman gave the yard a quick survey. It didn't seem to hold much interest.

"Hi, Ted," he called, holding up a hand in salute. "Charlie." He walked in our direction. "It looks like this yard is a highway for the kids!" He was rather loud, wasn't he? The man practically shouted.

"For me, too," I admitted.

"I would not mind that. I like people around." He turned back for another look. "If I lived here, I would put in a walk for them."

Before I could comment, Al continued. "I hear you peeped through those glass doors last year and discovered a body."

"I did. Junkies were camping in there, it seems." I wasn't going to go into all of that. By now, he probably knew the story anyway.

He nodded slowly. "I would tear them out and put real windows and doors there. Not that I am planning to buy the place!" He winked for our benefit.

"I have plenty of other houses I can show you," interjected Dick Warner. "This *is* the closest to the beach, anywhere near your target price."

"Still high," remarked Al.

"It is," I added, just to be aggravating. And because I still wanted the place myself.

"It would be nice to have Marty next door," said Charlie, not helping my cause at all.

"She would like that too." Guzman stated, in quite a serious voice, "It could help her career."

That baffled me. "Career?"

"As a surfing champion, Ted! Where better to live than next to a surf shop?"

"You know I don't sponsor that sort of thing myself."

"Ah, but maybe you should, eh?"

Unlikely. No, it simply would never happen. "Shaper is too cheap for that," Charlie told him. She gave me an up-and-down look. "Maybe too lazy too."

"That's me, just a beach bum. Now your mom has a good job I may quit working altogether."

I think Al was almost inclined to take us seriously. "Well, Dick, let's go look at those other houses on your list," he said. "Later, Ted. You too Charlie." The man headed for Warner's Caddy.

But to me, Dick whispered, leaning in close. "Remember the place on your south side is still for sale. Guzman completely turned up his nose at it. Wouldn't even take a look."

But maybe I should. "Let's make an appointment," I told him.

Chapter 36

I saw Jan's Malibu pull in at her parents' house, a bit after One. That meant she could have stopped back by the hospital after her morning classes at the community college.

Neither of us — Charlie and me, that is — should bother her now. She would be more in need of a bath and a nap than our company. We could pester her later.

"Phone, Shaper," called Charlie, hanging out the back door. When I came closer, she confided, "It's Chief Cotton."

I went up front and picked up the receiver. "Hello, Bill."

"Ted, hi. You know about Blake, right?"

"Yes. I've been to see him. He's doing all right."

"That's good, that's good." A pause. "Do you mind if I stop by tomorrow?"

"Any time, Bill. I'll probably be in most of the day."

"First thing in the morning, while it's still dark. I'd just as soon no one knew you and I were meeting. Ted, if they hurt Dave because of me, they might not be willing to stop there."

"Oh. Okay, Bill. I'll just follow my regular routine in the morning, then, and watch for you."

"Great, Ted. Thanks." He hung up.

Charlie obviously wanted details. "We were making Mardi Gras plans. He asked me to ride on his float."

The girl made a rude noise. "No one is ever going to throw beads to you, Shaper." The phone rang again.

"*Cully Beach Surf Shop*," answered Charlie. "Oh, hi, Mrs. Bell."

She listened a while. "Sure. I'll tell them to be there." Charlie hung the phone up and informed me, "You and Mom are eating dinner with the Bells."

"She knows your mother is working late, doesn't she?"

"Sure, that's part of why she invited you. Be there at Seven-ish." She grinned. "And tell me *everything* tomorrow."

Right. Charlie would be at class this evening.

She was long gone, off in John's truck, by the time Michelle made it home. "Kay is fixing dinner tonight," I informed her. "Whenever you feel like it we can go on over."

"Oh? Well, okay." She sounded tired. "I can definitely use a hot shower this evening. Even an outdoor one."

It was Seven-ish, indeed, when we showed up at our neighbors' back door. I noted that Jan's car was not parked by the house. Undoubtedly back at the hospital.

"Mashed potatoes?" I asked, sniffing the air. "With olive oil and garlic." That brought a memory. "That's just what we had the night you first told me about Michelle moving in."

"Who are you, Proust?" asked my girlfriend. I'm not sure any of the Bells got that, not even Kay. But Michelle was a reader. I hadn't fully realized how much of a reader until she moved in.

Richie was setting the table. Three wine glasses, one juice glass, five plates. Rick had a bottle of beer in hand, some inexpensive brand or another. I should've thought to bring over a Beck's or two.

"I'm ready to start in on a board for you," I said, pulling out a chair. "I'm thinking big-guy thruster."

"Big-guy?" That was from Richie.

"Yeah, my regular production board but a little longer, a tad thicker. Little adjustments here and there."

Rick considered this. "Sounds great," he said. "Go ahead. When you have time, man, when you have time."

"Lots of that right now. Things are definitely slowing down. So guys," I asked any and all, "what's the word on Dave?"

"He gave an official statement today. Jan heard some of it." Kay retrieved a tray from the oven. It smelled like seafood of some sort. And lots of seasonings. "He is being released in the morning."

"Two guys attacked him," offered Rick.

"Yes. You eat these, don't you, Ted?" she asked, placing what I could now see were crab-cakes on the table.

Richie had a ready answer. "If he doesn't, serve him more veggie-burgers!"

"Not if I have to sleep in the same room with him," objected Michelle.

"These are fine, Kay." I didn't really care for them but that was beside the point.

She sat down and directly addressed me. "Jan will be there when they discharge Dave tomorrow. I don't think it's a good idea for him to go back to his apartment, do you?"

"You thinking of taking him in?"

"It's one possibility."

"I don't have any room. Yet." I turned to Michelle. "By the way, I made an appointment with Dick Warner to look at the house on our south tomorrow morning. We might as well."

"I'm willing. Was Guzman interested in the other place?"

"Not sure." I looked at our hosts. "I believe we steered the conversation up the wrong stream. Where do you think Dave should stay?"

"Away from Jan," stated Rick. "I don't want her in any danger."

That was certainly a good point. One I might agree with. "Someone on the force has probably thought about this."

"That's true," said Kay. "We shouldn't be the ones worrying about it."

"Yeah, let's celebrate," said Richie. "Tomorrow is Mardi Gras!"

"Is there any celebration here?" asked Michelle. "Charlie loves Mardi Gras." Then, introspective of a sudden, she added, "She may have loved it too much in the past."

"No parade or anything," Kay told her. "But they do party a bit up by the pier."

"And then Ash Wednesday, right, Ted?" came Rick's question. "You have to fast or something."

"Ted eats like it is Lent all year 'round," Michelle told him.

"As long as I don't have to give up you," I told her, "I'll be okay."

It was sappy enough to make Richie snicker. But I think Michelle bought it.

Chapter 37

"I should have taken the retirement offer. I didn't want anyone to get hurt." There was no regret nor bitterness in the chief's voice. He was just stating a fact.

"Is it too late?"

"The offer is off the table. The DA intends to prosecute."

"Is he, um, do you think he is involved in any way? In the frame-up, I mean."

"No. He just wants to make a name for himself. Harbin intends to handle the case himself instead of assigning an assistant to it." Bill sipped his coffee. "Back to your regular brew, huh?"

"Can't afford to keep serving the good stuff to anyone who happens to walk in." We both drank coffee in silence for a few seconds. Bill had waylaid me on my morning walk and, parking his car at a good distance from the shop, had accompanied me home.

"This is still fairly good stuff," he said. "I've had really bad coffee."

"I can imagine. Part of being a policeman, isn't it?"

"That's the truth."

"So is facing danger, Bill. You know that and Dave knows that. Part of the job."

"But you're not a policeman. You're just a, um —"

"Successful businessman?"

"Not quite what I had in mind but it will do. You shouldn't be placed in danger, Ted. Neither should this family you just acquired." He was dead serious now.

"Well, I'm not really involved very deeply." I was no more than a messenger boy of sorts.

"That might not be obvious to everyone."

"Let's hope no one notices me at all! Have you heard the official report on Dave?"

He shook his head. "I'm completely out of the loop, Ted. No one tells me anything."

"Hmm, I've only heard bits of what he told Jan. I do expect Trejo will stop by and fill me in sooner or later."

"We'll have to depend on Jim now, with Dave out of the picture."

I had to chuckle at at sudden thought. "Or Bob Redding. He says he wants to help."

"The 'Brick?' I guess he's trustworthy but I don't know how useful he would be." He stood. "It's getting light out. I'd better get out of here now." Bill extended his hand. "Thank you for every-thing, Ted. Um, I guess I should contact you — yeah, I'll call in a day or two. We should stick to the phone from now on, maybe."

"Good enough." We both stepped outside. It was fairly light. When Daylight Savings hit us in couple weeks, things would be different at this time of the morning.

I truly detested DST. Possibly loathed, abhorred, and despised it as well.

Bill headed north along the sidewalk, towards where he had left his vehicle in the convenience store parking lot. I stood there a moment, watching him, and then turned south to look at the house next door, mostly hidden still in the shadows of the bushes and trees that surrounded it. It had a charm, didn't it? Well, we would look at it more closely later.

Both Michelle and Charlie were eating breakfast by the time I got back inside. They had been waiting for Cotton to leave, I would suppose. This morning, I was glad they did.

I really shouldn't meet him here again. Not until this was over and his only reason to come in was to buy a Hawaiian shirt. I would not put these two women at risk.

"Shall I make more coffee for you, Ted?" asked Michelle.

I guess I sat there a bit long before shaking my head. "Had enough. Thanks." I could see mother and daughter exchange a look.

They worried about me, didn't they? Just as much as I worried about them.

"I feel like starting on Rick's board," I announced and headed out the back door. I didn't really feel like it but I didn't feel like sitting in the kitchen either. There was Jan's car over at her folks' house. She'd be going to pick up Dave soon, I would think.

And take him where? I couldn't even guess.

I spent more time penciling lines on the blank than actually cutting foam. The blank itself was designed for a fun-board sort of shape, fuller in the nose and tail. I would have to trim some there. That inevitably weakened the board, as the foam in the core was less dense and less sturdy.

But I wouldn't take much away through the middle, which got the bulk of wear and tear in everyday surfing. I quite lost track of time and was surprised to look up and see Dick's Cadillac pulling to the curb.

Michelle popped out the back door. "I ordered Charlie to stay and hold down the fort. She's nosy enough to want to see the place too."

"It's not even opening time yet, is it?" But if she didn't want her daughter along, so be it. I rinsed the gritty particles of foam off my arms with the hose. No time to shower all of me, though I could feel bits of it down my shirt.

A minute later the three of us stood in front of the old bungalow. "It certainly has a lot more character than the other house," remarked Michelle.

Even our place had more character than the ranch-house to our north, which epitomized bland Sixties homes. Our flat-roofed Fifties 'Florida house' might be nothing special but there was a certain charm to it.

"Not as practical for us, though." She nodded in agreement.

I could see the peeling paint, the cracked concrete walk. Yes, the porch's low concrete floor had a deep crack running diagonally across it, too. But I could see that floor didn't support any weight of the house or the roof — there were brick piles along the front that served in that capacity.

The place needed work. That was for sure.

Dick unlocked the heavy front door and stepped aside to let us enter. Real estate agents knew to do that, the good ones, never go in ahead of the buyer — let them see the room, not you. I had been in that front room once, while the DEA agents had rented the place as their surveillance headquarters. It looked the same.

Smelled the same too. "This place needs thoroughly aired out," remarked Michelle. "And all this shabby furniture belongs on a bonfire."

"There are two or three bedrooms," said Warner, "depending on what one does with this space." He led us into a surprisingly airy room to the left, which also opened onto the porch. "The computer business that was in here used this as their showroom."

"I could see French doors there," I whispered to Michelle.

"I can see uneven floors," came her reply.

"Bedroom that way," continued our guide, indicating a door on the west side of the room. "Master bedroom, I would call it, and consider this space more of a family room, maybe."

And another bedroom beyond and a bathroom and turn right into a kitchen of more than decent size. Then we circled back through what was probably used as a dining room, returning to the room where we had entered.

"A double-barreled shotgun house," I remarked.

Dick chuckled. "Yes, I guess you could call it that."

It wasn't all that much footage, really

The high-ceilings made the place look airier, and bigger than it really was. A bit over twelve-hundred feet, maybe? Having grown up around builders, I could guess-timate that sort of thing. "What's the square footage?" I asked Dick Warner.

He pulled out the listing slip. "One-thousand three-hundred and forty-four feet under roof. That's not counting that big porch. There's a utility area around back that doesn't open into the rest of the house.

"There's a shed back there, too, that should be knocked down. If the termites don't do it first. Want to look at it?"

"We might as well," said Michelle. We followed Dick around the north side of the house. The tall hedge that separated this property from mine encroached on the rather narrow pathway. This place was a little deeper and a little narrower than my house, but fitted on the same size lot.

Well, no, if one counted the wrap-around porch it was just as wide. Maybe a bit wider, even. I shouldn't forget that. The shed was definitely falling down and definitely termite-riddled. That explained what Agent Field had told me. He wouldn't have realized that the sturdy cypress house was sound.

Very overgrown. "It's a jungle out there!" joked Michelle.

"There was a drive here," I noted as we looped back around the south side. Never a paved one, though, and unused for a long time. I could see the oyster shells that sometimes were used for driveways in an older Florida.

The steps up to the south side of the porch had crumbled into broken concrete and sand. There was a lot that needed fixing here but the important thing was that it could be fixed. That didn't mean I could see myself doing it.

"I'll be honest, Dick," I said. "I love the place. It's also completely impractical for us."

Michelle's expression told me I shouldn't have spoken for her. I think she pretty much agreed, however.

Warner shrugged. "I expected as much. If you do know anyone who is interested, send them my way, will you?" We shook hands and parted, him to his Caddy, Michelle and I toward the now-open front door of the surf shop.

Michelle leaned in and whispered. "I wonder what sort of critters live under that place." It was raised above the ground, with a crawlspace below.

"Raccoons. 'Possums. Lots of rats, maybe. And snakes that come to eat the rats."

"As long as they are making themselves useful. Do you think we should make an offer? Even if it's far from perfect?"

"I would rather make one on the other house. But not if Guzman or someone is showing a lot of interest. The owners would be less inclined to deal then." The owners were 'the bank.' Not the bank where Michelle would be working, unfortunately.

"Okay. We can wait. As long as you keep improving the plumbing here." With that she stepped on into the shop.

Chapter 38

"Dave is staying with John's family," reported Jan. "He was a bit surprised by the offer but he took it."

Not a bad place for him to convalesce. "How long will he be out of action?"

"At least two weeks." Jan then stated, with considerable determination in her voice, "Dave may be out of action for now but I am not."

"You aren't planning to get involved in his investigation, are you?"

She lightened up, perhaps hoping to disarm my obvious concern. "You said you could see me as an intrepid reporter, didn't you?"

"But there is no Superman around to protect you, Miss Lane."

"Oh, Shaper, I'm going to be careful. After all, who would suspect me of anything?"

"I've been keeping my eye on you since you were twelve. Who knew what devilry might be in that cute little girl?"

"More like, keeping watch over me and all the surfer kids around here. Our very own Superman." She giggled. "Our Shaperman!"

"Oh no, my secret identity has been revealed. Are you going out to the Brody house?"

"Yeah. Charlie and John will be going down to the pier for the Mardi Gras festivities, but I'm going to spend the evening with Dave." A wry smile, a shrug of resignation. "No partying for us for a while!"

"What are you two jawing about out here?" Kay had come to her back door.

"Gossiping about you, of course," I told her. "I've learned all sorts of interesting things."

She laughed. "I'd like to know about them too!"

"I'm going to hit the road, Mom," called Jan, rising from her seat at the picnic table. "I'll be late, I think.

"Bye, Shaper." And then the girl was off, a rumble of exhaust following her north.

I hadn't grilled her at all about Dave and his encounter, nor had I intended to. That information would get to me soon enough, from somebody else.

"I think she'll be okay," mused Kay, coming to stand by me as we watched the Malibu disappear up the highway.

"I hope so," was the only reply I could think of.

I had both an afternoon employee and Michelle to keep an eye on the shop, so, after popping in to check on things, I went on back to my glassing room. There should still be time to laminate Rick's board today.

I was busy on that when I heard Charlie's voice outside. "This is where I do my art." She didn't even notice me until she was a couple steps into the room. "Oh, Shaper, didn't know you were in here." Marty Guzman was behind her.

"Don't mind me," I told her. "I'm just laying up the glass on Rick's board. Mr. Bell's board." Layers of four and six ounce cloth, saturated with polyester resin.

Marty came up beside her friend. "Kim uses a glassing contractor," she said.

"That's fine, if you trust them not to mess up your lines. This is more cost-effective for me." It saved time, too.

She come over closer, but not close enough to get in the way. Marty had been around board builders before. "Flat into vee?" The wet cloth made it a little hard to see the nuances of the shape, but she was right.

"Yep. Better for the intended rider, I think." I chuckled. "A tad easier to shape, too."

Marty was now eyeing Patty's board, lying on the other rack, with some curiosity. "I still need to do some sanding on it," I told her. "That's for an older surfer too."

"Miss Singer?"

I nodded. "Oh, that's Patty's board? asked Charlie. "It's different."

"It is. But not a whole lot different from some of the first I ever shaped." I had to stop for I moment when I thought about how long it had been. "Thirty years ago."

"Thirty? Wow." Marty was impressed. That was quite a bit longer that Kim Timble. As long as her father had repaired jet engines.

"Thirty-two, to be precise. In Sixty-nine, I stripped down an old longboard and reshaped it. That was my first." If one didn't count DIY bodyboards as a kid.

"I'll bet it sucked," was Charlie's comment.

"Somewhat. I was imitating the deep-vee boards out of Australia and they had their shortcomings."

They didn't know what I was talking about. "Is John with you?" I asked. I assumed he had brought them.

Charlie shook her head. "Marty's dad dropped us. John's coming to pick us both up in a bit."

"And take me home while you two go party," grumbled Miss Guzman.

"You'll have to complain to your dad about that," Charlie told her. "It's not our doing!"

"I know. Shaper?" Marty turned to me. "Do you think you could teach me to do this? Kim doesn't have the time and she's not that close."

Caught me by surprise with that one, young lady. But why not? "As long as your sponsor doesn't object, sure."

Charlie laughed. "You don't have to tell her, do you?"

Chapter 39

"I slipped last night. Someone handed me a drink and I thought, 'why not,' you know? I took a couple of sips and saw John looking at me and dumped it out! The look on his face —" She shook her head. "I felt so ashamed of myself."

"He's your Jiminy Cricket."

"Huh?"

"Haven't you ever seen *Pinocchio?* Jiminy was appointed to be his conscience by the Blue Fairy." I thought I had that right. If I didn't, she wouldn't know the difference.

"Hmm, okay, Shaper. I won't always have John nearby when I'm tempted. And I liked that rum and cola. I wanted to drink the whole thing and then I would have wanted another."

"You didn't and that's what matters. It's certainly nothing to beat yourself up over." That was for sure, but I think I understood why the girl would be hard on herself. I knew that mind-set too well.

"I'll always be this way. And now John is disappointed in me."

"Did he say so?"

She started to sniffle. "No. John never — he's always —" A sob escaped her. Just one.

No, John would 'never.' Maybe he needed to, but I wouldn't know. "I think the only one disappointed is you, my girl, and that happens to all of us. Just call it a learning experience." I gave her a grin. "Enough of those and you'll be old and wise like Shaper."

"That's really something to look forward to! Oh, Mom's out of the head. I'd better claim it." She rose and disappeared into the empty bathroom.

It was less than a minute before her mother came into the

kitchen. "I could hear all that," Michelle quietly told me. She filled a mug with coffee and came to sit at the table. Two teaspoons of sugar, a sip, a nod of approval. "Well, strictly speaking, I was purposely eavesdropping."

I could picture Michelle with her ear to the bathroom door.

"John didn't stick around last night," she continued.

"I noticed. Maybe because Dave is at his folks' place."

"Or they felt awkward about what happened."

That, too, was possible. "Charlie has done well."

"She has. Moving here worked out better for both of us than I had ever hoped." She raised her eyes to mine. "You're a big part of that."

"Worked out well for me, too." I wasn't going to let things get mushy so I asked, "You have an early shift, right?"

"Uh-huh." Michelle sipped some more from the cranberry-red mug she preferred. "My last day. I need something sweet to go with this."

"I'm right here," I informed her.

"Nah, Ted, you're more like a bowl of oatmeal."

"I've been compared to worse. I'll be taking off, too."

"Church or surf?"

"No waves to speak of, so it will be *Our Lady of the Seas*."

"Ash Wednesday. Is that one of those, what do call 'em, holy days?" She got up and rummaged in a cabinet.

"Not exactly. If we had time I'd bake scones." We probably did have time. Scones could be ready in something like twenty minutes.

"This will do," said Michelle, lifting out a loaf of raisin bread. She popped a couple slices into the toaster. "No early mornings for me from now on. But," she continued, "we shall have to be sociable some evenings. That kind of goes with the job."

"Just tell your friends I'm on surfari to stay. I'd better get going if I intend to make the early service."

Did I need to change? No, nobody cared how I looked. And I had been sporting a beard for a few weeks so shaving wasn't necessary either. Oh, Michelle's van was parked in my way.

I cranked up the Dodge and backed it out to the street, then retrieved my own truck. We should work out a better system, especially now that she would be going to work later.

Up A-1-A I went, Ocean Avenue, past the pier, past Scott City Road, through the gray morning. A few joggers were out, and surf fishermen heading home. Too early for beach goers and nothing to bring surfers out this morning.

Left at Third, back a block. *Our Lady of the Seas* rose like the prow of a ship, which I think was the architects' intention. A fair number of vehicles in the lot, the faithful popping in before work, mostly. Snow-birds and tourists? They were sparser in Cully Beach by the end of February and had little reason to come early anyway.

Was that Jim's car? It looked like so many other little sedans, I couldn't be sure. But Jim Trejo was inside, in uniform. I will admit that I had come as much in hope of running into him as for any concerns about my soul.

The end of the service was receiving the ashes, a smudge on each forehead, and then we proceeded out into the parking lot. "Let's talk," said Jim, coming up beside me.

I nodded. "In my truck." We were almost next to it.

He climbed in the passenger side. "What have you heard about what happened to Dave Blake?" he immediately asked.

"Very little. I wasn't going to press his girlfriend for details."

"There wasn't much to her statement anyway. Miss Bell found him in his apartment, going in and out of consciousness, and called Nine-One-One."

"Mid-morning, right?"

"Yes. He told us he was jumped around dawn when he went out to get his newspaper. Two men, ski-masks. They hit him with something but we're not sure what. Maybe bats, maybe pipes." He stopped and looked directly into my eyes. "They could have done much more damage, Ted. This was intended as a warning."

"If any of us had any doubt of Chief Cotton being framed, this should remove it."

"But it's not going to convince the prosecutors. Too easy to say Blake made enemies in the course of duty."

"Have you seen his notes? And Cotton's?"

"Uh-huh." He looked out the window for a moment. "Bob Redding brought them over to my place."

"He's not the ally I would have expected in this. Or recruited."

"You never know someone till he's tested, do you, Ted? Jay Johnson is suddenly leery of getting involved in all of this." He shrugged. "I've filled in Millie and she wants to help any way she can."

Good for her. "I don't suppose there is much I can do, but let me know, okay? Oh, and —" I should mention it, shouldn't I? "I am afraid that Jan — Jan Bell — might try to play detective. Keep an eye out for her, will you?"

"Certainly. You have your own battle to fight anyway, right?"

"Battle? Oh, you mean the zoning thing? Yeah, I'm in on that, sort of."

Jim didn't say anything for a while, maybe thinking, maybe deciding whether there was anything more *to* say. "They may be the same battle, Ted. There seem to be ties between people involved in both of them. Especially that law firm." With that, he got out and went to his own car.

A connection? That seemed, well, a stretch. But there was no way I could know, was there?

Chapter 40

Sure enough, a notice of the variance request arrived in Saturday's mail. They must have been mailed out as soon as it was filed on Thursday.

And the notice was in the Sunday paper, too, along with an opinion piece that put forth arguments about 'best use' and 'progress,' while not directly addressing the request. The author was one of our city councilmen, Bernie Robinson.

I don't normally read the paper — unlike Officer David Blake — but I picked up a copy at the convenience store on the way back from my early morning surf check.

One thing I did note was that the official hearing before the Board of Adjustment had not been moved up and would be on the Twenty-eighth, the normal fourth Wednesday of the month. I should probably go, even though I was unlikely to say anything. People like Doris or Howard Deland would be better at presenting the case.

A yawning Charlie joined me, later than usual. No sign of Michelle at all. I guess I would see her when I got back from church. That's right, there was no surf this morning — I wouldn't have stopped to read the paper if there was.

The attendance at the early service was growing ever sparser. Father Paul was likely to suspend it after Easter and I would have to find a different time to miss mass. There were the Guzmans, father and daughter, up front. That Alvaro was an early riser did not surprise me at all.

No chance of making my escape without speaking to them.

Alvaro Guzman, his voice as loud as ever, greeted me on the church steps.

After pleasantries, he informed me, "We are going down to Vasco to visit Miss Timble. Your competition!"

I mildly objected. "Friendly rivals, more like. We're far enough apart for that."

"She told me you shaped boards for other shops in her area," said Marty

"True, both my own brand and stuff sold under other labels, at shops up and down the coast. I need to do another run of stock boards soon to send off." She would want to watch, I suspected. I winked at the girl. "You can be my spy and bring me back info on Kim's operation."

Al laughed uproariously. "I think it might be the other way around, Ted! She will be spying on you all the time if we move in next door."

I spread my arms. "No secrets here. Really thinking of buying the house?"

"Yes. You are too, aren't you?" With Charlie and Marty hanging with each other, that was bound to reach him.

"Considered it." I shook my head. "Too expensive." Best Guzman think I wasn't too serious.

"It is," he agreed. "We are in no hurry to buy."

Marty told us, "If you two don't decide, Miss Singer might steal it right away from both of you."

"Oh. I didn't think she was that interested," I replied. That would be problematic, wouldn't it? "Did Charlie tell you this?" The girl nodded.

"Anyone could come along and snatch it up," said Al. "That's just how it goes."

"Yes, it does," I agreed. We shook and parted ways, me to my well-worn pickup, the Guzmans to their big old pseudo-wood-paneled Buick station wagon. I could see at least one surfboard in the back.

"So how do we spend your last day of freedom?" I asked Michelle when I came in the back.

"We are going to visit the Brodys," she informed me. "And don't give me that expression, Mr. Carrol! It's a done deal."

I did give her that expression, didn't I? She was likely to see it a lot more times if she stuck with me.

"We can visit Dave," said Charlie. That was so.

"Will Jan be there?" I asked.

The two looked at each other, before Michelle said, "No, not today. She's going to come over and watch the shop." They were hiding something more, obviously, and would know that I could tell. No point in saying anything, however.

"Okay. Tell me when and we'll head out."

Chapter 41

"Marty's dad is a little deaf from being around jet engines for so long," came Charlie's voice from the back seat. "It lets her get away with all sorts of things!"

"That explains why he shouts, huh?" We were in the van this Sunday afternoon, rolling west on the Scott City Road. "You'll have to direct me once we turn."

Right on Greenwood Road. Michelle's former place of employment stood on the opposite corner. "It's only like a mile up the road," Charlie informed me. "Big place on the left."

Not only was it big but there was a sizable sign out front telling us it was the location of *Brody Services*. I knew Stan Brody and his older sons had a multi-faceted business going, pumps and well-drilling, electric, painting, and undoubtedly other stuff I didn't know about. There was also a paint and hardware store just east of the bridge in Cully Beach, in one of the very old brick buildings along the Scott City Road.

A long shed lay off to the north of the house, with four — no, five — large trucks parked in front of it. Nothing going on there today. The Brodys were the sort to take their Sabbath seriously.

And the house. Yes, it was sizable and, I would think, relatively new. It certainly didn't look like an old farmhouse, which was sort of what I had expected. The two-story brick facade whispered 'McMansion' to me.

"Park over there," directed Charlie, pointing.

"By those trucks?" A pair of big Dodge Rams, both bright red.

"Yep. John's brothers drive those."

"Oh. Are we, um, going to be intruding on the family's Sunday dinner or something?"

"We are *invited* to Sunday dinner, Shaper." I am not sure Michelle was any more aware of this than I. But in we went, following the knowledgeable young Miss Jackson, and were introduced to the extended family, John's parents, Stan and Adele, his older brothers and their wives. Shannon, who I think was John's sister. People who were friends or worked for them or something. From there out, Charlie pretty much was attached to John — or vice-versa — and left us to our own devices.

I did see her give Dave a disapproving look when he came down the wide, winding staircase to join us. I wasn't going to figure that out.

"I still have a sore jaw," complained the policeman, "and maybe a loose tooth. I'll have to stick to soft stuff." He gazed over the long laden table as we entered the dining room. "You're going to be limited too, my vegetarian friend."

I could get by. I'd done it plenty of times in the past. Michelle and I were directed to chairs close to the family patriarch.

Knowing families like this, I was certain that they would say grace before dinner. I also realized there was a possibility that I, the visitor, would be asked to deliver said grace.

Sure enough, I was. And I was prepared, having composed and committed a rather generic blessing to memory years ago for just such occasions. You see, I worry and I plan and sometimes it actually pays off.

"I didn't expect that," whispered Michelle. "And I certainly didn't expect you to handle it so well."

"You're Catholic, aren't you?" asked the woman on my other side, Ralph's wife, I think. "That sounded Catholic." I nodded, as she passed me the sweet potatoes. It probably did.

Brody, at the head of the table, was a rather gaunt, sun-burnt gentleman in a plaid shirt, a full head of graying hair atop his broad shoulders. "Come on out on the porch and sit," he said to me, after the pie — both pecan and apple — had come and gone.

"My older boys here," said Mr. Brody, indicating his sons, "help me run the business but John is going a different direction."

"He's the brainy one in the family," Stan Junior told me.

"Not that that is saying much," added his brother, Ralph.

"You boys let the three of us sit a while, okay?" They immediately went inside, leaving Blake and me with their father, and no one else came out. "They're good boys, but not very adventurous," Stan told us. "So, let's talk about this thing."

Dave started in. "It seems that I am still sort of coordinating this — thing, as Mr. Brody called it. Jim has been by to compare notes and so has Chief Cotton."

"The big fellow, too," Brody reminded him.

"Right, Bob Redding, but that was only to check on me. I think he has appointed himself my bodyguard. Anyway, it wouldn't be a good idea for us to all be here at once and raise suspicions. It wouldn't take much to get one or another of us suspended for not following orders. I've been getting news from both Jim and Mr. Brody, here. Stan seems to hear quite a bit of what is going on."

186

"I know a lot of people who know a lot of people," said Mr. Brody.

"The big news is that the DA is finally going to move to indict Bill."

"The evidence was too weak before," was Stan's opinion. "Not that it's much stronger now."

"They have found a woman whom they claim the chief was paying off. A Harmony Bozeman." He shook his head. "Millie recognized the name. She was on the force years ago and made a harassment claim against the department and the chief. Nothing came of it."

Stan added to this. "I haven't heard one thing that indicates they actually have her available as a witness."

"Anyway," continued Dave Blake, "it is likely to happen this week or maybe next. The grand jury, that is. When and if the indictment will come, who knows?"

"And there is one other thing," he continued. "It seems there is someone on the inside for us. Bill spilled who his original informant was. Sally Stuart."

Unexpected. "Then maybe the law firm is involved somehow? Um, Carver and Whomever?"

"It seems possible. But I can't imagine why."

I shrugged. "We don't know why Bill was framed in the first place. Until we learn that, nothing will make sense." I stopped myself. "Until *you* learn that. I'm no investigator!"

And I intended to keep it that way. I rose. "I should be on my way, Stan. Thanks for the hospitality. And for keeping an eye on this guy." I nodded toward Dave.

My standing up was apparently a signal for Michelle and Charlie, because both came out onto the porch. A few seconds later, pretty much everyone else started coming out too.

"I'm going to hang here with John," the girl told us. "He'll bring me home later."

That was neither new nor unexpected to either Michelle or myself. "Sure, Charlie," her mom murmured, and turned to me. "Is it time to hit the road?"

"Yeah. Let's go."

John's parents followed us out to the van. "It's not like we don't know what those two are up to," spoke Stan. "We don't exactly approve but we know what it's like to be young."

"And we would not object if they wanted to get married," added Adele.

Michelle was taken aback. Me, not so much. "They're much too young," she objected.

"We were younger when we got hitched," Stan said, turning his eyes fondly on his wife. "I'm all in favor of marriage."

"Me too," I announced. "Ready to go?"

Chapter 42

Lo and behold, the surf had arisen. Therefor, I was not around to send Michelle off to her new job. I am sure she understood and did okay and I did kiss her goodbye before heading out the door.

It was a shifting easterly swell, nothing special, but we had gone without for too long. Too bad Rick had work. His new board was ready to be ridden. But then, it wouldn't hurt to let the glass job cure a little longer, get a little stronger before it was taken out in the waves.

I would have to remind him that he owed money on it, too, even if I was only charging for materials. It was the pier this morning, as usual. Maybe I should change things up more frequently, ride other places.

A slight haze obscured the edges of my world. A faint smell of smoke, maybe? I knew it had been a dry Winter and was heading into a dry Spring. Florida had been in drought conditions for some time and there were forest fires popping up inland. That wasn't uncommon during these months but this year was worse.

I shared the waves with a handful of other surfers for a couple hours before heading in. I hadn't really needed that much rubber this morning. Lighter wetsuit from here out. No sign of anyone I knew as I rinsed off under the cold beach-side shower. No bicycle cops. Nobody.

Go on home, Ted. I didn't really want to for some reason. I felt restless.

But I drove home and showered and put my board away. Charlie looked up as I dripped my way into the kitchen. "Hey, Shaper." She turned her attention back to the books on the table. Class tonight.

SHAPER

Past Ten. I need to go up front and unlock the shop. Nothing on the answering machine, I noted, as I passed by the desk and went to open the front door. Mondays were always dead.

Maybe I should get back to fixing the pipes, getting Michelle her shower stall. Maybe I should. Or get to work on a batch of production boards. Did I have enough blanks on hand? Not sure. I jotted down a note to remind me to check. Or to order more, if needed.

Back into the kitchen. Make tea. Yeah, I could use tea.

"Want any?" I asked Charlie.

"Sure, thanks. I need a break." She closed her textbook, leaving a pencil in it to mark her place, and pushed it aside.

"John has quite a family," I commented, as I waited for the water to heat.

"I like them." She paused, hesitant. "It feels like I'm home when I'm there. Not that this isn't a good home, Shaper, and I really appreciate living here, but it's — well, it's not the same."

Maybe that was something I couldn't give her. "This wasn't a home at all until you and your mom moved in. Just the back of a surf shop." I turned to the kettle, rattling on the stove top. "That's almost to the boil. I'd better pour."

"Oh! Oh, I forgot to tell you. Patty called. I told her there was an epic swell and you were riding the wild surf!" She frowned. "Then she said you were just a ho-dad but I don't know what that means. For a moment I thought she meant I was a ho!"

I think Charlie knew better but I let her have her joke. "A ho-dad is someone who poses as a surfer," I told her. "All look and no moves."

Charlie snickered. "A lot of them come in here, don't they?"

"If they didn't, I'd go out of business. I'll give that a couple minutes more to steep." Sitting down across from the girl, I asked, "So what else did Patty say, besides insulting me?"

"She's coming back this weekend. Rented an apartment but she plans to look for a place to buy."

I wasn't sure how I should feel about that. Not that it would make any difference — Patty Singer was moving to Cully Beach and that was that.

"Hey, she says the next weekend is Pat's birthday and she plans to drive over to Ruby to visit him."

"Yeah, Saint Patrick's Day. That's why his parents gave him that name."

"Do you think maybe I could go? She invited me."

"Up to your mom. You know that."

"Yeah." Of course she did. I would never object, nor had I any right to.

We sipped tea for a while and Charlie turned her attention back to her studies. I sat where I could keep an eye on the shop and front door and eventually went up when a customer wandered in. And back out. But I could go over things, inventory or whatever. I almost wished a salesman would drop in.

How did Michelle like her new job? I wondered. I thought I hated it and wished she were here. It was edging toward noon when I heard voices in the kitchen.

Jan. She must have come straight home from her morning classes. She looked up as I entered the room.

"You didn't tell him, did you?" she asked Charlie.

Her friend shook her head. "Huh-uh."

"Is something wrong, Jan?" I asked. She looked tired, but maybe worrying about Dave did that.

"That depends on how you look at things, Shaper," she replied. "Dave broke up with me." There was a catch, as if she were just holding the line against crying.

"Aw, *man*." I couldn't think of anything more profound. It was probably what her dad would have said.

"I know it was to protect me. But maybe it was just as well. Could you see us together in the long term?"

I had to sit down at the table with the two. "Honestly, Jan? I thought you were about the best couple I had ever seen." I glanced at Charlie, who, believe it or not, was a bit misty around the eyes. "But maybe he was right. I can't say."

"I think he's the worst kind of chicken-shit coward," proclaimed Charlie, no longer able to contain herself. "He's running away!"

And maybe that was true, too.

Chapter 43

"I told Mrs. Boone that Patty was coming back," said Michelle, kicking off her shoes. She had gotten into the habit, already, of referring to Doris as Mrs. Boone. The woman was her boss, after all. "She wants us to get together at her place."

She looked up at me, while massaging her instep. "I think she wants an opportunity to talk about the zoning thing with you. Damn, I hate heels!"

"Why wear 'em?" Michelle was already fairly tall. She didn't need extra inches.

"Because," she answered. "Go fetch me wine, and stop asking stupid questions."

"*All* shoes are the invention of the devil," I told her. "Red or white?"

"Yes!"

I scurried off to do her bidding. I'd better get that indoor shower installed soon if evenings were going to be like this from now on. And this had only been Michelle's third day at the bank.

Exactly what she did there, I wasn't sure. I did know it wouldn't interest me much. I like work with physical results. Making things. I could almost sympathize with the developers' plans for across the street. If I were them, I would want to see my building go up.

But I suspected that all the Burkhardt company really cared about was profits. I carried a bottle of zinfandel into the house, lighter stuff, not old-growth. That should go down well.

"This job entails more driving around than I had expected," Michelle told me as she sipped her wine. "I'm almost like a real estate salesman, except without any hope of commission."

"You would have to be licensed for that." I knew how that worked. Michelle could only handle property as an employee of the bank.

"I'm spending time at city hall, too, looking up records." She sighed. Her sip was more akin to a gulp this time. "And tomorrow, I'll have to go over to Scott City and do the same thing at the county courthouse."

"Aren't they doing that sort of thing with computers, now?" I'd read that. One of these days, we would probably need to buy a computer, though I wasn't quite sure why.

"That's coming," Michelle agreed. "Not to Cully Beach yet."

"Speaking of the county courthouse, the proceedings against Bill Cotton started today," I told her.

"That sucks."

Nothing to say to that. I nodded in agreement.

"I'm going to okay Charlie's jaunt over to, um, Ruby. That's an odd name for a town." Charlie was off at the Wednesday GED class at the moment.

"Named for the river that flows through town. But I don't know why they gave the river the name." Neither did the folks who lived there, I had discovered.

"Maybe it's red."

"Nah. I've seen the Ruby River. It looks like any other Florida river, pretty much."

"All I've seen are Pat's paintings of it. Fill me again, won't ya?"

"Sure." I had barely finished half my glassful. That glassful would be my limit.

Michelle took another sip before asking, "So what have you been up to all day?"

"Building boards this afternoon. Marty Guzman has been watching me. Even when Charlie gets bored and wanders off."

"Sending these ones off to other shops, right?" She didn't wait for an answer. "You don't like doing that, I know."

"It helps pay the bills. I might end up ahead if I just closed this place down and only shaped for other shops."

"But you would be miserable. That is one thing I know, Ted. This shop means everything to you."

"It used to. Maybe not so much now."

Chapter 44

Bill might have been officially arrested and charged now, but there was not a judge in the county who would have put him in jail. He had remained free on his own recognizance.

And I wasn't surprised that he remained so after indictment. The grand jury had delivered for DA Harbin on Thursday afternoon, despite the somewhat sketchy evidence, despite no testimony other than a written deposition from the woman he supposedly had paid off.

Trial would be a while yet. But if whoever framed the chief wanted him out of the way, this was just as good as having him in jail.

Nothing I could do about it — nothing but wait and hope Cotton's friends were making progress with their investigations. The broken Jan-David connection was kind of keeping me out of the loop there, but somebody would talk to me eventually.

It was Saturday morning when someone from Warner's realty office came and replaced the sign next door with a 'sold.' So, I — we — had held off too long. Maybe I was a little relieved that I no longer had that expensive decision to make. I'm not sure I ever would have.

Michelle came to stand by me at the window. "Do you think Patty bought it?"

It was possible. "Don't know," was all I was willing to say. "No one applied for a loan at your bank, I would guess."

"I might not have heard," she admitted. "But Patty is banking there and they know we are acquainted." Her voice trailed off a little. No, probably not Patty, then.

"Too bad Charlie is off. If it was Guzman, she would certainly know about it." Charlie, not surprisingly, was somewhere with John. Apparently, her misgivings about their relationship had evaporated. But he still wasn't staying the night, even if his folks might have turned a blind eye to it.

And even if his folks would not have objected, I definitely did not expect him to propose!

Anyway, it was Al Guzman. Within the hour, a bright yellow Mustang, vintage sometime in the Sixties, pulled in and the man himself stepped out of it, going to the front door with a key. He opened it, nodded, and locked it back up. The process was repeated at the side door, the one in the carport that faced my shop.

"That must be what he drives when he isn't carting surfboards around," surmised Michelle.

"He seems to like old cars," I replied.

She nodded. "I wouldn't be surprised if he likes to work on them too."

Yeah, probably. "We should go out and welcome him to the neighborhood."

"He's coming over here."

The front door stood open, this being business hours. Indeed, a half-dozen potential customers were roaming the shop. Alvaro came in, stopped, and surveyed the place. It probably seemed pretty small to him.

"Hi Michelle! Ted! You have guessed I am your new neighbor, I think."

"We suspected something of the sort," I told him.

"We have not closed but I was told I can move some things in. I will have to wait to move Marty and myself!"

His brief pause was apparently for dramatic effect, as he didn't wait for a reply. "I heard that Miss Singer was coming back and thought I should make an offer before she arrived." I had no doubt he had heard that from Charlie. Or from Marty who would have heard it from Charlie. "I could put down plenty of cash, which helped my cause!"

"Well, we're happy to have you moving in," Michelle told him.

Yeah, we could have done worse. Assuming Al was no more than a bit annoying. "The last people over there," I told him, nodding in the direction of his new home, "tried to operate a business out of it. The ones before them, too, for that matter. You have any plans, Al?" I didn't want to be surprised.

"Ah, maybe, Ted." I had not seen the man reticent about anything before. "I like to fool around with fishing tackle and I might do some repairs or something of that sort."

That sounded pretty good to me. "But I am retired," continued Al, "and not inclined to work very hard. Except," he stated, "when it comes to Marty."

"As long as you don't stock surfboards," stated Michelle.

"Or sell smelly bait," I added.

"Nothing smelly," he agreed. "I have to live here too!" Al headed for the door. "I'll be back later with a wagon full of boxes." With that he headed out.

We stood on the front step and watched him back out and head north. "Jan won't have the only muscle car in the neighborhood now," I murmured.

But Michelle was looking southward now. "I think we should make an offer on that place," she said.

I agreed.

Chapter 45

I am sure I mentioned hating Daylight Saving Time. It messed me up on Sunday morning, with me getting out and checking the surf at altogether the wrong time. Or the right time, except the clocks were wrong. Whatever. I would get acclimated eventually. Until Autumn when my routine would be sabotaged again.

At any rate, the waves were only ankle-high so I headed back. Patty would supposedly roll in sometime today, maybe as soon as noontime if she took off early. We were certain to see her, whenever it might be.

Whenever turned out to be late afternoon. "I stopped and got a room and cleaned up some before coming over here," she announced. "So who bought the house?"

"Alvaro Guzman," Michelle told her. "Marty's father."

"Oh, the surfer girl, right? My, it is still so light out. You won't have an excuse to close early anymore, Ted."

"That won't stop him," said Michelle. "Where are you staying? And come on back to the kitchen where we can sit."

"I'm at the little motel down the street, the one where Pat and Betty stayed. Just until I can get into the apartment." Where the apartment might be, I didn't hear as they disappeared through the door and there were customers in the shop who needed my attention.

Half an hour later it actually was closing time so I shut the door and made my way to the back. There was wine on the table; Michelle, of course, had her own key to the fridge and, to make it all the easier, my workshop was standing open. "Hey, we looked at

Patty's board while we were out there," Michelle told me. "She wants to test drive it before buying."

"I knew I should have asked for a deposit." I plopped down in the empty chair. There were supposed to be four of those, but I kept one of them up in the shop. Handy for changing light bulbs.

"It looks fine, Shaper," said Ms. Singer. "Can I leave it here for now?"

"As long as you want. You said you're getting an apartment?"

"A condo. It will be available in a couple days when the owners head north. I'm going to take it by the month until I decide on something else." She giggled. Or maybe it was a snicker. Not sure. "Or if I procrastinate, until they get back in the Fall!"

"Up north of the pier," added Michelle.

"Then you're looking for a place to buy. Too late to be our neighbor." I was *not* going to mention the house on our other side.

"I don't think it would have suited me. I'd rather not be on the highway, but I guess your Mr. Guzman doesn't mind."

"I think being somewhere with surf right across the road for his daughter was what sold him. As long the access over there isn't closed."

"That's part of this zoning thing you're fighting, isn't it? I'll be sure to ask about it on Tuesday."

"Tuesday?" I wasn't certain what that meant.

"When we go to Doris's, dummy," Michelle reminded me.

"Oh, right. Doris." She had told me. "It isn't, um, dressy, is it?"

"Dressy?" laughed Patty. "Who says 'dressy?'"

"Guys who are never dressy," was Michelle's response. "No, you can be casual, Ted. But not flip-flops and board-shorts."

"Awww, Mom, why not?"

"Yeah, why not?" asked Patty.

"Suit yourselves. Just don't stand near me."

Patty sipped some wine. White. What were they drinking? I turned the bottle to see the label. Without my reading glasses, it took me a moment. Chenin blanc? Yeah. I would pour a glass for myself, if I had a glass. They wouldn't appreciate me drinking from the bottle.

"Thanks for letting Charlie travel with me," said Patty.

"If you're willing to put up with her, why should I object?"

Sounded reasonable. I got up to find myself that glass. "Ruby is a whole other world," I informed her.

"I want to see what its attraction is for Pat. Solitude? The scenery? A mistress he has tucked away?" She grinned. "Also I hear the fishing is good so I'm taking a rod."

"Charlie and I came very close to heading there in December." Michelle spoke quite soberly. "When — when our lives here fell apart." Then a touch of mockery entered her voice and a smile touched her lips. "This kindly gentleman took us in."

"Only so you could work for me. I made that clear at the time."

"Yes, Ted, you let me save face when my pride was driving me away from — from here. And from you."

"And I was being just as unbending. It's a miracle we aren't hundreds of miles apart right now."

Patty looked from the one of us to the other. "I've never heard

202

this part of the story," she mused. "No need to fill me in though. I have a whole weekend to pump Charlie for intel."

"I can't believe she's willing to part from John for that long."

I agreed. "Yes, incredible, isn't it?"

Patty laughed, and then told us, "I've been parted from my stuff too long. I do need to find a storage place and have it moved here!"

Chapter 46

"This must be it," I announced, pulling up to the curb.

Patty gazed out the window at the home of Doris and Don Boone. "Not a bad place. Maybe I should look for a house in this neighborhood."

"Some of them are on canals," Michelle told her. "They have access to the river."

"Oh, then I would have to buy a boat." I think Patty rather liked that idea.

The Boones' house was one of those canal-front properties. I had wandered around the subdivision a bit before locating it, as the roads in this neighborhood wound rather than being laid out in a grid.

Patty slid open the van door and stepped out. "Oh, I see they have a dock. And a boat."

The house itself was a nondescript ranch. It could have been built anytime in the last thirty years or so. Doris and Don lived in an older development not far north of the bridge, on the east side of the river. Originally laid out in the Sixties, I understood.

Doris came out to greet us. "Come on around to the patio," she said. "Everyone's there. Welcome to Cully Beach, Patty!"

Everyone meant her husband and attorney Howard Deland and a woman I assumed to be his date. An assumption that proved correct. Chances are I won't mention her again.

"No kids," whispered Patty. I think she was disappointed. I was, too. Hate to have to spend time with the adults!

"There will be some other folks along later," said Doris. "Wayne said he might show. Wayne Davis." He was a councilman. I knew that and that he tended to side with Doris on the issues. "Want a drink? Don is mixing."

I had not had a mixed drink nor hard liquor in, well, decades. "I'd prefer a beer," Patty told her.

"Or wine," added Michelle.

"Okay, we have plenty of both. How 'bout you, Ted?"

"I'm with the girls. Wine or beer is fine." Not much, though. I needed to designate myself the designated driver.

"Girls?" asked Patty. "You know that comes off as a tad sexist."

"Okay, sorry. I'm with the old ladies." I hurried off to say 'hi' to Don before they retaliated.

Other visitors filtered in over the next half-hour or so, some of whom I knew, some pretty much strangers. I didn't go out of my way to meet the latter or learn names. Didn't care; in fact, I kind of wandered over to the canal and spent time looking out across the dark water. Lights shimmered up and down the channel, in houses, on docks.

I knew places like this. My father had built plenty enough houses in them for people like the Boones. We never lived in one ourselves, and never wanted to. Mom and Dad needed their elbow space.

"There he is," came Doris's voice. "Might have known he would be hiding." The small woman beside her looked familiar. Oh, of course, she was my own district's representative on the city council. Vicky Ward, one of us south-enders that the rest of Cully Beach tried to ignore.

"Come on up," Doris told me. "We have things to discuss."

"Not street lights, I hope," quipped Vicky. She knew well that I kept complaining about those.

A group was seated on the patio, occupying plastic chairs. Not everyone there tonight had come for politics, of course, and socializing continued all around us.

Doris began, addressing me. "We have your young friends to thank for the hearing not being moved up. There was way more publicity about this than they expected."

"Yay, Charlie," came from Patty.

"We only won a little skirmish, there. This whole thing is a skirmish, maybe, with the true battle to come."

"Burkhardt wants their five stories, certainly," said Deland, "but their ultimate goal is more ambitious."

"So it seems," Doris agreed. "The hearing will be on the usual fourth Wednesday. That's the Twenty-eighth, One in the afternoon. We need to get as many people there as we can."

There were murmurs of agreement. I would try to be there, certainly, but unlikely to say anything.

She continued. "Their law firm is working on this, but they know better than to send in a lawyer to present their argument. Donna Burkhardt herself intends to do that."

"We can be sure *Carver, Carver, and McGee* will prep her thoroughly," remarked Howard Deland.

That name again. The firm where Sally Stuart worked, that might be mixed up in Bill's case. I would mention this to someone, when I got the chance, Dave or Jim.

"Wayne, do you want to take it from here?" asked Mrs. Boone.

"My pleasure, Miss Doris," said Councilman Wayne Davis. "The variance is not the big thing here. This fight is going to shift to the City Council soon, with higher stakes." The old gentleman let his gaze go from one face to another. "The proposed street closure would just be the first step toward expanding the *Sand Castles* south."

"But that is city land!" objected Vicky. "What do you know, Wayne?"

"There is going to be a push to sell it to Burkhardt, who also intend to buy the property south of it." That would be the aban-doned filling station. Maybe the older two-story condo beyond that, too? "Bernie is all for it, and probably Lana. No telling where Rouse stands."

"And there would go our park," I commented.

Vicky Ward nodded. "I'm glad you know what it going on, Mr. Davis. I just don't know enough insiders." Vicky was something of a political novice. Davis had been in and out of city politics for forty years or more.

"So that is something we need to be ready for in the future," announced Howard. "But right now, we focus on the hearing, okay?"

"As always, some board members are predisposed in one direc-tion or the other. I would not suspect any of ever being corrupt but they are capable of being pressured."

"Who appoints them?" asked Patty. A sensible question, to which I knew the answer.

"City Council, right?"

"Yeppers," replied Doris, "from names recommended by the Community Development Department, for the most part. Not that there is a big pool of applicants for the duty."

"Cantankerous retirees," I commented.

"Some of them," she admitted.

"It's still two weeks," Howard Deland told us. "We'll be ready and we'll be organized. And remember, all board decisions are supposed to be final but they can be appealed to the Circuit Court within thirty days. Just in case it doesn't go our way."

So we could at least slow them down. Or, if there was something underhand going on, evidence might be found and presented.

"So that is that," stated Doris, rising. "Plenty of food and drink, folks, so dig in and enjoy yourselves. The night is young, even if we aren't!"

Chapter 47

"We have waves," I informed Charlie. "Decent little northerly swell." I had pretty much expected it, having looked at weather patterns for so many years.

"Patty can try out her new board," she said. "Should we call her?"

"She can see the beach." Maybe not from her apartment, but she was certainly close enough to check it out. "If she stops by, her board is in the workshop."

"But no way to carry it." Charlie giggled. "Unless she stuck it in the passenger seat."

Yeah, why hadn't I even thought of that? A Miata was not a surfer's vehicle.

"She needs to buy a pickup. When are you guys taking off?" I asked. "Tomorrow?"

"Yep. Pat reserved us a room for Friday and Saturday night."

I nodded, as I poured myself a cup of coffee. Maybe I should fill my travel cup and take off right now. No, no hurry. It was still mighty dark out, what with the time change.

A couple muffins later, I was loading my own board into the truck and heading off. With the new schedule, it worked better to park Michelle's van ahead of my truck.

I turned south, down toward Jumento. It was unlikely to be better than the pier but why not? Change things up, Ted. Cully Beach petered out pretty quickly this direction, in part because the strip of land between ocean and river grew increasingly narrower.

To my left, unlimited beach access, though one really shouldn't go hiking across the fragile dunes. To my right, wetlands. Ahead, I saw the Jumento Inlet bridge rising. Some specks in the water on both sides.

Hmm, south side. There was a wedging peak working off the north jetty, but the angle of the swell wasn't ideal for that today. Maybe a half-dozen guys out here. I could handle that.

Most were probably from Vasco, or even Ormond. Ah, there was a familiar Cully face, and riding one of my boards. That was good to see.

Nice sunny morning, not too cold. A couple hours, mostly on the less-favored, mushier lefts, then back to duty. Michelle would have long since headed off to her own duty.

Charlie was gone too. I had the place to myself.

Just before Ten, I went up front to open the shop. The phone rang almost immediately.

It was Patty and she started right in. "Hey, I figured you would be there by now. I stopped by but you were surfing and Michelle was about to leave and was going to drop Charlie off somewhere."

"Sorry I wasn't here. Did you want your board?"

"Nah, I'm busy looking at houses and storage units and generally taking care of business today. You'll see me tomorrow when I pick Charlie up for our cross-state jaunt."

"Unless there is surf again," I warned her. I much doubted it.

"Yes, you have your priorities, Ted. I'm surprised you never competed like your little neighbor-to-be. Charlie told me she is off to another contest this weekend."

"Aw, you know I was never that good."

"But steady. And fearless in the big stuff."

"Some people would say I was just foolhardy. Or crazy."

"Oh, we knew about the crazy part, Ted. I won't lie."

That made me laugh. No, Patty wouldn't sugar-coat my problems. Past problems. "You could have headed for the Islands," she continued.

"But I didn't. I'm in the right place for me."

"I hope so. See you tomorrow morning."

I said goodbye. And I hoped Patty was now in the right place for her.

My slow Thursday morning was slowing down further when Trejo and Johnson, bicycle cops, pedaled up to my door.

Both came in. I gave Johnson a questioning look.

"Jay's okay," Jim told me. "He's with us now."

The younger police officer looked a bit embarrassed about it all. "Man, I didn't want to take a chance of messing up my career. We were ordered to keep out of this."

"So what changed?"

"Well, Deputy Chief Saunders asked me to look into whether some of the force was flouting that and report on what was up. I'm sure he thinks Jim is in on it or he wouldn't have come to me. Knows about Blake, of course, but doesn't have proof."

"That is *Acting* Deputy Chief. Saunders is reporting directly to the mayor," added Jim. "We all know that."

"And what she hears goes to the DA. They're all one club. It's one thing to try to not get involved and another to be a spy. I won't do that." Jay's voice had grown more resolute.

"But you said you would?" I asked. I could see where he was headed.

"Yeah. Double-agent Johnson, at your service."

As long as he wasn't truly Triple-agent Johnson. I was not inclined to suddenly give him my full trust.

Jim Trejo had little news for me, but we jawed about the case and Chief Cotton for a few minutes. Not long — these guys were on duty, after all. Then I had to tell him what I heard about the Burkhardt company and their lawyers.

"That law firm keeps popping up, doesn't it? I think we need to sit down with Sally Stuart and try to get to the bottom of this. All of us." I wished he didn't look at me when he said that. "I'll talk to Dave about it. He's going to move back into his apartment this weekend."

"Even though everyone thinks it's a stupid idea," said Jay.

Maybe. But his assailants had made their point. Why go after him again?

"Let's loop down a block and head back north," suggested Jim, and the two headed their mountain bikes down the highway. The rest of the day disappeared, leaving no trace, as most days tend to do.

Michelle and I were both in bed, both reading, when we heard Charlie come in. Hushed voices — John was with her. That was not unexpected.

"John-boy is going to have to miss his girl the next couple nights," I remarked. "Maybe the next three."

"It will be good for him," yawned Michelle. "I'm at the end of a chapter. Ready for lights out?"

"Yeah. Can't keep my eyes open. She and Patty took to each other awful quickly." I reached for the lamp on my side.

"She's stealing Charlie right away from that boy." She sighed and switched off her light. "I sometimes fear she is going to steal both of you."

Chapter 48

"Don't you ever clean this mug?" Michelle held up the cup I had rinsed and left to drain.

I looked up from the Sunday paper. "It is rather stained, isn't it? That's from the tea. Been drinking more of it lately."

"Good excuse. Well, I'm not washing it, Mr. Carrol."

I did pretty much all the cleaning and dish-washing and such anyway. "Can I fix you anything?" I asked. "Pancakes? French toast?"

She poured herself of bowl of Cheerios without answering. Well, not really Cheerios but a generic equivalent. I was also doing the grocery shopping again, now that Michelle now longer worked at the *Winn-Dixie*. "Anything interesting in there?" she asked.

"An opinion piece by our mayor, railing against public corruption. She doesn't mention Chief Cotton by name but it's pretty obvious whom she means."

"She really believes Bill is guilty?" Michelle sat down and began gobbling her little circles. Not even a cup of coffee first — must be mighty hungry this morning.

"She wants to believe it, I am sure. Parish has wanted him out of office all along." He represented the old guard to her, those who stood in the way of her ideal Cully Beach.

"The paper as a whole isn't very sympathetic toward Bill," I continued. "They are pretty much prejudging him."

I folded *The Courier* and put it down. Yes, it just comes natural for me not to leave it messy. "Want to do anything before I have to open the shop? We have a couple hours." Well, an hour and a half, anyway.

"Just spend time with you, Ted. I've been missing that lately."

"Me, too," I readily admitted. "You must be missing sleep, also." She hadn't appeared until after I got home from church.

"It's just the new routine. The time change, too."

"Yeah." I heard a car door slam. "That couldn't be Charlie back already, could it?" It was only a matter of leaning back and looking out the window to find out. "Oh, the Guzmans."

"I wonder if Marty has a new trophy." Al had shown us the boxes full of them, among the belongings he was moving into the house.

"We could go ask her."

"Let's wait until her father stops carrying boxes in. We would have to help him."

I had to laugh. It sounded more like something I would say than Michelle. "Good enough. I'll make us some coffee while we wait until it's safe."

"Make it the good stuff. The coffee at work is pretty miserable."

The first thing Marty said when we sauntered out fifteen minutes later was, "Is Charlie is back yet?"

"We don't expect her till evening," I informed the girl. "How did yesterday go? You would be competing in a new district, wouldn't you?"

"I'm in a new district *and* a new division."

I didn't follow the competitive scene but I couldn't help picking up a little knowledge of its workings. "Junior Women, right?"

"And she took a second," said Al, returning to the now-empty station wagon. "That is good."

"But not as good as first," stated Marty.

215

"Remember that world titles have been won with a string of second-place finishes," I told her. "Consistency counts for a lot."

"Very true," agreed Mr. Guzman.

"But consistently finishing first would be better!" the girl declared, laughing. Then she asked, "Shaper, do you think I could leave my boards at your shop until we move in? It's a hassle keeping them at the apartment."

"Sure." Bicyclists coming up the road. Yeah, the Cully Beach bike patrol. I waved to them as they passed by — Jay and some other guy. Must be new.

Of course. Another rider was necessary since Dave was out of commission. He had been sort of the alternate, filling in when needed.

Al looked at what had caught my attention. "Ah, the bicycle police. Jim is a good man." He shook his head. "It is too bad that they had a crooked chief."

"That is unproven and I do not believe it at all," Michelle objected.

"Nor do I," I stated, perhaps a little too vehemently.

Guzman eyes went from one of us to the other, before he smiled and said, "Then I will will not believe it either. Come, Martina, we need to go home and get cleaned up for mass." I wondered if that would be the evening Spanish service. I wasn't even sure if Marty could speak the language.

Chapter 49

"We stayed at a little motel called the *Hilltop Lodge*," said Charlie, sprawling in a kitchen chair. "Mr. Edwards had made reservations for us."

Patty, who looked even more exhausted, offered, "The owner is a fishing guide. I might just go back someday and charter his boat." She looked over to where I was standing at the stove, preparing a late meal for us. "But I definitely wouldn't want to stay in Ruby for very long!"

Charlie took up the narrative again. "The boy there, the owners' son, really plays guitar great! He says he's going to play at the Florida Folk Festival, whenever that is. Martin. That's his name."

"Pat and Betty go to that event, too. White Springs is pretty close to Ruby, isn't it?"

"Reasonably," I said. "An hour and some away. The festival is on Memorial Day weekend." About two months from now. Man, time was moving.

"They invited us a while back," added Michelle. "Now that I don't have to run a motel, maybe we could manage it." But I still had the shop to consider, and that would be a busy holiday.

"We visited the Edwards's house and Pat's studio. I messed a little with his weights." Charlie ostentatiously flexed her bicep. "If I'm gonna be a cop, maybe I should start working out."

"You could help me dig up the drain pipes," I told her. "That would build some muscles."

"That's no fun, Ted," admonished Patty. "Is that chow ready?"

I spooned up a 'bow-tie' and nibbled it. Yeah, that was done. "Coming up." Drain the pasta, drain the veggies. Toss with butter and olive oil, some Romano and Parmesan, herbs, garlic. To the table with it.

I grabbed the kitchen stool, as the three women occupied the three chairs. Where was the pepper grinder?

"This is basic Ted cooking," explained Michelle. "I like it from time to time but he would be willing to live on it."

"Simple and nutritious. Like Ted himself," said Patty.

"Bland and healthful, Mom calls it," chimed in Charlie.

"And I got that description from Kay."

"It is the impression he gives," stated Patty, without elaboration. "I didn't have the opportunity to mention it before leaving town, but I met Donna Burkhardt, quite by accident. Donna *Todd*-Burkhardt, I should say."

"If the accident was you hitting her with your car, I'm glad it happened."

"No such luck, Ted! I was checking out the golf community across the river. Yeah, I know I said I was leaving that lifestyle behind and I will, but I looked at some houses and the country club. Just to see what was there, you know?"

"We'll forgive you. Don't let it happen again."

"I'll try to behave. It turns out she is staying at the hotel there and we were introduced. Maybe because I hinted that I might be interested in a beachfront condo." Patty smirked in a rather self-satisfied manner.

"I didn't know what to expect. Maybe the solid businesswoman in a conservative suit or maybe some cliché of a gold-digger-done-well, with careful coiffure and manicure." I nodded. I knew just what she meant. I could visualize those women myself. "But instead, it was more like looking in a mirror!

"I ended up playing a round with her. With borrowed clubs — those were among the things I sold when I left Atlanta. I will tell you that she is *very* competitive!"

"Are you competitive?" Charlie suddenly asked.

"Yes, I'm afraid so. I might have been happy painting these past thirty years if I wasn't."

That seemed to satisfy the girl, so Patty continued. "She complained about her work here being obstructed. Especially," she said, looking directly at Charlie, "by certain surfer kids who were being a nuisance."

"Wow, I'm a nuisance!" crowed Charlie.

"Like a cockroach," said her mother. "Make sure someone doesn't step on you."

"I would not put it past Ms. Burkhardt," Patty said. "Not at all."

Chapter 50

"She knew about Sally Stuart," said Dave. "Jan was helping me with my notes up until — until the incident." He was not going to say 'breakup,' was he? Easier to refer to the attack on himself.

Dave was pretty well recuperated and back in his own apartment, even if he had been advised otherwise, but not reinstated to service yet. "I expect to pass my physical next week and be back in uniform," he had told me.

We were not in that apartment. That would not be wise, even if it was unlikely Dave was being watched. Dave Blake faced me across a checkered tablecloth in *Mama Toni's*, where he devoured a barbecue sandwich while I nibbled on bread sticks. For me to go anywhere for lunch was pretty unusual, but the man had called and asked, and Charlie was available to sit in the shop.

"And she will only talk to Jan now? That is what you are telling me?"

"So it seems. Oh, I understand why. Stuart doesn't want to be seen with anyone connected to the police. She's paranoid and I don't blame her after what happened to me!"

He wiped some sauce from his chin. "And she will talk to you, apparently. You know her from some time back, right?"

"Uh-huh. Sally used to work for a friend." Dave might or might not know about our one-and-only pretend date. Jan could certainly have told him.

"And Jan knows her, um, live-in girlfriend from the college. She teaches English, I think." I had no idea. "All I can tell you is that you have been once again drafted as the go-between. It's a lot to ask, Ted, I realize that."

"I'm willing," I told him. "But if you hadn't split with Jan, it might not have been necessary."

"That was to keep her out of all this. Here she is, jumping right back into the middle of it!" Chagrin, frustration — they were there, even if Dave tended to keep a tight lid on himself.

"That shouldn't surprise you," was all I had to say.

Nothing I could do about any of this, I told myself as I drove home. My mind was more on the zoning hearing in a week. I still couldn't see any link between that and Chief Cotton's predicament but maybe Sally Stuart could shed some light on all of that.

Charlie ambushed me at the door. "Hey, Shaper, what's a good hair color for Spring? I thought I'd change it for the official start of the season."

"There is no official first day of Spring," I informed her. This was, admittedly, a pet peeve for me. "Starting the season on the equinox is sort of a new-fangled idea. Some of our ancestors would have seen this as the center point of Spring."

"That's being pretty picky, even for you, Shaper. Okay, what color for the middle of Spring? I'm tired of black." I knew the current Elvis-black of her hair to be the result of dye. The girl's natural tone, as far as I could figure, was a dark brown like her mom's hair.

"Well," I began, "you went with that bright red for the Christmas season. Maybe a greenish tone now? Oh, or lilac!"

"No, no, nothing too unnatural. I don't want to shock John's parents. Not too much, anyway," she giggled.

"Then be a blond, but not that bleached white you were before.

You know, if you got out in the sun more, your hair might end up sun-bleached."

"Maybe I could fake that. I may stop and get some dye on the way to class."

I'd best not comment.

"I went around the house next door," she said, as we stepped into the shop. "I'd like to see the inside sometime. You are planning to buy it, aren't you?"

"We intend to make an offer."

"If John and I got married, we could live there."

What was she getting at? Going the long way around, whatever it was. "I suppose so."

"Well, we probably won't. Not anytime soon. Never maybe. I was just thinking about it."

"His parents seem to think you're mighty fine marriage material, miss."

She burst into laughter. "Don't I know it?" Then she added, "But John needs to get his degree first. Maybe I do, too."

"Still," I said, "if we do purchase the place, it might not be a bad idea to have you listed as a co-owner." I couldn't resist adding, "But you would have to come up with a third of the price."

"No problem, Shaper. Stan Brody would lend it to me!"

Chapter 51

"Sorry to be bothering you like this, Mr. Carrol. We had a complaint and we needed to check it out."

"About my remodeling?"

The inspector walked over to where I was working on the pipes. I had just completed building a wooden form so I could pour a small concrete pad. "This isn't a problem," he said. "Nothing here that even needs a permit. Hooking up a new drain, aren't you?"

"Yes. Moving the washing machine out here."

He nodded. "I'm certainly not going to call the building department on you. The complaint was about the work you do back here. The, um, manufacturing."

'Light industry' had always been permitted here and no one had complained in the past, including city inspectors. Why now? Had Al Guzman called them on me? I couldn't think of anyone else who might be interested in what I did.

"You can see what I do." The door to my shaping room was wide open. The man came in and gave it cursory survey.

"Is there any machinery employed in the business of this, um, surfboard making?"

"Nothing I can't hold in my hands. Power planer, sanders. That's it." He could see them on my bench.

"Okay. What's in the other side of this building?"

"Storage, mostly. I also do my fiberglass work over there."

He sniffed the air and smiled thinly. "I can smell it, but barely. That's allowed here. As long as you store the chemicals safely." He turned to me. "You do, don't you?"

SHAPER

"Certainly." That wasn't any sort of fib. I was careful about that kind of thing to the point of obsessiveness.

"Good enough then." Apparently he didn't feel a need to look at it. "We're not supposed to say who made the complaint and, to be honest, I don't know. I do understand one of our city councilmen brought it to us personally and asked us to come down here." The inspector reconsidered that. "More than asked, I guess."

I couldn't expect him to say which councilman might have made the request. I could, however, figure out that this was petty harass-ment, probably over the zoning thing.

Of course, Al had nothing to do with it. I shouldn't even have thought of him.

By the time my official visitor had departed, it was Ten-ish so I opened the shop. All by myself on this Friday morning. I was, oh, upset some by this. Not really angry. I'm not inclined to get angry. I should tell Doris, maybe, or Vicky Ward.

I had Ward's number, didn't I? She didn't live all that far away, either. One of the nice beachfront houses down south of me.

Later. Customers were already coming in, the beginning of our weekend traffic. That had slowed down from peak tourist season and would continue to do so over the next month, before picking back up as Summer approached. April was pretty much the slowest month here.

But kids — and grown-ups for that matter — bought surfboards year round. I wasn't going to go out of business. I would expand this showroom if we bought that house over there. My eyes went to the tall hedge, not far from my south-facing windows. That was some sort of evergreen, wasn't it?

Podocarpus, maybe. Whatever it was, I would definitely trim it back. Maybe take it out altogether.

Don't get ahead of yourself, Ted. There's no guarantee you could swing the deal. We could swing the deal. I needed to include Michelle. Without her, I really couldn't do it — and probably wouldn't want to.

I wasn't completely sure I *did* want to.

Chapter 52

I recognized Sally, of course. There was no reason for Jan Bell to elbow me when she entered the *Cully Beach Surf Shop*. The slender woman accompanying her must be the girlfriend. The two browsed a minute or so, attempting to appear inconspicuous, I assumed, before coming over to the counter.

"You know Sally," said Jan. "And this is Karrie Goodpaster." The fact that Karrie wore an aloha shirt was a definite point in her favor. She didn't offer to shake but gave me a rather distracted nod of the head, before turning away altogether to gaze around the shop.

"Probably writing a poem in her head," Sally confided in a near-whisper.

Jan had been in on enough of what was going on to know about Sally Stuart and had approached Karrie. So here the pair was on this early Sunday afternoon, Sally having quite firmly insisted that she would meet with me and me only.

"I'm going to go look at the Hawaiian shirts," said Ms. Good-paster, and wandered away.

"She always wears those shirts. Everywhere." I don't think Sally Stuart completely approved.

The first thing I asked Sally was, "Are you certain you want to get involved in this? I mean, it could cost you your job."

"I'm the one who tipped off Chief Cotton in the first place so I might as well see it through. In for a penny, you know?"

Bill's insider information. We already were aware of this. "So I would guess, um, your law firm was in on this."

"Someone there is. Not the senior partners, I'm sure."

"They are all in Daytona, aren't they? That's all I know about them."

"One or other of the girls comes up here on occasion." She stopped. "You don't know what I mean by that. Carver and McGee are the daughters of the firm's founder, George Carver. He doesn't go anywhere. In fact," said Sally, "I've never laid eyes on the man.

"But as I was saying, I don't think they are involved. Certainly not directly. Whether there was implied approval, who can say?"

"Approval of what?" Let's get to it.

"Bribery. Someone in the city government is getting paid off and that goes back to what I first told Chief Cotton. That is why evidence was planted to frame Bill."

"By someone who works for the law firm?"

"I think so. Or maybe for the client that is involved. I don't have any evidence as to who that might be," she confided, "but I have suspicions."

"The Burkhardts," I guessed.

Sally seemed surprised. "You've been thinking about this."

Ms. Goodpaster was holding up one of the good silk shirts to the light. She had taste. I turned my eyes back to Sally.

"I know they have a motive. They want the city property across the street." It would have to be someone on the City Council who was compromised, wouldn't it? No one else could deliver that to them.

"My Aunt Jean knows what is going on. I've told her most of what I told you."

That would be easy enough for her to do. Sally's father would be

Acting Chief Jean Miller Stuart's brother-in-law, right? The Stuarts were an old family around here.

But Jean getting together with the officers involved in this illicit investigation would be more difficult and raise suspicions. Hence, the need for someone like me or Dave to pass info along.

Jan added, "And I have written all this down, with copies of what evidence there is, so you can pass it on to, well, whomever."

We both knew whom she meant but would not say it. To Sally, I said, "You might want to come in the early morning if you need to see me again. One Sunday afternoon shopping here is not remarkable but repeated visits might arouse suspicion."

"Good idea."

"Shaper is almost always up and about by Five," Jan told her. "Be quiet and the jealous girlfriend won't notice." To me, she said, "I'll bring over those notes later."

"Let's hope they lead us somewhere," I told her. "This investigation seems to proceed in sudden jumps."

"Punctuated equilibrium," stated Karrie Goodpaster, who had a couple shirts over her arm. "You have nice stuff here, Carrol"

Being an Art History major — even if all that was years in the past — I knew what she meant by that bit of postmodern jargon. It might even be applicable.

I was glad I had dodged an academic career. "I try to, Miss Goodpaster. You'll be taking those?"

She held them up for her partner. "What do you think, Sals?"

"They look like Hawaiian shirts," was Stuart's reply.

I shook my head. "Not a connoisseur, is she? I pick out all the designs personally."

"I'll have to come back, Shaper — I can call you Shaper, right?" I nodded. "Maybe I need to take up surfing!" She snickered. "And then write bad poems about the experience."

She leaned forward, saying in a theatrical whisper, "I am really good at writing badly!"

"That's better than being bad at writing well," I responded. "Cash or credit?"

Chapter 53

I simply closed the surf shop, even if it was the middle of the day. This was more important.

And Charlie had a right to be here, too. I wouldn't ask her to stay behind. I would just be moral support, of course, I wasn't about to get up and argue anything. The more bodies that showed up at this hearing, the more the board would know we cared about it.

City offices had moved to new buildings up north years ago, before I had arrived in Cully Beach, from their original location just south of the Scott City Road. Only the police station remained down there, and some of the utility services. I knew enough to park at the rec center, a block over, and walk to City Hall.

Al Guzman was at my side, having seen me pull in. "It surprises me," he spoke, as we approached the crowd outside the building, "how few blacks there are in this town."

"I had the same reaction when I moved here," I told him. "There are plenty of black families on the other side of the river. Just not in town." The divide was money. I knew this. The wealthy moved in and forced out the ordinary folk of every color. What was going on today, at this hearing, was a part of that.

"When I was growing up, I knew what I was — Puertorriqueño . We had our own neighborhood and no one confused us with the blacks. Here," he said, "people see me and most think 'black.' I know this is so."

I could only nod in agreement. "There's Charlie," I said. Patty had given her a lift and both were with a group that included Doris Boone. When you are Senior Vice President, you can take the afternoon off occasionally.

Michelle, no doubt, had to remain at work.

I introduced him. "This is Alvaro Guzman, my new neighbor. He's come to help us out. Doris Boone," I said. "Patty Singer." I didn't know any other names.

The courtly Mr. Guzman greeted both, as well as Charlie. "We will win today, will we not?"

"That's the plan, sir," Mrs. Boone told him. "I've been told by some of the board members that there has been pressure to approve this." Her voice remained steady. "But I have hopes. They may be beholden to the council for their positions but they tend to be pretty conservative about changing the rules. And most don't have a stake in growth."

"There's Burkhardt," said Patty. "I'd just as soon she didn't spot me." She kind of slid to the back of the group.

Donna Todd-Burkhardt. She did look someone you would have a drink with at the golf club, didn't she, in her casual slacks and pastel blouse? Certainly not a cut-throat businesswoman. The young fellow with her was assuredly a lawyer.

They headed directly in. It must be close to One and the start of official business.

"Is John coming?" I whispered to Charlie as we went up the steps, toward the glass-enclosed entry.

"No, he needs to be in class, but he's going to pick me up. I saw Jan somewhere. Kay, too."

Seven members, most old or at least old-ish, near equal in gender. Obviously, with seven, they couldn't be exactly equal. There were a couple of other requests first, little things, but they took their time and heard the cases out, listened to any comments from those in attendance. Fortunately, few had anything to say.

I think I would have fallen asleep by now if I were on the board. This very room, with its bland beige walls was slumber inducing.

"I've never seen this many people jammed in here," remarked someone behind me.

Case something-number was announced, Burkhardt Development Group, Inc. requesting a variance, etc. etc. That's when it started to fall apart. Donna Burkhardt was greeted with boos when she stood to present her case. And she did not like that one bit.

Burkhardt began in about 'best use' and 'growth' and what was good for Cully Beach's future, and 'fairness,' and so on. No mention of how it would affect her company financially, of course. If she had hoped to charm the board and the crowd, the plan fell apart almost immediately, as she spoke ever louder and more angrily over the noise of the crowd. There were repeated calls for quiet.

To their credit, the audience never really got out of hand. They were just a bit vocal at times. Someone from the Community Development Department spoke. I couldn't quite figure out which side he was on.

Then the floor was opened to comments, and there were plenty of them, one after another, lines of folks waiting their turn. Almost all spoke against the variance.

As it grew late, people inevitably began to slip out. Not everyone could hang on all afternoon. I hoped that would not hurt our cause. Our cause? I guess it could be called that, yeah.

It was closer to four than three when the board finally voted. The old codgers looked pretty tired of it all. Nay. Nay. Aye. Nay. Nay. Nay. Aye. That was pretty conclusive.

"The request for a variance is denied."

Chapter 54

"Donna was seething. It's a good thing she didn't know which side I was on!"

Patty and I sat at a cast aluminum table in front of *Coastal Coffee*. It had been painted to look like cast iron, but the real thing wouldn't hold up well across the street from the ocean.

"I wouldn't even have approached her," I admitted. "She's kinda scary."

"Oh, someone to commiserate with over that gross miscarriage of justice was just what she needed." She sipped her tea. "It wouldn't hurt for me to remain friendly, huh?"

"No, not at all." Patty knew little of the other part of this affair, the part involving Bill Cotton. Maybe I would let her in sometime. "That won't last if you keep hanging around with me."

"I like hanging around with you Ted. Always did."

For the moment, I was at the proverbial loss for words. Fortunately, Charlie came out and joined us right then, mocha in hand. John should be showing up shortly, to take her to her Wednesday evening class.

"It's light for being so late," remarked Charlie.

"It's the same as ever," I grumbled. "They just fouled up our clocks, like every year."

"Was he always so cranky?" she asked Patty.

"Definitely. He should have had a career as a critic."

We all sat and watched the ocean for a while. Tiny wind-blown waves broke at the fringe of the beach.

"Al is Marty's father, right? The one who bought the house next door to you?" asked Patty.

"He is and he did," I replied.

"Okay. That's what I thought." She turned to me. "Just making sure. And you are considering buying the place on the other side, aren't you?"

"Thinking of it." I was unwilling to admit more.

"Maybe I should take a look at it."

Oh, great.

Charlie gave us a heads-up. "Bike patrol coming."

Patty turned to look. "I like to watch them go by. I'm eager for summer when they only wear the spandex."

"Dirty old lady," I muttered. "Hi, Jay." He pulled up by our table.

Johnson was riding alone. "Hi, Ted. How ya doin' Charlie?" He turned toward the third in our party.

"Patty Singer, this is Officer Jay Johnson."

"Pleased, ma'am." He returned his attention to me. "Blake has been cleared for duty. He's going to be back with us on Monday. And," he went on, "he, um, got us up to speed on everything." Meaning all the things Sally had told me.

"Great." I rose. "I'd best take off. Michelle will be home shortly." I shook Johnson's hand. "Good to see you, Jay."

"I'll hang here with Charlie till her boy comes to get her," said Patty. "Take care."

"Bye, Shaper." I headed toward my truck, parked on the other side of the highway, as Jay peddled on southward. Probably on his last sweep of the area and ready to turn toward the station a few blocks down.

I doubted I had missed many customers, closing the shop on this afternoon. I used to close up for a day and take off, maybe to do business somewhere up or down the coast, maybe just to go surfing. Not so much, more recently. I drove homeward.

Park the truck out front so Michelle can pull into the drive first. There was Al's Mustang parked in his own driveway. The man hurried out to greet me.

"Ted, I saw someone behind your house when I drove up. Two of them I think."

"Kids?"

"No, I wouldn't have been too worried about that. These were men. I could not see that they did anything."

"Well, let's look." We walked around to the back. Windows looked good. Locks were in place on my workshop. Check the shed attached to the back of the house. Oh man, my boards.

Al looked over my shoulder at the bashed surfboards. "The only thing they could get at easily," I said, mostly to myself. It was a good thing I'd kept Patty's board in the glassing room.

"Why?" was all Guzman could ask.

"Retaliation," I answered.

Chapter 55

There had been a message on my answering machine. "Next time it might be you," was all it said.

Did I call the police? Darned right I did. Not that they could do anything but I wanted this to be out there, for anyone and everyone to know about it. That this was in some way tied in with this whole Burkhardt business was certain. The real question was whether it was only venom over the zoning or someone knew I was involved in trying to clear Bill Cotton's name.

Would Donna Burkhardt hire thugs to do something of this sort? I doubted it. But there would be underlings, hoping to please her, to keep things running smoothly. All she would need to do is express her displeasure.

Anyway, Burkhardt had left town. "I would have liked to talk to her about it," said Patty, on hearing the news. "See what she thinks of such goings-on in this town."

The boards? A total loss. So I would build new ones; that wasn't a big deal but I did regret losing the board Charlie had painted on, her first effort, with its portrait of Michelle. That rankled.

Naturally, it upset Charlie too. To make matters worse, the girl thought her activism was the cause of it. "You would never have gotten into this fight if I hadn't given you a push," I told her. "I was no innocent bystander." She may have bought it.

Otherwise, things pretty much settled down. Bill's trial was once again postponed. Seemed the prosecution was having trouble locating their witness. If that kept up, they might not have enough of a case to go through with it.

But Cotton had been kept out of the picture. That might have been the objective of whoever set him up, not a conviction. If Bill were offered a retirement deal again, I had no doubt he would take it this time. He'd had enough.

Or that was the impression I got when I briefly saw him on Saturday morning, at Stan Brody's place. Charlie said I needed to be her taxi service for some reason or another but I think it was because he was there. We didn't have much to discuss.

It was Monday morning when Dave Blake came by, back in uniform. "I'm supposed to be on light duty for a while," he informed me, "so Millie assigned me this follow-up visit. That's the official reason." We both knew why she really chose him.

"The department isn't tying your incident to mine, but I have little doubt it was the same two guys."

"It seems likely," I admitted.

Dave looked at his notes. "So the boards were worth a thousand dollars?"

"Loose estimate. I figured two-hundred for each of the five boards." I couldn't sell them for that much, used, but it would cost way more to replace all five. "It's not like I'm going to be making an insurance claim on them."

"No matter what they were worth, it sucks to feel vulnerable like that. I know from personal experience." A rueful chuckle. Then, more seriously, "You need to keep safe, Ted, you and those around you. Planting those yuccas under your windows was a good idea."

"I was burglarized once when I first moved here," I told him. "That's when I put those in." It was time to get the hibiscus I'd talked about last fall, wasn't it? Kay had bugged me about my meager landscaping. I should go over to Joy and Susan's nursery, and see what they had.

"Unfortunately, your neighbor's description was no better than my own — two white males. But the good news," Officer Blake told me, "is that we were able to get some fingerprints this time. These guys weren't careful — it was just luck that they didn't leave any evidence behind at my apartment."

"You know who they are?"

"Not yet. We'll get them, Ted." He put down the report he had been holding. "Let's talk about Sally Stuart. Can we really trust her? I mean — she does work for the, um, other side."

It was a thought that had occurred to me, too, I had to admit. How could we be sure she was not getting information from us, from her aunt, and reporting back to her bosses?

"For all we know, she might have been the one who blew the whistle on Chief Cotton," Dave continued.

"Why, when she gave him the tip in the first place?"

"They could have found her out and made her an offer. We can't ignore that possibility."

"I don't think you will solve this without her help. You'll never get a look at anything from inside that law office on your own."

"True. Millie needs to make this an official investigation so we can go after evidence."

"Secretly? Could she get away with that?" The prosecutor's office would not approve. That I knew.

"If she had the ear of the right judge. Good thing most of them like Bill." Dave rose from his stool. "We need more proof of all this first."

At the door, he finally seemed to ready to ask, "How is Jan doing?"

"Well. That is something you could have learned on your own, if you were willing." I didn't really approve of their breakup any more than Charlie. Not that it was my business, but — well, you know. They were my friends.

"I stand by what I did. I don't want her in the middle of this."

Good luck stopping her, I said, only to myself.

Chapter 56

"Yes, we have closed," Al Guzman informed us. "Time to move in!"

Charlie was not interested in that, not at the moment. "You have your driver's license?" she asked Marty. The girl had been at the wheel of the Buick.

"Learner's permit. I'll take the test this summer." She glanced sideways at her father. "Maybe."

"If all goes well with school," he announced. "You must have good grades."

"I should be able to get mine back this summer," said Charlie. "But I need to get some good grades too. That has priority and I'll worry about driving later."

"Oh, you'll do fine, kid," I assured her. "You'll pass and get your GED and we'll all go out and celebrate. Shoot, even if you don't pass we'll go out anyway and celebrate Cinco de Mayo."

"Why do, um, gringos celebrate a Mexican holiday?" asked Al. "I have never understood this."

"We need an excuse to party?" I asked him, and shook my head.

"I guess not! Let's get this stuff inside, Marty, before the truck comes with the furniture. We sleep in our new house tonight!"

"Can you keep an eye on the shop for a few minutes, Charlie?" I asked. "I want to finish up here."

"Okay, Shaper. You gonna put in these bushes somewhere?" I had a half-dozen potted Rose of Sharon hibiscus lined up by the driveway, picked up that morning at the *River Road Nursery*.

"Along the front. Not likely to get at them today." I wanted to finish up out back. Rick had helped me slide the washer out of the utility room and it now rested on the new concrete pad outside. No roof over it yet, but that would come. A tarp would do for a few days, or even weeks.

Now I could finally start on the inside shower. As soon as I finished hooking everything up out here.

I had added a padlock to my surfboard shed. Reluctantly. I had always let friends borrow boards from it in the past or stow their own there temporarily. Now I had to start refilling it, an entire new 'quiver' of surfboards. Until I got something built, I could grab a board off the 'used' rack in the shop.

All seemed proper. I turned on the water briefly, both hot and cold. Good. Drain was working too. What was that? Oh, moving van pulling up out front. I threw the tarp over the washer and went to watch the show.

It wasn't a big van; I don't think the Guzmans owned a lot of furniture. They might be done unloading before Michelle got home.

And there was Patty, pulling up in front of my place. "Hi, Al," she called, waving. "I see it showed up." When had the two gotten so friendly?

Patty came and stood next to me, watching for a moment before saying, "It's a nice little house. I think I could live in a place like that." Then she turned to me and confided. "But if I had the money, I'd want a house like your friend Vicky. Right on the beach!"

Vicky was my friend? Barely knew her. "You've been there?"

"Sure. Her husband is really loaded, you know. No wonder she can make politics her hobby."

I didn't know. I didn't even know his name. And I would have to honestly admit I didn't care.

"Didn't you say you wouldn't want to live on this busy road?" I asked her.

"It's not so bad down there, and they have a lot of yard between them and the highway. It's practically at your door!"

"Yeah, that's true. If they widen it to four lanes someday, I won't have a yard at all."

"So have you made an offer on the place next door?"

I suppose I sort of grimaced. "The listed price is kind of high. I'm not sure how much to offer." I looked toward my new neighbor's place. "If Al had bargained a bit it would help my cause. The owners' will think they can get more now."

"Hasn't it been on the market for a long time? I'd go really low. In fact, I will if you don't"

"You don't want to live there." I hoped.

"Maybe for a while, to see how I like it." She smiled wickedly. "Then sell it to you at a profit!"

"I won't have any more money later," I warned her.

"That's not surprising, Ted. But I would be willing to, say, invest if you don't have enough. Seriously, it could be turned into a nice place. A real Florida home in the old style."

"That is true. Before they started building places like that." I nodded toward the Guzmans' house. "Or even mine. But I'm not interested in turning the place. I just want room to expand. For Charlie, especially."

"If she sticks around."

"Yeah. I think she will. She seems committed to college now." I chuckled. "And to John-boy."

"The country boy surfer. He seems like a good kid."

"He is. I'm not sure what kind of place Charlie would be in now without him."

"I can hear you, you know," came from the window behind us. Dang, I'd forgotten they were open on this warmer Spring day.

"We knew all along," lied Patty. "That's why we were making up good things about your boyfriend."

"We don't really like him at all," I added. "My true fear is that he would move in if I bought that house."

"Not unless we're married, Shaper. You know that."

Patty raised her eyebrows at that. "She doesn't plan to be, does she?" she whispered to me.

"Not ready yet," I told her. More loudly, I said, "We could put the two of them to work remodeling the place."

"That's not at all a bad idea. I need to run. Bye, Al," Patty called, waving in Guzman's direction and heading for her sports car.

As she pulled out, Michelle pulled in. "Patty here for any particular reason?" she asked, climbing out of the van.

"I think she was mostly checking on our new neighbors, but also asking about our plans for buying the house."

"She needs to keep her pointy nose out of our business." She didn't sound overly serious, but I wondered if Michelle did resent Patty hanging around here.

I had to laugh. "It does stick out a bit, doesn't it? She used to joke that we could use her face as a sundial."

Michelle joined me. "I guess I'm no one to be criticizing noses, am I?" she asked, fingering her own prominent protuberance.

"You've discovered my secret turn-on. Girls with big noses!"

"They just remind you of surfboards. Still, I wish she wasn't quite so — so nosy!" She laughed again at her own joke.

"Give her time. She'll find new friends to annoy."

Chapter 57

There was someone parked just south of our place, along the curb, where the overhanging trees made the predawn morning even darker. John sometimes left his truck there but I knew he had gone home hours ago. Had it been there when I walked over to check the waves? Maybe I simply hadn't noticed. A figure — I tensed up, if only for a second.

"Hi, Ted." A woman's voice. Sally Stuart, I could see as she approached.

There had been waves, but they could wait this morning. "Come on in," I told her. By the light from my kitchen windows, she could see the potted hibiscus, as we went up the drive.

"Time to plant? Rose of Sharon, aren't they?"

"Yes. Picked those up at the *River Road Nursery.* Come on in." I held the back door open.

"Oh, Joy and Susan's place."

"You know them?" I wouldn't have expected them to move in the same circles.

"Sure. See them at the monthly meeting of the Lesbian League." I had to laugh at that one, and Sally joined me.

No sign of Charlie. That didn't mean she wasn't awake.

"I do, well, envy them," continued Sally. "They've stayed together."

"That can be hard for any couple."

"Yeah." She was quiet for few seconds, before telling me, pretty much out of the blue, "Karrie cheated on me with a guy. I don't know if that's better or worse than a woman."

I don't know why she chose to unburden to me. Maybe she had

no one other than nonthreatening Ted. "'Bout the same, I would think."

"I suppose." There was resignation in her voice. "The thing is, I know she'll do it again. But I know what to expect, you see? No surprises."

She paused before adding, "It's who she is."

"Is it who you are?"

"Oh, Ted, you would come up with a question like that."

"Well, here's an easier one. Cup of coffee?"

"Sounds good. And let's get to business." I handed her a mug. Sally added neither milk nor sugar.

"You understand that I don't have access to any sort of accounting records. I do see some of the expense account items that go across the lawyers' desks however, and I know some of those are off-the-record payments." Sally savored the aroma of her brew and took a sip before continuing. "A fair amount of petty cash goes to what could only be called informants."

"Is that illegal?" I asked.

"Mostly, no. Not really. Information helps with cases. But if the informant happens to be a public employee — well, then it is definitely a no-no." Sally glanced quickly to her left. "Was that your girlfriend darting into the bathroom? I'm not intruding, am I?"

"Her daughter, more likely, and it is not a problem. Public employees? Such as people at City Hall?"

"Yep. And I have no doubt whatsoever that we break that rule now and again." She leaned forward, her voice lower. "Most likely someone there — probably someone who deals with records — noticed Cotton's snooping."

"And that could have been the same individual who planted the evidence, couldn't it?"

"Quite possibly. Or facilitated it."

I knew what Bill was looking over — questionable actions by elected officials, a vote here, a bit of pressure there, that sort of thing. He was looking for a pattern because this woman had suggested something of the sort might be going on.

How did she know? I decided that wasn't actually important at the moment. She had noticed something and that was good enough. But it was a thing we should learn, down the line.

"So what we need to find is a money trail to whomever was being paid off. And paid off more for planting evidence, wouldn't you think?"

"Exactly," answered Ms. Stuart. "This person would have been getting little payoffs for some time but possibly a larger one, suddenly. I would think that would be the best way to find him or her."

"If it was cash, that would be near impossible."

"Unless this individual was not careful and deposited it in a bank account. Especially that bigger payoff."

"Assuming there really was a bigger one. That's a guess."

She nodded and we both drank coffee in silence.

"I do think someone at the firm might be suspicious of me. If only I knew which one the lawyers was behind all of this!"

"Who was the guy that accompanied Burkhardt to the zoning hearing?" I asked her. "That was someone from your place, right?"

"Blair. That would be Blair Rainey."

"I think I might start with him," I said.

Chapter 58

"Redding messed up," said Jim. "He as much as admitted to Jack Saunders that there was something going on."

He shrugged. "Bob is just not suited to conspiracies. The good news is that we never clued him in on either of the Stuarts being involved. If Saunders takes it to Millie, it won't matter."

"But chances are he'll report to the mayor's office too," Jay Johnson reminded us.

"And they will also turn it over to the acting chief, most likely. We'll be safe for at least a while."

"Except for me," said Jay. "He'll know I've been stonewalling him now."

"Which also means we'll probably not be partners for a while. Millie will have to separate us for appearance sake." Jaime Trejo continued in his normal level, matter-of-fact voice. "I may be leaving the department anyway. I've had a job offer elsewhere, someplace with better chance of advancement and, well, more of the sort of responsibilities I want. But," he continued, "I would not desert while Chief Cotton is still in trouble."

"Tired of riding a bike, Jim?" I asked.

He gave a wry smile. "That's the best part of the job. I'll miss being by the beach every day." We all looked out across the Atlantic, across the decent swell rolling in by the pier, on this some-what overcast day. There was the smell of smoke again, hanging in the air.

And I had been out surfing, on one of the used thrusters from the shop. Not my preferred style of board, but it would do. Surf or not, we had chosen this as a good place to make contact from time to time — people were used to seeing me near the pier and the bike cops patrolled the area regularly. I had already filled them in on Sally's early visit.

"Chief Stuart has made a formal request for an audit of the department," stated Jim, getting back to business. "If money disappeared somewhere, she wants to know how. We don't know if it will be approved."

I wouldn't be surprised if she were doing one on her own. Or had already.

"I'd better get home and open for business," I told the pair. "I reckon you need to go pedaling about and looking useful, too."

"True," said Jim, looking at his watch. "North?"

Jay nodded and both headed in the direction of the pier and beyond. How far up that way did they patrol? Possibly further than they did south, toward my place.

There was a silver Miata in the drive when I reached that place. Visiting with Charlie? Or with Al? Both his vehicles were parked over there, the yellow Mustang inside the carport. He had mentioned an intention to enclose that space.

Whatever. I would find out where Patty was soon enough. Go get a shower, Ted.

As the warm water washed the sand and salt from me, I heard a voice. "Do you think we should peek?"

"No need for me. I've seen Ted without his clothes."

That one I could identify. Patty, of course. Who was the other woman? Darn, I should have brought something to wear out with me. I wrapped as best I could in my towel and stepped out.

"You'll have to tell me about it sometime," said Vicky Warner.

"It was not story material at all," my friend told her. That was true. "Let us in, will you, Ted? We're getting tired of Al trying to flirt with us."

"Won't Ted?" asked Vicky.

"Never. He doesn't know how," Patty assured her. She had changed her hair, hadn't she? It looked more like the bowl-cut of our college days than the styled, feathered pixie Patty had arrived with a few weeks ago.

"My surf shop is your surf shop," I told them, opening the back door. Where was Charlie this morning, anyway? "I'll be right back." Into my bedroom for a tee and shorts. No, too cool for shorts. I slipped into ragged painter pants instead.

"I started tea," was Patty's greeting. "I hope you don't mind." I guess she had learned where stuff was in my kitchen.

"No problem," I mumbled. "Gotta open up." I went up into the shop and did just that, leaving the front door hanging wide in invitation.

Vicky was seated at the table while Patty busied herself. Was she looking for something to eat, too? Make yourself at home, girl!

"You didn't hear what happened at the City Council meeting yesterday, did you, Ted?" asked Patty. "And doesn't anyone in this house eat cookies?"

"Cookies don't last around here. City Council?"

"I thought maybe Michelle had told you. Doris certainly knows."

"Burkhardt attempted to make a run around the board's decision by having the zoning laws changed," spoke Vicky. "Not that we can be sure they were behind it, but who else, right?"

I shrugged. How would I know?

"It was Ronnie Rouse, of all people, who brought it up. We never know where he stands — the man's votes are all over the place!"

"I assume it did not pass."

"The council wouldn't even consider it. Even Bernie balked at that one."

Patty looked up from her pouring of hot water. "They all have reelections to worry about, I would think. The idea is obviously unpopular."

"But they might try to sneak something like this through later. A lot of people *are* sympathetic to these developers' ideas on growth."

"Even to the point of breaking laws," I threw in.

"Your broken boards?" asked Patty. "That's a lousy thing to happen to you but not very important on the large scale."

"It's way deeper than that." Suddenly, I felt like letting more people in on this. "The whole affair with Chief Cotton appears to be tied into it. The assault on Dave Blake is linked. There is some serious stuff going on, and hardly anyone knows about it."

Ward looked skeptical. Was she even capable of believing that her friends and colleagues might be involved in bribery and corruption?

I sat down with the pair over cups of pekoe and pretty much gave them the whole story. "Acting Chief Stuart is going to need friends on the council," I finished. "I hope you will be one of them, Mrs. Ward."

Chapter 59

Yield! Yield!
Shipbuilders hiring
welders. Marineland!
Three-point-four miles
to next exit.

And so on.

"A lot of her poems are what she calls *bricolage*," said Jan. "She finds words here and there and sticks them together, signs or stuff from books. It doesn't matter." She slipped the page back into a dark blue folder.

"Maybe not to her," was all I could say.

Charlie laughed at that. "Oh, you can be mean, Shaper. Patty was right — you should have been a critic!"

Perhaps I had unfairly chosen to dislike Miss Goodpaster, due to the things Sally Stuart had told me. Those confidences would not be shared, of course. "It's not my thing," was all I did say.

"She's one of your professors?" Charlie asked.

"Instructor. Not professor. And yes, I'm in her writing class this semester. That was a last minute choice, after I finally chose my career path." Jan gave us a crooked smile. "I don't think it's helping me much with that."

"You might be surprised," I told her. "It has shown you new things and that's the best part of college."

"That and having a degree when you go job-hunting," added Michelle, who stood at the door into the kitchen, coffee cup in hand. "I could use one of those."

Sleeping beauty had joined us at last. Michelle did not rise early on weekends since starting to work at the bank. "Degrees are over-rated," I told her. "Mine is quite useless."

"But you went back to college and got it anyway."

I couldn't argue with that, so I didn't. The front door was already hanging open as an invitation to shoppers at half past Nine — didn't hurt to open a little early on Saturdays. "So you two are going to leave us to ourselves today?" I asked.

"You can handle it, Shaper," Jan replied. I could. It was nice to see her and Charlie spending time together again, too. There had been less of that lately.

The phone. Michelle picked it up before I even turned around. "Certainly, Mrs. Stuart." She held the receiver out to me. "For you. The police."

I took it from her, the long coiled cord trailing across the counter. "Hi, Jean." It was mostly just touching bases but she relayed one piece of information before we said goodbye.

"They found a match to the fingerprints," I announced. "One, only. It seems these guys were wearing gloves but one of them had a hole worn through on one of the fingers." The man must not have thought through the ramifications when he pulled it on. If he were the sort that thought at all.

"Are they going to arrest him?" asked Charlie, maybe with just a little too much enthusiasm.

"No. That is the main reason she called me, to tell me they want to watch the guy for a while before letting him know they are onto him."

Jan nodded knowingly. She was in on a lot more of this than Michelle or Charlie. "Did she give you a name?" She asked.

"Actually, yes. Donald Pruett. Meant nothing to me."

Did the young woman's eyes light up? I suddenly realized I had given her something to investigate. "Don't let her go getting in trouble now," I told Charlie, as the two headed out.

"Where are they going?" asked Michelle.

"I haven't the slightest idea. And that may be a good thing."

"Do you at least know when Betty and Pat are coming?"

I had to admit I didn't. "Pat implied that he wanted to stay home for the Easter weekend, even though break starts on the Twelfth. Thursday."

"So not until Monday, maybe. Betty gets the whole week off, I know. Okay." Michelle seemed satisfied with that. "You'll be doing church stuff this week, won't you?"

"It's possible." I might or might not make some of the services. "Maybe Thursday evening. Maybe Good Friday afternoon."

"And tomorrow is Palm Sunday, right?"

"Yes, Michelle. Even heathens like you know that."

Chapter 60

I did come home with some palm fronds the next morning, as did my new neighbors. I wasn't going to be able to avoid them, was I?

I never knew what to do with those fronds when I got them home. Sometimes I stuck them in a vase somewhere. For the moment, I just tucked them behind the visor in the truck and went on in without them.

Who knows how long they might stay there?

My family — I can call them that, can't I? – had newspapers spread across the kitchen table, dirty dishes pushed to one side. The passive-aggressive guy inside me wanted to clean up the mess while giving them dirty looks, but I kept him in rein.

"Any coffee left?" I asked. No, I could see that. They hadn't cleaned the coffee maker either.

Michelle looked up. "Could I make you some, Ted?"

"No thanks, kid. I think I want tea." I filled a kettle and started to assemble the makings. "So, tomorrow — still good after sleeping on it?"

"Yep, tomorrow," agreed Michelle. "I haven't changed my mind. What about today?"

"Nothing planned. Maybe I'll get onto board building." Including one for me, my first replacement for those that were destroyed. "Did you want to do something?"

"It's such a nice morning." She turned to her daughter. "How about hanging out on the beach for a while?"

Charlie looked to me. "Sure, if Shaper doesn't need us."

"Go ahead. I'll hold things down here." Half an hour later,

Michelle was backing her van out and I was cleaning up the kitchen.

There was still about an hour until my official opening time. Maybe I could go back to the shaping room and do some preliminaries on a board or two. I barely had the garage door open before Patty pulled into the drive.

"Not riding around with your new friend today?" I called to her.

Patty slipped out of the Mazda. "Vicky? That was, ah, networking. Not someone who is ever likely to be a close friend."

That didn't surprise me, I'll admit. "I hope you are making some of those here."

"A few. Toni and I hit it off right away, for some reason." She seemed to consider for a moment or two. "Well, I guess you're my best friend here, really, Ted. Despite not seeing you for nearly thirty years."

She continued, "I do consider Michelle to be a friend but that is mostly because she is attached to you. We would be an unlikely duo otherwise. I've never been good at having girlfriends. You know that, Ted. I rub 'em the wrong way, somehow."

I wasn't going to argue. "And you've been just the opposite," she went on. "I know how women confide in you, I saw it even when we were in college. I did it myself." She smiled, shaking her head. "Now I'm doing it again!"

It was true, I knew. I had always had more female friends than most guys. And fewer male friends, for that matter.

"Not that you interacted much with anyone back then," Patty said. "You were really shy, Ted, or really introverted, or something."

"I used to think I was an introvert. Then I realized I really just didn't like people."

"Hmm, sure. Hey, I know you were having trouble and the rest of us didn't see it. And I'm not going to poke into that — it's just good that you're happy now."

"Happy? Maybe so. For a long time it was enough for me to just get along without being *unhappy*." That was pretty much my life before Michelle.

Patty nodded. "I get that. Not being happy and being unhappy are two different things."

She did get it.

I had several blanks laid out on the driveway pavement, deciding on my course. "Customs or production?" Patty asked.

"No custom orders at the moment but I want to build something I can ride. Need to run off a few production boards, too."

"Feel free to ride mine," she said. "I'm terrible for not getting onto it yet."

"Haven't been a lot of opportunities. Just remember you're a surfer now, not a golfer." We both chuckled, not that it was all that funny.

"Speaking of golf," she said, "Vicky mentioned that councilman, Rouse, remember?" I nodded. "I think his wife was one of our four-some when I played with Donna Burkhardt. They must be pretty friendly, hmm?"

"Maybe. I know zip about golf and foursomes, you understand."

"Lucky man. Where are the girls?"

SHAPER

"Deserted me to go lie on the beach," I told her. "And that is fine with me. Michelle needs to get away from here and unwind."

"Maybe she should take up golf," was her deadpan response.

"Yeah." I picked up a longboard blank. "This one, I think, for my board." I could do a near-replica of the much-missed 'Big Red.' "And I'll start the production boards with, um, this one. I could do a Five-eight."

"Really short."

"I sell a lot of boards to little kids." I started to replace the other blanks on their storage racks. "And I need to sell more of them. We're making an offer on the house tomorrow."

Chapter 61

"It wasn't really hard to find out who this guy is," reported Janice Bell. "And where he lives."

"I'm sure the cops would have done all that," was Charlie's opinion.

"But did they check out the woman he lives with?" She continued without waiting for an answer. "Her name is Suellen Wyatt. And can you guess where she works?" Jan did wait for a reply this time.

I caught on. "City hall."

"Exactly, Shaper. She's a records clerk."

"This is something I absolutely have to tell — um, someone. Jean Stuart." I wasn't going to say Dave Blake, even though that was who I would probably contact. Maybe Sally should know, too. She might be familiar with the woman.

"The man has a criminal record too. That's easy enough to find out." She addressed herself to Charlie then. "You need to get a computer and get connected to the web," she told her. "It's going to be more and more useful for gathering information."

I was skeptical but, as you know, I hate change.

"What I really need to do," said Charlie, "is take detective lessons from you and Shaper. You guys made a jump I wouldn't have thought of."

"But you know a lot of stuff about real life that I don't," Jan told her. It was true; Jan Bell had lived a sheltered life.

"You'll have to hire Jan to investigate for you," I said. "She could be Charlie's angel." I was lucky they didn't throw anything at me.

Charlie did glance up at the wall clock. Again. "What's keeping that boy?"

"Sunday dinner with the folks?" I asked. That didn't require any intuitive jumps whatsoever — more often than not, John and Charlie were at his parents' house on a Sunday afternoon.

"Uh-huh. John had a shift this morning."

"So he would only have gotten off like ten minutes ago," said Jan. "You expect him to rush over here?"

"Absolutely!"

The young man's truck pulled up out front a couple minutes later and Charlie herself rushed out to it. Jan stood at the front window and watched them drive away.

I could guess at the sort of thoughts that were in her right then. There was nothing I could or should say.

So I went back to her investigations. "I'd like to tell someone about your findings as soon as possible." But whom?

"Call Dave," she replied, her voice flat. "Do you need me in the shop, Shaper?"

"I don't think so. It's pretty slow this afternoon." I might just close up. "Heading home?"

"Mm-huh." The girl managed a smile and asked, "Should I send Michelle home?"

"She can gab with your mom as long as she wants. See you, Jan." As soon as she was out the door and headed up the sidewalk — being leery of traipsing across our new neighbors' back yard — I was on the phone.

"I'll pass this right on to Millie," Dave told me. "And thank Janice for us, okay?"

Yes. I would do that.

Chapter 62

"Aunt Jean called me last night and told me about the new information. She says this was just the sort of evidence they needed to get a judge on their side."

Sally had once again waylaid me on my morning walk. Now we drank coffee in the kitchen behind the *Cully Beach Surf Shop*.

"Still pretty sketchy, I would think." Circumstantial, any lawyer would say.

"That's true. But she thinks it will be enough to let them look at bank records."

I nodded. That might be all they needed, at least to move things forward.

"I wondered how you became suspicious in the first place." I made it a statement, not a question. It was not my intention to put Sally on the spot, nor my right to interrogate her. But I was curious.

"It was just a little thing. I almost ignored it," she began. "I was asked to draw up a contract for what was essentially a 'sweetheart' deal. No names on it but it was very generous, practically a giveaway. Well, no, it *was* a giveaway. I could see that — a piece of one of Burkhardt's developments for some ridiculously low amount.

"I had to wonder, why would something like that come through our office, instead of Daytona? And the answer had to be that someone local was doing them favors and, most likely, illicit ones. Oh, I considered ignoring it, not causing trouble, not jeopardizing my own position. But it could be hurting the firm, which would hurt me and the people I work with, right? So I took it to Bill Cotton. I didn't know who else to go to and I've know Bill for years."

"And Bill took it seriously."

"He did. I thought that would be the end of my part in all this."

Her cup was empty. "More?" I asked. Sally nodded.

As I poured, I commented, "I see that the trial is finally starting." It had been in the Sunday news.

"After the Easter break," she said. "Jury selection should start on the Twenty-fourth."

At the courthouse in Scott City. "And the prosecution finally rounded up their witness."

"Yeah. Harmony Bozeman. Aunt Jean says that she was passed over for promotion when she was with the department and that nothing came of her harassment claim." She chuckled. "Normally, I might see that as a stock sexist response but I am inclined to believe Jean."

"Bozeman's claims do sound shaky," I said. "It comes down to the supposed payments, doesn't it? Maybe Jean's audit will help clear all this up."

"You didn't hear? The City Council put her proposed audit on the back burner until after Easter. But she and Dave Blake have been going over everything on their own." Sally leaned forward, speaking as though to a fellow conspirator. Which I was, sort of. "Cotton's attorney could request her findings as evidence. He wasn't officially informed of any of this, of course, but word gets to him."

I could imagine it would. She put down her mug. "I'd better take off."

Charlie could come out of hiding now. "Okay. I'll walk out with you."

Sally had parked just down the road, as before, in front of the house I would be attempting to buy today. For a moment, I thought maybe I saw movement in the thick shrubs around that house. Just a trick of the darkness, no doubt. I watched her drive off.

There had been no mention of Karrie Goodpaster this time, and that was okay with me. I'm no one to give relationship advice.

Chapter 63

"There will be a counteroffer," warned Dick. "You know that, of course."

"We're ready to deal," I replied.

"And I think you will get a reasonable deal, considering how long the house has been on the market. Do you have your financing lined up?"

"Michelle is taking care of that." She did work at a bank, after all.

"Good enough then. I'll present this to the owners." Warner gathered up his papers. "Between them not living locally and the holiday, we might not hear back right away."

"That's all right." We were moving forward. That would suffice. I rose. "I'll be on my way then, Dick." We shook, I headed home. It was only a few blocks from his office.

So that was done. Late enough to open for business, not that there was likely to be much on an April Monday. Well, no, some people were already on their Easter break. Or Spring break. And this week was traditionally the last one spent in Florida for many of the remaining snowbirds. There would be shoppers out, visiting the stores one last time before heading north.

Charlie was hanging in the kitchen, studying. "Classes tonight? When do you get your Spring break, girl?" The community college campus was shut down, and Jan and John and all the other kids I knew who studied there had a couple weeks off.

"Next Monday, only," was her somewhat distracted reply. "I don't mind. I need to learn this stuff."

"Okay. Keep at it." I went up front and opened the shop door. Gorgeous, sunny day, with a deep blue sky. That meant not much moisture in the air — none of the rain Florida needed would be coming anytime soon.

I chafed a bit at sitting here, minding a mostly-empty store. I could be working on something, shaping boards, getting that shower stall built.

A slender woman in tan slacks and an aloha shirt, with unruly straw-colored hair, came in around One. Karrie Goodpaster. Of course, the instructors at the college would be off also.

She was younger than Sally, wasn't she? Or maybe she just acted younger.

"Hi Shaper," she called, and waved to me, before turning to the rack of Hawaiian shirts. I hadn't added any new stock but there was no reason to tell her that.

"I want to buy all of them!" she declared. "I don't have very good impulse control, I'm afraid."

"We don't object to that here," I told her, walking over to where she was sliding hangers back and forth.

She might have laughed louder than that deserved. "How could someone like me take up surfing?" she suddenly asked. "Do you give lessons or something?"

"Lessons are overrated," I stated. "The best way is to just get in the water and learn by doing it. Maybe start on something like a bodyboard, though." I gestured toward the several I had for sale. "Charlie is learning on one of those."

"Janice's friend? She's cute." She looked from the boards to me. "So are you, Mr. Shaper."

Before I could think of any response to that, she continued. "She's your girlfriend's daughter, right?"

That I could answer. "She is. Charlie's in the back right now, studying. For her GED exam." I don't know why I felt the need to add that.

"Right. I learned quite a bit about the girl from one of Janice's writing assignments." She shook her head, more dramatically than at all necessary. "Ms. Bell will never be a writer, I fear. But maybe a good journalist."

"That's what she wants."

"I know. I may seem a complete scatterbrain, Shaper, but I actually remember things pretty well." Karrie tapped her forehead. "A steel trap," she claimed, and sort of chortled.

"Mine is rusty," I replied.

"Self-deprecating," she mused. "That's something I know about. I either go too far one way or too far the other!"

I nodded. It was something I knew about too. "Just don't rock so far one way that you capsize."

"Right!" She turned back to the shirts. "One only. Moderation in my madness!"

Karrie picked out a rather lovely powder-blue shirt with a floral design in shades of tan.

"That's going to be all?" I asked. "Anything for Sally?" Maybe I shouldn't have but I was only thinking of making a sale. It was the sort of thing I said to customers all the time.

"I wouldn't know what to get her. Isn't that an awful thing to admit?" She looked thoughtful for a moment, then blurted, "You pick something out. Sally will be so surprised if I bring *anything* home for her!"

I wouldn't know what to get her, either. "Jewelry?" I knew she wore some simple ornaments. Karrie wrinkled up her nose and shook her head. Okay. "Oh, here we go." I held up a *Cully Beach Surf Shop* tee-shirt. "And I get free advertising if she wears it."

"In red," said Karrie. "She likes red." She giggled. "And make it small so it's tight on her boobs."

"Great." I put both shirts in a bag and rang up the sale. Whether Sally Stuart would even wear the tee, I didn't know. But I suspected she would appreciate the gesture.

"Thanks for suggesting it. I don't think about Sally enough." She frowned. "I don't do enough for her."

I attempted an encouraging smile as I handed her the bag. "Consider this a step forward in your relationship."

"Our relationship." Karrie sighed, and it was both more and less than a dramatic gesture this time. "She's the stable one, the one I depend on, but lately something has her distracted. Distant. It makes me feel like I don't offer enough. That I'm not good enough."

"Then show you are good enough."

"Some of us will never be good enough, Shaper. That's just life."

Chapter 64

No waves this morning. Lots of stars to be seen, though, even with the glare from the new security lights over at the *Sandcastles* construction site. It looked like they were finally ready to build — three stories, I would assume, even if the sign still portrayed five.

No fence yet. My way to the beach was unobstructed. I knew well enough that might change. I turned to head home.

To my left — two men. I couldn't make out faces in the dark. Oh, no faces to be made out. Ski masks covered their heads.

You're in trouble, Ted.

But I saw them coming. I wouldn't be jumped the way Dave had been. And I was in good shape. Fight or flight?

I chose flight, but one had moved to block my way. I would have to go through him. The smaller of the pair, he was probably the quicker.

I attempted to take him with my shoulder and get by. And it almost worked except that he swung the bat he held as I slipped past, catching me with a glancing blow to the lower back, enough to make me stumble, almost fall.

And then both had caught up to me.

"Get him," one hissed. Hands grabbed at me. They would have been smarter to use their clubs again but I doubt they were the brightest guys around. We were almost to the edge of A-1-A when one caught the back of my leg with his bat and sent me sprawling.

A flashing blue light. Even with the mechanical resonances of his bullhorn I could recognize the voice of Officer Bob Redding. "Halt. Hands up!"

They did not obey him but took off running. He should have expected it.

Across the highway they went, with Bob in pursuit. I didn't think the large policeman would have much hope of catching them. A cacophony of barking came from the Bells' house as the pair of thugs cut across their lawn and onto Al's, Redding doggedly following.

If they got beyond my place, it would become relatively easy to elude him, hide in one of the dark, overgrown backyards of my neighbors to the west and south.

Someone over me. Rick. I was up on one knee now, without actually realizing I had done it. "Are you hurt, man?"

"Uh, yeah, Rick. Guys hit me with baseball bats." What was happening? One of the fleeing assailants was on the ground, Redding and someone else standing over him. The other was not to be seen.

"I think falling down hurt more than the whacks they got in," I told Rick. My hands and knees were skinned from sliding on the rough pavement. There would be bruising for sure. "I can walk. Let's go over there."

The scene was illuminated by the floodlight in Alvaro Guzman's carport. It was a bathrobe-clad Al who was standing by, as Redding cuffed the man on the ground. That man groaned from time to time.

In Al's hand was a tire iron. That explained much. "I rise as early as you, Ted," he said as we approached, "and saw the flashing light." He looked toward the miscreant on the ground. "These men attacked you?""

"That they did."

"Ah, then I wish I had hit him harder!"

Officer Bob was attempting to read the man his rights from a little card. The light wasn't really quite good enough for that.

Rick leaned in and whispered. "Are these the same ones who beat up Dave?"

I nodded. "Most likely, Rick."

"Then I wish Al had hit him harder, too. Why don't we get you inside?" He escorted me to my kitchen. Alvaro remained to super-vise the arrest.

Of course, Michelle and Charlie were up, what with all the commotion. I'm not sure which one grabbed hold of me the harder, and I didn't complain.

But Rick did. "He's hurt, girls. Let him sit down." He directed me to a chair. "You got a first aid kit?"

I chuckled. "It's in the shaping room. That's where I'm most likely to hurt myself."

Charlie grabbed a set of keys and went to retrieve it. "There's a couple more squad cars out there now," she reported on her return.

"They'll want to talk to me," I said, and attempted to rise.

"Sit yourself down, Edward Covington Carrol!" demanded Michelle. "The police can come to you."

Which they did. A rap on the back door — I didn't recognize the officer who entered. "Do we need an ambulance?" was his first question.

I shook my head. He looked at my bleeding knees. "They got in some whacks with a bat, right?"

"Yeah. Here." I pointed to the back of my right leg. "And here." And to my lower back. That one didn't hurt much. I'd been hit harder by loose surfboards.

"Okay. I won't call a bus but you should go to the hospital, if only so they can give us an official report on your injuries. Can someone drive you?"

"I will," volunteered Rick.

"Oh, man, that's like ten miles," I complained. And a waste of money, I added to myself.

"We can't force you, sir," said the officer.

"Good," I replied, considering it settled. "Do you know who the guys are?" I already was certain that one was Donald Pruett.

The man smiled. "I was going to ask you the same thing."

"Two thugs in ski masks," I answered. "Probably the same two that busted up my surfboards a little while back."

"Very well, sir. Someone will come to take a full statement later today." He gave me a somewhat disapproving look. "Preferably after you visit the hospital."

Chapter 65

"Roy Left is the man's name. Known as 'Lefty' even though he's right-handed." Officer Church looked up from her pad. "Quite a record of petty offenses but nothing like this before." She turned over a page.

"Do you think they intended to rob you?"

"No. They intended to beat me up." I thought maybe I could get a smile out of her with that one, but no luck. So I went on. "Your acting chief will know why. She will also have a good idea of who the other assailant was, so there is no point in asking me."

I didn't feel like playing games of secrecy today. I really had nothing to add to them.

She raised her eyebrows but didn't press me. "Okay, Mr. Carrol. We need to go over your injuries. They were cataloged this morning, right?" She checked her notes again. "Yes. But I should follow up."

I held up my bruised and scraped palms. "These from when I fell. Same on the knees." I rolled up the right leg on my sweat pants to show her. "And a bruise on the back here from a bat." I turned my leg to show her. "That's not much."

"And then," I finished, "a bat to the lower back." I stood and hiked up my shirt to display the bruise. "Not that bad, either."

She made some notes. "Away from the kidney," she remarked. "That's fortunate."

I returned to my chair. "Yes, it is. And it was very fortunate that Bob Redding drove by or I would have a lot more damage to show you." I chuckled. "Probably from a hospital bed. I need to thank the man."

"All right Mr. Carrol. Thank you for your time." Officer A. Church — that's what it said on her name tag — rose and departed. I could see through the window that she went next door to the Guzman house. No doubt needed to follow up with Al too.

My leg was a little stiff but I got up and went into the shop, where Charlie was taking care of business.

"Everything okay up here?" I asked.

"Sure, Shaper. Mom's been calling a lot to check on you."

"You may inform her I'm struggling to hang on. I'll tell you," I said, holding up my palms, "these would really hurt if I got into the salt water."

"I'll bet. You're going to have trouble using tools for a few days, too."

"Yeah." That sucked. No doubt about it. "I'll have to put Marty to work shaping the boards."

"Can you believe she slept through all of that this morning?"

"Maybe I should have. Too many bad things happen on my morning walks." As soon as I said that I regretted it. One of those bad things had been coming on the body of Charlie's father. But she showed no reaction and we both let it pass.

"Miss Goodpaster thinks you're cute," I said, to make a complete break in the conversation.

"Oh, great. I'm not just enticing school boys into your shop now."

"Be happy that you are useful in some way. She was flirting with me, too." I could recognize that.

"Jan says she does that a lot without thinking about it."

276

"A good way to get in trouble," I commented. "If you want to go anywhere, I'll stay up here a while."

"Okay, Shaper." She hopped down from her stool. "I'll just go get a snack and clean up a little."

I wasn't sitting there that long before the phone rang. Yes, it was Michelle. Yes, I'm fine, I told her. We'll discuss it all over wine in, um — I looked up at the clock — three hours.

Nearly Three already, I thought, as I hung up. Did I have a part-time employee coming in? Easter break messed up everybody's schedules, including kids. My question was answered when Joan Keaton came through the door a few minutes later.

I was about to leave the place to her when the phone rang again.

"*Cully Beach Surf Shop*," I answered.

"Good afternoon, Ted," came a familiar voice. "It's Jean Stuart. Wanted to follow up a few things with you."

"Fine with me." I leaned back against the counter. That hurt. I returned to standing up.

"You're okay, aren't you?"

"Okay enough. But curious about some things."

"Explanations, then. We've been keeping an eye on Don Pruett and knew he had been in your neighborhood yesterday."

They could have warned me. "Oh?"

"Yep. More importantly, Sally suspected that someone was onto her, and might have seen her at your place. That was why I asked Bob to patrol the area."

"And I am very thankful that he did. I take back every thing I have ever said about the man!" And some that I had thought.

"I'll let him know you are grateful. Not that you had been maligning him."

"That's good. I don't suppose Sally should come here again."

"It may not matter anymore. We'll have to see where things go now."

"Uh-huh." I guess we would. "Anything more, Jean?"

"That covers it, Ted. Thanks."

"All right. Bye."

"Was that about this morning, Shaper?" asked Joan. "The news is all over school."

"It was. I shouldn't talk about the investigation." I didn't know if that were so but figured it would keep her from asking questions. "School is still in? When's the last day?"

"Tomorrow. Then we have a week and a half free!"

"Lucky you."

Chapter 66

I looked at my new row of hibiscus and hoped that legions of surf rats cutting across the lawn wouldn't trample them. I had not had good luck in the past.

Would you believe that, despite everything, I got up at Five this morning and walked across the street just like yesterday and pretty much every day for ten years past? A couple of bat-wielding thugs weren't going to mess up my routine. No sir!

There was news of those thugs on the radio when I got back. I wasn't inclined to turn it on so much in the mornings since the women had moved in, and even less since Michelle had started her employment at the bank. But I did this morning.

A manhunt in progress for Donald Pruett, it announced, suspected of assault. Had 'Lefty' talked, implicating him? Otherwise, the only thing they had on Pruett was bashing my surfboards. I would probably find out eventually.

Now, here I was, alone, standing at my front door. Michelle at work. Charlie off early with John and not coming back until after her evening class. Al was doing some sort of remodeling work next door. I could smell paint.

I had gone so far as to sit down on my front steps when Patty Singer drove up. She came and plopped down beside me.

"Up to anything, Patty?" I asked her.

"I've been looking at places over toward the, uh, river. Isn't that what you call it? There are some bigger lots with old houses back there. Near where your friends have their nursery." Her eyes went to my hibiscus.

"You could find far worse areas. But you wouldn't have a canal like Doris."

"Waterfront is nice. It's also expensive. I have some money but I'm not going to throw it away!"

"Sensible. This house over here." I gestured toward the south. "Would be considerably cheaper were it a couple blocks further west."

"And just as good a place to live."

"Yeah." I looked out across the highway before going on. "I'm no idiot, Patty. In ten years these lots may well be too valuable as development property for me to remain here. And I might be ready for retirement."

"So they are an investment. In part, anyway."

I turned my head, looking up at the sign above the door. "And all this would be gone, like the *Cully Beach Surf Shop* never existed."

"But it did exist, Ted. That won't change."

"Like your design firm?"

"That was a monster I created, like Frankenstein. I was lucky to escape it."

"But you accomplished something with it."

"I think you've accomplished a lot."

"Some days, convincing myself to stay alive has been accomplishment enough." I chuckled. "Morbid Ted. Don't mind that."

"You still live with that, don't you? The depression."

"I always will, just like Charlie with her alcoholism. It's in me."

"If that is so, Ted Carrol, then you are damned lucky to have put together such a great support group. I envy you this — this family."

She paused, gathering what she wanted to say. "Not just Michelle and Charlie, but your neighbors and friends and all the little surfer kids who call you Shaper. I — I want to be part of that family, Ted."

"You always have been, kid. Always have been." Hadn't she?

"Thanks." She leaned over and kissed my cheek. "I need to get going. More houses to look at!"

Chapter 67

We looked over the counter-offer Dick Warner brought by.

Charlie asked, "Shouldn't Mister Warner be trying to get you a good deal?".

"He's working for the sellers, dear, not for us," Michelle informed her.

"Right. And, naturally, the higher the price the bigger his commission."

"So who's looking out for you?"

"We can depend on our own keen business sense," I stated.

"And lawyers," added Michelle. "Okay if I take this with me and let some of the minds down at the bank give their opinion?"

"Go right ahead. Oh, I may not be here when you get home."

"Church?"

"Right." There would be an evening service on this Holy Thursday.

"Ready to go, Charlie?" she asked. Dropping her off someplace — the girl would find her own way home eventually, I assumed. Charlie nodded her head of imitation sun-bleached hair and away they went.

Alone. Were my hands in good enough shape for me to attempt shaping this morning? Maybe not. I needed fine control when running a planer across a foam blank. Better to make the start on the indoor shower.

I stood at the utility room door — well, it used to be the utility room — and pondered the project. Would it be cheating to buy one of those ready-make plastic shower enclosures? Nah, don't do that, Ted. You're supposed to be a craftsman.

So, the existing floor was terrazzo, common enough in houses from the period. That was good. But I would need to put in a curb and to raise the floor a little in the shower stall for better drainage. The pipes were not a problem at all — everything was ready for them.

Tile. I would need tile. I started scribbling a list. Some bags of concrete mix. A shower head, of course. I bet Charlie could pick up this stuff for me, maybe at the Brody's hardware store. Yeah, I could put her and John on it. What was it called? I had driven by frequently enough I should remember the name.

Enough of that. Time to open the shop.

It wasn't really a slow day, considering that it was a Thursday in the off-season, but there wasn't a lot of traffic either. Tomorrow would be about the same, most likely, and perhaps a good crowd would come through on Saturday, the day before Easter.

Easter Sunday itself would be dead, I knew. Betty and Pat would be coming in that afternoon; I might just close early.

I told my afternoon employee to close up. That wasn't really necessary anymore, as Michelle would be home before Six, but I liked to give the kids some responsibility. Than I got cleaned up and headed off to *Our Lady of the Seas*, through late afternoon traffic. Such as there was in Cully Beach.

A few acquaintances at church had heard of my scrape on Tuesday morning and offered well wishes. Beyond that, nothing much to report. We remembered the last supper and went our ways.

I ran into the Inezes on the way out. Sam gave a quick hello and went to get their vehicle, while Liz waited at the curb.

A few pleasantries. Then, I mentioned, "I've made an offer on the house next to my place. I may need your services soon."

Liz Inez gave me a sly look. "We can do prenuptial agreements too."

"I'm not sure which one of us would need protected."

"Both, of course, but you are the one who owns a business and a home. This is no time to talk of that." Certainly not. She couldn't bill me.

"Coming tomorrow?" I asked. I hadn't decided whether I would.

She shook her head. "We're leaving first thing, going down to Tampa to visit Sammy's parents. Ever spend time in Tampa, Ted?"

"Not exactly. Apparently I was, um, conceived there." I sort of regretted saying that as soon as it came out, but figured I might as well follow through. "My folks lived there in the late Forties."

"I don't think that counts. Ah, here's Sam. See you." She slid into their deep gray Volvo. The automotive choice of serious-minded rich folks everywhere.

I couldn't say what sort of automotive choice old Toyota pickups are. It was dark enough to turn on the headlights as I headed home.

The lights were on in the kitchen too, I noted as I pulled in behind Michelle's van. Just her and me this evening. Probably a bottle of wine, as well.

Hopes dashed. Or knocked slightly askew, anyway. Al Guzman sat at the table with Michelle. "They caught the other man who attacked you," he immediately announced.

"Chief Stuart called a little while ago with the news," said Michelle. "Not surprisingly, all they had to do was wait at his girl-friend's place."

"Dames is always gettin' us mugs in trouble," I told her. "It's enough to drive us to drink."

She took the cue and poured me a glass of merlot. "Suellen Wyatt's apartment, right?" I asked. I knew from Jan's digging where she resided.

"She didn't mention that. Just the guy, um, Something Pruett."

"Don Pruett. Let's hope he or Left talks. Wyatt is the person they really need to get." Michelle knew what I meant.

Al didn't but, to his credit, did not pry. Rather, he said, "I like to go to the City Council meetings now that I am retired and have time to fill.

"This morning," he continued, "the idea of selling the land across the street was brought up by, uh, Robinson. That's the name. No mention of who might be buying it but we know, don't we?"

I nodded. Michelle sipped wine. He had probably told her this already.

"I think maybe some of them wanted to vote on it right then! Mayor Parish put a stop to that, to her credit."

Perhaps trying to prevent the political damage caused by ramming something like that through without prior discussion. She favored the idea, so far as I knew.

"There will be hearings, maybe, and they will take it up again later. This is something that must be prevented, I say."

"And we agree," said Michelle. "Don't you need to get going?"

285

Al looked at his military wristwatch. "Yes, I must go pick up Marty at the rec center."

A hurried goodbye and he was out the door. "I talked to some of my, um, coworkers and they mostly agree on what would be a good counteroffer," Michelle told me. "Pretty much what we already planned." She rose. "I'd better stick our supper in the oven."

"My lovely leftover lasagna?" I had set some out to thaw before leaving.

"Yeah." She slipped it in and set the temperature. "Do you fast tomorrow or something? Al said so."

"Supposedly."

That was apparently answer enough. "Patty came by," she continued. "She wasn't completely surprised you were at church."

"I guess she knows me."

Michelle came and sat again, pouring another glass of red. "Knows you pretty well, considering how long it's been. I guess people don't really change."

"I would say we are all changing constantly. Even though some of us fight it!"

She only shrugged. "Patty has made an offer on a house too. Somewhere out west of us."

As she had told me she might. "Now we shall be able to go to her place and hang around and pester her."

That finally brought a smile to the unusually subdued Michelle. "Turnabout, huh? Except we're both too busy. Well," she added, "I am anyway."

"Maybe Patty will have things to occupy her too," I suggested, "once she settles in. Painting."

"As long as you aren't one of her occupations."

Chapter 68

My involvement with the whole Chief Cotton affair was pretty much out in the open now, wasn't it? That is, whoever was behind the scenes knew of it, or they would not have set Pruett and Left on me, probably through Suellen Wyatt.

But all the more reason to be careful of whom I met with, maybe. Were there more henchmen out there? Someone of a little higher caliber than those two?

Jay Johnson had an opinion about those two. "I would have called them white trash, once." He glanced at his partner. "I've had training since!"

The new partner was not only white but also female. I recognized her from our previous encounter. Jay introduced her. "This is Anna Church. Newest addition to the Cully Beach bike patrol."

"I've met Officer Church." I nodded an acknowledgment toward her. "But are you sure she is a cop and not playing truant from high school?" The compact blond-haired woman blushed quite red.

"Now Ted, she gets enough of that from us," said Johnson.

"Then I apologize. You guys — um, not guys — are you officers just starting your patrol?"

"Yes, sir," replied Anna. "I hope I can keep up!"

"Jim is on desk duty for a while." Jay smiled broadly. "Supposedly it is some sort of discipline but we know he is actually helping out Millie." Once again he looked toward his partner. Trying to be on best behavior for her. "Er, Chief Stuart."

"Well, that's who I am here to see. Later, Jay. Anna — okay if I call you Anna, isn't it?" She nodded but I don't know how okay it really was. The pair peddled off and I entered the police station.

"Not surprisingly," said Jean Stuart, when I took an uncomfortable chair in her office, "Pruett and Left were more than willing to turn on each other. Getting them to admit Wyatt's involvement took a little more time." She shook her head. "It was the boyfriend who actually gave her up."

"So they've admitted to everything? Me? Dave?"

"And your surfboards too, for that matter. We have Miss Wyatt in custody now but we're not getting anywhere with her." Jean raised her narrow face from a paper she was holding. "There are powerful people involved and I think she trusts them to take care of her. She already has a lawyer she could never afford on her own."

"But not from the Carver firm, of course."

"No, they would not get directly involved." She took a moment to remove her glasses and wipe at the lens with a tissue. "Not that we should assume the firm itself is a part of this. We think a single ambitious attorney there is just as likely."

I nodded. The more people who were involved, the harder it was to keep something like this secret. "So you are going to look at Suellen Wyatt's financial records," I said.

"I can't divulge information like that to you," she replied, and winked. "I couldn't tell you we are looking at Pruett's bank account either."

"Okay, I'll just remain in the dark. Do you need anything from me while I'm here?"

"We could let you look at a lineup of men in ski masks," she joked. "Nothing else I can think of right now. Blake is a couple offices over if you want to talk to him."

"I might do that. See you, Jean."

They had Dave in an office? I realized why when I found him, surrounded by ledgers and file folders. "Hey, come in, Ted. I'm not as busy as I look."

He did look busy. "That's a lot of material to go through."

"But Millie and I have both been through everything, over and over, and we can not find any missing money. It had to have been changed in the records at City Hall."

"That's what Sally thought, too," I noted. "Some regular expenditure labeled to make it seem suspicious."

"Unless there is an official audit, so we can compare, we won't know." He closed the folder he held and tossed it onto a table. "How are you doing, Ted? Not banged up quite as bad as I was, I hear."

"You need to learn my secrets of self-defense. They involve running really fast in the opposite direction."

That set something off in the man. "Jan should learn that lesson."

"Jan is independent. She's not someone you can order to keep out of things." I'd known her since she was a little girl. She had always been that way.

"I just wanted to protect her."

"Janice Bell doesn't want to be protected."

"But if she is going to be with a policeman, she needs to be," he argued. "If she can't accept that, I can't see us as a couple."

If Dave was going to have that attitude, I couldn't see it either. I didn't say so but just maybe I should have.

Chapter 69

It was past opening time but I assumed Charlie was in the shop. If not, it didn't matter all that much.

Yes, the front door was open. "Shaper! The police are trying to get hold of you."

"I just left the station."

"Something happened to your friend Sally right after."

"Number?" She handed me a slip. Good work, Charlie. That's the front desk number, isn't it? I rang it up.

Jean Stuart had left the station, I was told. That was to be expected. Her niece had been in a hit and run was about all the information available right then. That and the fact that she was on her way to the hospital, the local one in Scott City. That was probably good news. If it were really critical she might have been airlifted to a bigger facility.

"I'm going to the hospital," I told Charlie. "Can you hang here? If not, no big deal, just lock up." I didn't even wait for an answer but ran for my truck.

No need to stop at the front desk and ask anything. There was Dave Blake. He must have accompanied the acting chief.

"Ted," he greeted me, "you know her, um, partner, don't you?" I nodded. "She's on her way here and a familiar face might help."

I might as well be useful. "Okay. How is Sally?"

"Broken leg, some contusions and cuts. Someone ran her bicycle off the road and into a ditch."

"On purpose."

"Seems likely, doesn't it? Someone with connections further up the food chain than Suellen Wyatt, I would think." There was exasperation in his voice. "No description of the vehicle, of course. Sally never saw it coming."

So she was talking. That was good. "There's Karrie Goodpaster," I told him. Jim Trejo escorted her.

Karrie seemed dazed. More dazed than usual. "Shaper!" she exclaimed and ran to give me a hug. "Thanks for coming." Not 'how is Sally?' or 'what happened?'

But we all handle things in our own way. Or maybe we don't handle them at all. Karrie might fall into that latter category.

"She was still in the emergency room last time I checked," said Dave. We headed that direction, not that they would let a crowd of us into the ER.

"Moved to a recovery room," said one of the nurses. "She should be good to go home in a little while." The direction was pointed out.

And the door was open so we slipped in. The room was empty except for Sally, who sat up and asked, "What kind of world is it where a girl can't enjoy her day off?"

Karrie took a look at her, turned, and ran from the room. I don't know whether Sally or I sighed the deeper. "Let her go," she said. "Maybe she'll process it and find her way back." I wasn't sure she cared.

Jean Stuart came in a moment later. "I leave you for a moment and this mob breaks in." Then she added, in a more tender voice. "I saw Karrie crying down the hallway."

"Shall I?" I asked Sally.

"Sure, Ted, if you want. She likes you for some reason." She laughed and grimaced. Ribs must hurt.

Goodpaster was done with sobbing by the time I found her, sitting on a couch in reception. The slender form slumped forward, eyes fixed on the floor. She looked up as I approached.

"I can't handle this, Shaper. Not on top of all the crap that's been going on." She had complained about Sally's preoccupation. That, I assumed, had been due to our investigation.

As was this incident. "I could take you home if you would rather wait there. Her aunt will bring her to you."

She nodded. "Okay."

I went to let everyone know what was up and then accompanied Karrie to my truck. She rode silently as I searched out the address I had been given. "This it?" I asked.

"Yeah." It was a rather nice apartment complex out a mile or so west of the river.

She climbed out. "I'll be fine, Shaper," she said. I got the feeling she had pulled herself together, maybe made some sort of decision. That was good; Sally didn't need her falling apart, what with her own troubles.

Too late to head for church, take in the Good Friday passion service. Oh, perhaps not really, but I wasn't up to it. I drove on home.

Charlie and Jan were there, gossiping in the showroom, and probably waiting for my report. I gave them most of it. All they needed to know.

"Wow. More to investigate," was Charlie's enthusiastic response to the tale.

"Don't go getting in trouble," I warned. "Either of you."

"And don't you start sounding like Dave," said Jan. So the girl could joke about it now. That was good, wasn't it?

Everything needed to be repeated when Michelle showed up an hour or so later. Just the two of us, over wine, this time. The girls were still hanging up front, a few minutes before closing time, when I heard the phone ring.

Charlie's voice. I couldn't tell what the words were. Then both she and Jan came back into the kitchen.

"That was Mrs. Stuart on the phone," Charlie reported, "about Karrie Goodpaster." A pause. "She was gone when she got Sally home. All her stuff too."

I considered this news. I wasn't surprised, was I?

"A breakup?" asked Michelle.

"And a breakdown," I answered.

Chapter 70

That had been pretty serious, hadn't it? It was one thing to beat someone as a warning or to commit acts of vandalism, and quite another to plow into them with an automobile. Sally could have been dead rather than injured.

Why Sally? Why now? Someone feared what she knew, or what she might learn. Leave it to the police, Ted. Ha, every time I told myself that, I got pulled in again.

Lots to keep me occupied right here on a busy Saturday. Mind the shop, work on the shower, build boards. My hands were in good enough shape now, weren't they? The swelling had gone down.

Not church. If I knew Pat, he would make it to the evening service, with its lighting of the Pascal fire right after sunset. Early morning tomorrow was more my style.

First thing this morning, however, I was heading over to the Stuarts's place. Not intruding, you understand; Jean has asked me to stop by if I could.

I pulled up at the modest ranch, not far from where Doris Boone lived, as the crow flies. If one drove, it was a rather long and round-about way between the two. Buddy came to the door and waved for me to come on in. Hadn't seen Buddy in ages.

Nor visited their house. I and the Stuarts did not really move in the same circles. Sally rolled her wheelchair my direction. "Hi, Ted. Just when you think you're out, we pull you back in, don't we?"

"How are you, Sally? Sorry to hear about, um, your —" Darn, I didn't know how to put it. Shouldn't have started a sentence I couldn't finish.

"My Karrie. I thought at first maybe she had run off with you."

That I recognized as an attempt to cover her pain. I'd let her get away with it. "I wouldn't have guessed it when I left her. She was just gone with all her things?"

"It's my place, really. Karrie just sort of — stayed there. She didn't have many things."

Jean spoke. "When we found that woman had left, I told Sally to come and stay with her Uncle Buddy and me. It would be safer." Not just because of her injuries, I imagined. There could be another attempt to harm her.

"I could have gone to Dad's." She didn't sound enthusiastic about the idea.

"You and your father are much more cordial at a distance," said Buddy.

"I wanted to let you know some things that are going on in, ah, an unofficial setting. Buddy won't rat us out," said Jean Stuart. "The biggest news is that we have found checks connecting Don Pruett to *Carver, Carver, and McGee*." She looked to her niece. "Yes, dear, we have real evidence about your employers' part in this now."

"Who signed them?" was Sally's immediate question.

"The name is Marcus Bowes. He isn't an attorney, is he? I didn't see his name on the list I have."

"He does some kind of security work for the firm. I've never quite understood what." Sally shrugged. "Sorry I don't know more."

"That's all right. There seem to have been regular payments over a couple of years." She paused. "Then one rather large one a few months ago."

"That's what we expected, isn't it?" I asked. "Um, what you expected."

Jean laughed at that. "Yes, it is. Or what we hoped to find. It seems that Miss Wyatt was being paid for services rendered via her boyfriend, to avoid suspicion." She gave a rather self-satisfied nod of her head. "But the silly woman would transfer it into her own account. Presenting this evidence to her might loosen her tongue."

Loosen her tongue? Well, Acting Chief Stuart could phrase it as she wished.

"But we still don't know what attorneys might be involved," said Sally. "Or who was being bribed higher up. There was someone, that's for sure."

"I suspect a certain city councilman," I stated. "He seems kind of obvious to me." And the most obvious one is usually the right one, except in convoluted mystery tales.

"Not Bernie Robinson?" asked Jean.

"No, not Bernie. He's willing to do everything the Burkhardts want anyway, in the name of progress."

Buddy chuckled. "That's true."

"I mean Ronnie Rouse. I was told that his votes are all over the place but it looks like they only hurt other developers, not the Burkhardt company. What really caught my attention was when he introduced a resolution to sneak in a zoning change for them."

"And he is always sort of the swing vote," noted Sally, catching on. "Yes, the obvious person to bribe."

"But nothing that can be proven." Jean Stuart pondered. "I think you are right, Ted. At least it's a good place to look!"

"Then my work here is done. I'd better get home and open for business." I hoped that my hunch was right. I would feel rather silly otherwise.

Not that I didn't anyway, from time to time. "I'll roll out with you, Ted," said Sally. "This is a great way to get around. I may never bother to walk again!"

"We're going to put you on crutches next week, girl," warned her aunt.

She pushed herself along almost to my truck before speaking. "Karrie always had a lot to say about us, but in the end I guess actions speak louder than words, right? Every cliché has some truth behind it."

"Actions may speak louder than words but words can help us understand the actions, can't they? Even when they are lies."

"Maybe so. And maybe I'll understand in time."

"Or forget," I told her. "That works too."

Chapter 71

"I hope you don't mind if we go over to *Mama Toni's* again," I told them. "Patty wants to meet us there."

"No young folks coming?"

"Not this time. We wear them out, you know."

"You wear everyone out, Ted. I get tired just hearing about the things you've been up to."

I gave Pat my best squint. "You with your muscles? I'd get worn out trying to keep up with your workouts."

"Don't give me that. I know you do loads of push-ups and squats and stuff when there aren't any waves. You can't stay still, Ted. I know you."

He did know me. "You're all refreshed and ready to go?" I asked.

"As good as we're going to be after that drive," said Betty. "Let's go."

We piled into the Edwards's wagon this time, old-folks style, with me and Pat up front and the women in the back.

"So you and Patty are both buying houses?" came Betty's question, somewhere around Greenwood Road.

"It looks that way," Michelle told her. "We've made another counteroffer and are awaiting a response."

"We'll have a place for you to stay next time you visit," I added. "We'll send you to Patty!"

Then back to small talk. As we pulled into the little restaurant's parking lot, Pat asked, "Patty likes this place?"

"She and Toni are buddies now," I told him. "There's her car." The silver Miata was near the entrance.

"Isn't that your young policeman friend?" whispered Betty, as we entered. "But that isn't Jan with him."

I followed her line of vision. Yes, Dave Blake. And that was Anna Church sharing a meal with him. One shouldn't blame a young guy for moving on. But I did anyway.

"There's Patty." And Toni was sitting across from her. We headed their way.

"Oh, hi folks," said the tall proprietor, rising from her place. "I'll get you set up." She returned shortly with menus and water and bread sticks. Those, I think, were mostly intended for me.

Patty leaned forward. "Sorry to hear about your friend. And I was just thinking of buying a bike."

"No one is going to purposely run you off the road, Miss Singer," I told her. Of course, then Pat and Betty were curious and the whole story had to be told and all the rest that had happened since they last visited. Somewhere in the midst of that, we ordered our dinners. And a bottle of Italian red.

Our crime-solving adventures having been covered thoroughly — with special attention to my encounter with masked thugs — we moved on to houses.

Said Pat, "We'll have to go see the place you're thinking of buying, Patty."

"I actually considered getting a boat to live on," admitted Patty. "For a little while. But where would I paint? The house I made an offer on has great natural light." She laughed softly. "So I'll probably end up painting late at night with electric lighting."

Here came the pasta. Nothing extraordinary there, just decent

Italian food. By now, Toni knew my picky vegetarian ways and made sure I wouldn't find any unwanted meatballs or such in my meal.

Dave and date getting up. He would feel obligated to come over and say hello before leaving. I rose and shook his hand. "Hi, Dave. You know all these folks," I said, "and they know you. This is Anna Church," I said to my friends. A few pleasantries and they were out the door.

"How do you know Anna?" asked Michelle. "I can't keep track of your girlfriends!"

"She's Cully Beach's newest police officer. We need more like her, don't you think?"

"Absolutely," agreed Pat.

"Perhaps Charlie will be on the force in a few years," suggested Patty.

I nodded. "It could happen. It's only a couple weeks now to her GED exam and then she can go whatever direction she wants with her future."

"I'll drink to that," said Betty, raising her glass.

We all joined her.

Chapter 72

I didn't recognize the van parked by the Bell house. I might not have noticed it in the dark, returning from my morning surf check — flat again, darn it — were it not for a glimmer of light from inside.

Check it out? That sort of thing always gets you in trouble, Ted. But I went over anyway.

Hmm, Florida plates. Kind of a fancy conversion van, not particularly new, with airbrushed pictures. Unicorns?

"Hey, Shaper," came a voice. From the van? I heard the door slide open on the far side. By now, I could place that voice so I went around. Karrie Goodpaster, wrapped in a blanket.

Of course she had a van. With unicorns.

"Keeping an eye out for your neighbors?" she asked. "No plans to rob them or murder them in their sleep!" I could probably believe her. "Jan said I could park here. I'm living in the van till I find a place." She turned to look into the well-lit and well-appointed interior. "It's not the first time."

"It looks like you could do it indefinitely."

"As long as I have some place to park. And electricity is nice. I have my own extension cord!" One of her odd chortling giggles. "If the Bells tell me to move on can I park in your drive?"

"Oh, Rick and Kay would never do that." I hoped. I didn't need Miss Goodpaster's unicorns — I could see them gamboling across the side more clearly now — in my driveway. Or Miss Goodpaster, for that matter.

A thought. "But if I go through with buying the house south of mine, I wouldn't mind you parking there. In fact —" I started thinking rental income. "Well, that's something for later. It sounds like we woke up the dogs."

"You'd best run before they release the hounds! Later, Shaper." She slid the door closed. Well, Karrie didn't seem the worse for her recent breakup. Better than Sally. Or better at hiding things. I didn't know.

I rolled on home and filled Charlie in on our temporary neighbor. "I wonder how long she'll stay." She took a long pull on her mug of coffee. "I know her kind. If someone doesn't shoo her away, she'll never leave!"

"What would you think of me renting the house next door to her?" I thought it might be better to see what Charlie thought before running it by Michelle.

"Well, she does have a job." A sudden thought made her laugh and spray a bit of coffee. "And she thinks I'm cute."

"Yeah. I wonder when your mom will get up. She shouldn't waste a day off."

"Sheesh, Shaper, it's only Five-thirty."

"Why when I was a kid, Five-thirty came a whole hour earlier!"

That, she ignored. "You running around with Betty and Pat today?"

"More than likely. I may just leave the 'closed' sign up all day."

I wouldn't be alone in that today. Lots of businesses were taking the day off. Government offices too, of course.

"Then you won't need me. That's good 'cause I didn't plan to be here."

"That's not unexpected. Off with John?"

"Nope. Mr. Guzman invited me to ride along with him and Marty. They're going down to Cocoa to tie up some things."

"Cocoa's an interesting town. Lived there a while." I should bake something for Michelle's breakfast. I could run off my version of scones — a 'bland and healthful' version, naturally. I got up and began rummaging through the cabinets for what I needed. Flour, oatmeal, sugar. Two bowls, baking sheet. Raisins. Well, and so on — no need to bore you.

"Lemon juice?" asked Charlie.

"Yep. Flavor and acid for the baking soda."

"Hmm, I'll leave the baking to you, Shaper. John will have to learn to cook if we stay together. Or," she went on, "if we lived next door I could come over here for breakfast!"

"I'll have to ask John's advice on pricing." I had them mixed up and into the oven before it was even done preheating.

"You put apple sauce in there, didn't you?"

I nodded, and peeked in the oven. Rising nicely.

Charlie looked out the window. "They're up and getting ready to go. I'd better get my stuff." She disappeared into her bedroom.

One way or another, it might not be Charlie's bedroom much longer. Things do change.

And I would miss not having the girl in my place.

A few minutes later, she was in the back seat of Al Guzman's Buick wagon, heading south on A-1-A, and Michelle was sniffing the air in the kitchen. "They are almost ready," I told her.

"Coffee first," she muttered, pouring herself a mug as I removed the just-turned-tan scones from the oven. Onto a plate, onto the table. I would eat one — no, two.

As Michelle picked one up and began nibbling, a rap came on the back door. I did hope that was Pat, and not Karrie Goodpaster out wandering.

Neither. Patty Singer stood there. In she came before I could extend an invite. "Looks like I'm first. Did you bake those, Ted?"

"Help yourself." First? Had someone invited her?

Patty sat down and did, indeed, help herself. "You're with Ted for his cooking, right?" she asked Michelle.

"He pretty much broke the ice between us by baking me brownies."

Patty regarded me for a few seconds. "He would rather make things than talk. Hey, Ted, bring me a cup of coffee while you're up, okay?"

I pretty much emptied the carafe into her mug, and started a new pot. "I assume Betty and Pat are coming?" I asked.

"We want a tour of Cully Beach and you've been elected guide. I'll bet you've never even driven Michelle around just to show her things."

"I'm revealing its mysteries one at a time," I explained.

"Let's take the van," said Michelle. "We can all ride comfortably in it."

Except maybe the driver. But so be it.

Chapter 73

Up and down the streets we had gone, old neighborhoods, new neighborhoods. North through Doris's subdivision, up A-1-A and back, down winding River Road past the aptly named *River Road Nursery* at the junction with Seventh Street.

"Turn at the next corner," ordered Patty.

"That will take us home."

"Also past the place I hope to buy." East onto Eighth. "Over there." I slowed down.

"A stilt house," observed Pat. "We have a lot of those in Ruby." Considering how flood-prone that town was, it was understandable. The weathered wooden structure rose on a double lot, facing south.

"Big windows on the back and big rooms inside," said Patty. "I don't think I could find a better place."

"Want to stop?"

"No need. I'll show you around when I own it!"

And so, on down Eighth Street to the highway, *Kay's Korner* to our right. I noted that Karrie's van was gone. "Back to my place?"

"That would be sensible, considering our vehicles are there," observed Pat.

"Man, I could make you get out right here and walk. Don't push me."

Patty burst into laughter. "My god, you two are just as bad as when you were twenty."

"Now I'm fifty so I'm two and half times worse," I informed her, as I pulled into my drive. "It's still early. Can I fix you all some lunch?"

"Better yet," said Pat, "we'll run and get some food and bring it back here."

That would be okay. "Piggly-Wiggly is your best bet," I called after him and Betty. "You know where it is."

Patty surveyed what passed for my back yard. "Not much room for a picnic."

What had once been a bit of a postage stamp lawn had become half a stamp as my workrooms had expanded. But there was still a nice little space. Enough that I had to mow it occasionally in warmer weather.

One of Rick's picnic tables sat squarely in the middle of it. "Maybe we should bring out some chairs," said Michelle.

Patty had something to add. "Charlie says you have guitars. Bring those too."

We hadn't even pulled them out of the closet this past month. "Be grateful Pat didn't bring his banjo," I whispered to Michelle as we went about our errands.

The guitars. My own fairly decent classical, Michelle's inexpensive Yamaha. I remembered glimpsing it in the corner, the first time I visited her and Charlie at the now-gone motel. We had made music that night and, out of practice as we were, I had not enjoyed it that much in years.

Before long, our shoppers returned with an assortment of deli foods, some of which I was actually willing to eat. The shadow of the rear fence began to creep toward where we sat, but it was still a warm April afternoon, shorts weather at last.

SHAPER

I could have napped. Not permitted. "Play something," demanded Patty. "I've never heard you."

"You missed his rock-and-roll days," commented Pat. "You didn't even pick up a guitar until after college, did you Ted?"

"Nope." I could see curiosity in the way Michelle looked at me. Another thing from my past she did not know about. Could I finger-pick? The hands were still a bit stiff. I'd try something.

I launched into 'Careless Love.' Michelle had heard me do this one loads of time.

My tiny audience applauded but maybe they were just being polite. I noticed that some clapping came from beyond the hedge and I took a guess as to who was there. "Is that you, Karrie?" I called.

She slipped her slender frame between the bushes. There was already a bit of a gap from the DEA agents who had used that route. "You said I could park over here, right Shaper?"

"We don't own the place yet! But I don't think anyone would notice you." I introduced her to my guests. Karrie did not come near but only nodded in their directions, like some wary wild creature that had wandered into the yard.

"I like being able to park back where no one can see my van," she explained. "It's too open over there." She waved a thin but well-tanned arm at the Bells' house. "Strange people come around at Five in the morning!"

"Come on over and have something," invited Betty. "Nice shirt."

Karrie and I snickered simultaneously — it was the one she had bought from me a few days earlier.

I wondered for a moment whether Sally ever received her too-tight red tee. Then Karrie had taken a chair and was gabbing as if she had been part of our group forever. She seemed, well, pretty normal this afternoon. Even rather charming.

Our little group broke up as dusk approached, going our different directions. That was about the time Jim Trejo drove up out front, with Dave Blake in the seat beside him.

Chapter 74

The chairs were already there in the back yard, so we sat down to talk. Michelle chose to disappear inside; I think she did not really want to be involved in any of this.

"All the government offices are closed today, of course," said Dave.

"Except the police," came Jim's addition.

"Yeah, right Jim. That does not mean judges are inaccessible. Millie knew who to contact and went to lay everything out for George Grimsley." I had some vague knowledge that a judge by that name existed. Nothing more.

"What it comes to is that he okayed all the warrants she asked for. We'll be cracking this open tomorrow!"

Jim nodded. "By the way, Tony Milton — Bill Cotton's lawyer, you know — received copies of the records incriminating Bill. He had a right to those."

"Somehow," added Dave, "he also learned that Acting Chief Stuart had made an in-house audit and asked for that too." There were chuckles from both men. "An order has been issued for us to hand over copies."

Which was pretty much what we wanted. Now the two could be compared and maybe they could see where the records were altered. That would be up to Attorney Milton.

"I assume you two have been assisting Jean today."

"You would assume correctly, Ted. We thought you would like to know what's going on. We owe you that."

"Undoubtedly," I replied. "Do you know how Sally Stuart is doing?"

"She seems to be pretty good," replied Jim.

"But a bit down, I think. This would get to anyone," said Dave. "Intrigue and being run down by a car."

"And losing her lover," I said, lowering my voice. "The runaway girlfriend has her van parked over there." I tilted my head toward the south.

"So you *did* steal her," said Dave. "We should have known."

Jim nodded knowingly. "All the chicks love this old surfer dude. Even the lesbians."

Dave brought us back to our main topic. "I don't quite understand why Miss Stuart was targeted."

"If someone at the law firm suspected her —" I began.

"Which they obviously did."

"Yeah. Whoever is behind all of this couldn't just fire her, could they? Probably wouldn't even have the authority to do that. But they would want her out of there so she couldn't spy anymore."

"Or they might have thought Sally knew more than she did," conjectured Jim.

That, too, was possible.

"Another couple weeks and we won't be able to sit in the dark like this," I said. "The season of mosquitoes and no-see-ums will be upon us."

Dave nodded, somewhat disinterestedly. "We should go." Both rose, shook, and headed for their vehicle. As they pulled out, Al Guzman's wagon pulled in next door.

I started carrying the chairs inside. Michelle must be in our room.

Charlie at the back door. "Can Marty come in? Man, we're beat!

I could imagine. It was at least a couple hours down to the Cocoa area, depending on route and speed. "Sure. Help yourselves to whatever." I went to get the last two chairs.

"We stopped in Vasco and talked to Kim and her husband," Charlie told me as I came back in. The two already had a jug of milk and assorted snacks on the table.

"Buzz," added Marty.

"Not Berz."

"Who's Berz?"

Charlie pointed at me. "That was Shaper's old nickname. Short for 'berserk,' right?"

"'Fraid so." Marty didn't look like she believed it at all.

"From when he rode reeeeally big waves!" Charlie snickered; Marty merely smiled.

"It referred more to my stupidity than my courage," I informed Marty.

Charlie continued. "Then we went down to Patrick Air Force Base. It is cool how the planes take off practically on the beach."

"I surfed across the street from the base more than a few times."

"Oh? Me too," said Marty. "Did you ever surf by the old pier?"

"My favorite spot. There was a lot more of it left thirty years ago."

"We had some stuff in a storage locker down there and brought the last of it home. That means we are truly and completely moved in!"

"Good feeling, isn't it?"

Chapter 75

Tuesday started out low key. A rather small swell was rolling, possibly worth attempting to surf.

My neighbor would go out. I would bet on that. Her boards had long since moved from my workshop to her own house. I wondered if Jan would like a ride down to the pier, as I used to give her from time to time. Those times had gone. I hadn't given the girl a lift in months.

Another surfer girl growing up, moving away, maybe forgetting the magic of the waves altogether.

What the heck. I shouldn't forget that magic myself. My replacement for 'Big Red' was finished and it was time to baptize it. I put it in the back of my truck before going in.

Charlie didn't seem to be up yet. Worn out from yesterday? I could have some coffee before taking off. There were a couple scones left I could reheat, too, before Charlie got hold of them.

Wetsuit? Yeah, the water was still cool, and so was the early morning air. A shorty would work. Have to go out and get it from the shop.

I stepped out with my keys to retrieve it. "Shaper? Are you going to the pier?"

Marty. "I am. Want a ride?"

"If it's not any trouble. Dad says it's okay." I had no doubt Al was watching.

"Throw your board in. We'll take off in, oh, fifteen minutes or so." She hurried off, I slipped into my wetsuit and went back inside.

I guess Al thought I was trustworthy. I might not have, in his shoes, what with me being attacked and all. Who could know it wouldn't happen again?

Charlie was yawning in the kitchen now. "Goin' surfin'?" she mumbled.

"That I am. Marty's riding along."

"That's cool." She slurped coffee. "I'll tell Mom."

When I went outside, I found that I had not one but two surfers waiting. "Hey, Jan, you're coming?"

"Yep, Shaper. It's been too long. Is that Big Red Two?"

"That it is. Let's go."

"I saw Marty getting her board and figured what was up," said Jan, as she climbed in. "Did Dr. Goodpaster park over here last night?"

"Next door," I told her. "I think so, anyway."

"Okay. I was a little worried about her." That was Jan for you.

A southerly swell. Hadn't had one in quite some time. South-easterly, I should say; waves from an extreme southern angle were rare here, due to the Bahamas getting in the way of ocean swells.

North side of the pier didn't even look rideable. Maybe on low tide. The girls grabbed their boards and hit it, paddling into waves still gray, difficult to see rising in the early morning shimmer until they were almost upon one. I paddled out on — what should I really name this surfboard? Shoot, it was Big Red, just like the broken board it replaced, and that was what I would call it.

I'd even made sure to use the same deep wine-red pigment in its finish. And it rode pretty much the same. No matter how carefully one attempts to replicate a board, there are bound to be subtle differences. Still, it felt familiar.

While Jan and Marty traded waves over close to the pier, hitting the peak wedging off the pilings, I sat at a sandbar a bit further south, and rode the somewhat mushy rights. Fun, but a tad boring after an hour or so. Other surfers joined us as the sun climbed the sky.

I knew that Jan was good, and I could see that now. But Marty was better. Eventually, I paddled over to them. "I will need to head back soon," I informed the pair.

"We know," said Jan. "I can stay with Marty."

"Tell my dad to come pick us up in a couple hours."

Hmm. "Nah, he put you in my charge, Marty. I don't want to get off to a bad start with him."

Jan looked at her. "He's probably right. Let's all go. Another fifteen minutes, maybe, Shaper?"

"Good enough." I rode a left in — closed out most of the way — and stepped up onto the sand. Al probably would not have minded. I would have to talk to him about that sort of thing if I were going to be giving Marty rides.

And home without problem. Michelle was off to work, of course. No running about with our friends this day. Our friends? They had all been my friends, hadn't they? Had Michelle really made any connections outside my circle? I wondered if I were, well, stifling her.

"It was fun, Shaper," said Jan, grabbing her board and heading across Al's back yard. Marty was a little slower getting out.

"Thank you, Mr. Carrol," she said. "Jan is nice, isn't she? I hope she hangs with us more."

"I don't know about that, Marty. I am afraid she is turning into a responsible adult and won't play with us kids anymore."

I expected a laugh but instead she solemnly nodded her head. "That's what I thought too." Marty grabbed her board and headed for her house.

Charlie was still inside and once again seriously at the books. Her exam was close now. Three more classes? Maybe four. Best let her study and ask nothing more of the girl.

Not as slow in the shop as expected, mostly due to the kids being out of school on a nice day with a bit of surf. Youngsters popped in and out, rarely actually buying anything. Many were surfing across the way, at the Eighth Street access.

I wondered briefly how the whole investigation thing was going. My part in it was at an end. I recognized that. But I would still like to know what was happening!

Dick Warner came by a bit before noon, all smiles. There it was. An acceptance of our latest offer. I sat down behind the counter and carefully read through the contract. "That's great, Dick. Once I talk to Michelle we can get on with this."

I wished I had someone to tell. Don't bother Charlie. Call Michelle? If Karrie were still parked next door, I might even have run over and told her, but I had seen her drive away a couple hours ago.

It can wait, Ted. Don't even mention it to Pat if he comes by.

Michelle should be the first to hear. I slipped the contract back into its envelope and stowed it under the counter.

Betty and Pat did come by. "We spent the morning exploring the park down at the inlet," said Betty. "Jumento. We didn't know there was a nature preserve down there."

"It looks like a good place to fish, too," Pat added. "I'll bring a rod next time."

"See my new neighbor about that," I told him. "He does custom rods and that sort of thing." I was bursting to tell the pair my good news but succeeded in resisting temptation. "Any plans for this afternoon?"

"Just the beach," said Betty, "and maybe a nap!"

"We'll come by when your lovely Michelle gets home. Dinner somewhere?"

"If we're all up to it." I supposed we could go out again. "I have something to celebrate." Yeah, I know, I shouldn't have dropped that hint. I couldn't help myself.

To their credit, neither of the Edwardses pushed me on it.

"A party, then," said Betty. "We should include Patty." We should, though I doubt either Pat or I was enthusiastic about it.

"Okay, I'll call her."

Chapter 76

An answering machine at the number Patty had given me, with a confusing message. Oh, it belonged to the people who owned the apartment she was renting. I hoped Patty checked it.

I should include the Bells in this. After all, they were truly my best friends here. Later. Maybe we could all get together somewhere.

At Five, I had a wine glass and the contract sitting on the kitchen table and went outside to shower. I'd been puttering along on my remodeling project and was a bit grimy, with concrete splatters up my legs.

"Patty phoned," Charlie informed me as I came in. "She won't be coming. Says she has a date!" The girl didn't sound like she quite believed it.

It surprised me a little too. But why not? Patty had certainly met people by now. "Just as well. I think your mom has seen more of Patty than she wants."

"That's okay, Shaper. You need to make her jealous now and again!"

"Oh? Maybe I should start introducing young men to you, just to keep John-boy on his toes."

"I can find plenty of those on my own," she sniffed. "There's Mom."

Michelle needed only to see my little tableau to know what was up. "Our offer was accepted!"

"It was. This first." A long kiss. I missed Michelle when she was at work. I'll admit that.

And I would never have expected it a few months ago. I poured pinot grigio into her glass while she looked over the papers. "You'll need to go in with me to discuss the financing," Michelle said.

"No problem. We know we can swing this." I had savings, Michelle had her unexpected windfall. And I was a homeowner, a business owner. A loan wouldn't be a problem.

Except to me. I did not like being in debt at all.

"Let me get cleaned up," she said. "Betty and Pat are coming over?"

"Yep." I turned to Charlie. "Would you like to look at the place? I know the combination to Dick's key locker." There was still plenty of light for a quick tour.

"Sure, Shaper. But are you *supposed* to know the combination?"

"Of course not. Let's go."

O-C-N. I had used the mnemonic 'ocean' to help me remember it. In we went. "Oh, this will be my room," stated Charlie. She stepped into the next. "No, this one."

"Keep going," I told her. I had been thinking the smaller bedroom at the back for Charlie. She wasn't quite so enthusiastic about it.

Into the kitchen. "Whoa, this is big compared to what you have." She looked around. "But there aren't any cabinets."

"That was the way, back when it was built. We could get some shelves in here." Maybe a nice work-table in the middle, too. Out the back door. I hadn't gone that way before.

And there was Karrie's van pulled in behind the place. Karrie Goodpaster herself was sitting in a lawn chair beside it, smoking a cigarette and apparently quite at home.

Charlie and I exchanged looks that mingled incredulity with amusement. The absurdity tickled both of us.

"Hi, Shaper," called the woman. "Hi, Charlie."

"Good evening, Karrie. It's official now," I informed her. "We're buying this place. That means we can charge you rent!"

Karrie took that in the spirit intended. "Let me know when the electric is turned on. My extension cord is at the ready."

"Do you plan to stay that long?" asked Charlie.

"I suppose I should look for an apartment. But —" A pause. "I would rather like camping in this little patch of wilderness for a while longer." She hesitated again, then continued. "Till I sort things out some, you know?"

I was not at all sure how Michelle would feel about that. "By the way," Karrie continued, "would it be okay if I used your outdoor shower?" I suspected she already had.

"Might as well," I said. "'Long as you're here." Voices from beyond the hedge. Betty and Pat must have arrived.

"We'd better lock up," I told Charlie. We returned to the front via the dining room, which she had not yet seen.

"This would be a great room to paint in," the girl observed. It would, wouldn't it? Two large windows faced north.

"That hedge blocks the light. I'll be taking it down."

"Uh-huh. Good idea." Out the front and back to the shop, after returning the key to the lock box.

No, it wasn't the Edwards couple. Kay and Michelle were standing in the drive, discussing our news. "We'll have a party to celebrate all the changes," Kay declared. "You and Patty and

320

Alvaro." She thought a moment. "Saturday afternoon. Are Betty and Pat staying that long?"

"I think so," I replied. Pat had mentioned leaving on Sunday, hadn't he?

"Everybody," she continued. "You, Charlie, and your boyfriend." She frowned. "Maybe we need to find someone for Jan. She's been moping."

With that, she headed back to her own home, across Alvaro Guzman's backyard. I noted that his Buick had long black surf casting rods in the back.

Chapter 77

"I went evening surf fishing with Al."

"Fishing only?" A vulgar comment about rods came to my mind but I quashed it. I wouldn't say something like that to Patty. Nor anyone else, I suppose. Forget I mentioned it.

"He is extraordinarily straitlaced."

"What? Not a Latin lover?" I joked, but I could readily believe her assertion.

"Nope. But a good fisherman. Al tells me he likes to cast while his daughter surfs."

That seemed like a good use of the time — if one liked to fish. But I wanted to spill my news rather than gab about either fishing or Alvaro Guzman. "Our offer was accepted," I told her.

"So was mine."

"Then we both have reason to celebrate. We're going to do a backyard thing at Kay and Rick's again this Saturday and you are invited." I couldn't resist adding. "Al, too."

"I'll try to make it." She got up and poured herself some more tea. "I hope you will drop by my new place and I can fix you tea sometimes."

"We're close enough to walk," I observed. "Or maybe we should get those bicycles." That was one of those things I had thought of now and again but never got around to.

"That would be nice. I'll do just that, Ted." She laughed. "Maybe a Granny trike!"

That, I had to laugh at too. "It's good to have you here, Patty," I said. "I, uh, hope you don't take this the wrong way but you're sort of like, well, my sister. Do you get what I mean by that? You feel like family." Darn, Ted. Why did you blab all of that?

"Absolutely, Ted. I think I feel the same way." She giggled. "You can be my sister too!"

"Thanks."

"Really, I do feel like family with you. Even with Michelle, who I think resents me a little." I wouldn't argue that. "I'll tell you a secret, Ted. When I arrived and found you not, ah, formally attached, and all our past came back to me, I thought of stealing you away from her. Yes, I did."

She leaned back and regarded me. "You two compliment each other so well. When one makes sense, the other makes nonsense! Me, I just make nonsense all the time."

I kind of got what Patty meant by that. Not that she was nonsensical, but that we were two of kind, so to speak. We *did* act like siblings.

"Essentially," I stated, "I need adult supervision."

Patty furrowed up her brow. "And so does Michelle. That's what you give to each other. It's something I could never do." She grinned. "I would aid and abet."

"But you were a successful businesswoman on your own," I observed.

"And a completely miserable one." Patty looked at me across the top of her cup. "You've done okay for yourself, too, but you told me you weren't exactly happy."

No, not until Michelle. And now that happiness seemed to be slipping away, eluding me once again.

I nodded. "You know," I said, "sisters let brothers drive their sports cars."

"Never mind. I'm disowning you!"

She took off a few minutes later in that sports car. Where? Not my business, nor yours either. It was time to open for another sluggish April day in the surf shop, which was my business. On my own — Charlie was out running whatever errands she had and wouldn't return until after her evening class.

Betty and Pat did drop by for a few minutes, kids came in and out, but it was not until mid-afternoon that an older Ford LTD pulled up out front. I recognized the green sedan — with one of those ugly vinyl roofs — as a vehicle Joan Cotton normally drove. Today, Bill was behind the wheel.

And Bill was practically bouncing. "It's over," he told me, sitting himself down on a stool by my sales counter and making me feel a bit like a bartender. "Charges dropped. I should be reinstated shortly."

That was great news. "I have you to thank for that as much as anyone, Ted. You were willing to believe in me and to act on it."

"I didn't exactly do it by myself."

"No, but I wonder if Dave and Millie and the rest would have gotten it together without you. By the way, Millie believes Blake should be Deputy Chief once she retires. She doesn't think much of Jack Saunders."

"That's not soon, is it?"

"Seventeen months, Ted. Then you'll only be likely to see her at the beach with her grand-kids!"

"So, what happened?" I asked. "You've been completely cleared?"

"Once Tony Milton had the documents he requested, his people found what had been altered pretty quickly." Bill chuckled. "It was a legitimate recurring expenditure for office cleaning! Someone altered it so it looked like the checks went to Harmony Bozeman. It was quite well done, Tony tells me. Way beyond the capabilities of Miss Wyatt.

"Our district attorney could have asked for an official audit to confirm all this but I think Harbin knew he was beaten. Their witness recanted, I was told, when all this was made known. I'm not sure she was ever actually here."

"This still leaves a lot of loose ends. Like the motives for framing you."

"I think that will be tied up soon too. Suellen Wyatt is talking."

Chapter 78

Michelle and I had a Ten o'clock appointment. There wasn't much to it, to be honest, look at some figures, nod my head, sign by the 'X.' Yeah, and initial over there. Having a girlfriend who worked at the bank certainly facilitated things.

They might have gone even smoother were we legally married. I didn't mention that to her, however.

That out of the way, the sale could go through and the house would be ours. Mine, Michelle's, and, yes, Charlie's. We were putting it in her name too, although Liz Inez thought that was a bad idea when I had dropped by her offices.

But, of course, she didn't know that Charlie was likely to end up hitched to John Brody. It seemed inevitable to just about everyone now.

I wondered if John suspected.

But back to the bank — before I left, Doris Boone beckoned the both of us into her office. "I doubt you have heard," she began. "I just got the news. Ronald Rouse has resigned from the City Council!"

So things *were* being tied up. And my hunch had been correct.

"Can you run to replace him?" asked Michelle.

"Wrong district. I think Howard Deland might announce."

"I wonder if he will face criminal charges," was my addition to this.

Doris shrugged. "Who can say?"

As long as I was out and about, and in the neighborhood, I stopped by the police station. That would make me later getting into the shop. No biggie. There were interesting things going on!

Admittedly, things that were not my concern, not anymore. But if Jean or someone was willing to take the time, I would like to hear about them.

No one would talk. But a rather harried Jean Stuart said, "Stop by my place on Saturday morning, won't you? Sally would like to see you."

"Is she back to work?"

"She is, albeit on crutches." She watched an officer escort a tall black man in thick prescription glasses and dark suit into a room. "That would be Marcus Bowes," she said. "I need to speak with him."

Home again. Not that late and Charlie had opened up for me. Betty and Pat were sitting in the shop, gabbing with her. Jan, too.

"There he is," said Pat. "Now we can blow this joint!"

"We're all going on a shopping spree," Charlie explained. "In Saint Augustine!"

"Have fun. See you all later?"

"A lot later, maybe," said Jan. "There's a lot to see in Augustine."

"We'll spend time with you tomorrow, Ted," promised Betty.

"I'll hold you to it."

And then I was alone, with a Thursday afternoon to fill. No one coming in to relieve me later, either, what with my young employees' Easter break schedules conflicting with my own.

Michelle seemed distracted, thoughtful when she got home. With the loan and everything else that had been going on, I thought I understood. I suppose I did understand; not completely but some.

We were already in our bedroom when we heard Charlie

coming in, back from her jaunt up the coast. She rattled about in the kitchen a while before going to her own room.

"Are we going to move her into the new place?" I asked. "Do *you* want to move into it?"

"We can certainly move some of our overflow over there. We have a lot of stuff sitting around, Ted."

That was true. The place had been crowded when it was only me. "Or we could rent it out while we make repairs," I suggested. Though probably not to Karrie Goodpaster.

Michelle closed the book she had been holding. "This is a big thing, Ted, a way bigger commitment than anything up until now. Why, it's practically like getting married!"

Despite her misgivings, the woman couldn't help making a joke. One of the things I loved about Michelle. We both smiled.

Then her voice grew serious. "Is this the right thing for us?"

"It's life," I said. "We move forward."

"Towards what? The rest of our lives together? Is that going to happen?" Was there something akin to resignation in her voice as she continued? "Isn't someone like Patty what you have really been looking for all your life?"

Oh. Maybe some part of me still yearned for a surfer girl, a part that had dreamed and idealized that perfect woman for so many years. Michelle might see herself falling short beside that dream.

"Once, she might have been. Seeing her after all these years showed me how wrong I was about that. Patty would never need me and I would never need Patty."

"Do you need me?"

"As much as you need me," I answered.

"That's a lot."

Chapter 79

"I hear Karrie has been camping out in your neighborhood," said Sally Stuart, dryly adding, "I have cop friends who notice these things."

"It's true. She has parked her van here and there."

Sally sighed. "I'm moving back into my apartment today. Without her. I don't know what the hell went wrong."

"She might have been looking for an excuse to break it off," I conjectured. "Maybe not even consciously."

"Perhaps so, Ted. Karrie is nothing if not unpredictable. Ah, but she was something different, something wild." A pause, a reflection. "Something that had not been in my life before."

"We all need that sometime. Maybe only the once."

"Did you have that?"

"Yes. Unfortunately, more than the once. But I've learned." Yes, I had learned.

The doorbell rang, the Stuarts's dachshunds barked, someone answered, muffled conversation. It was Jean who escorted her guest into the room. A striking woman — or was she? Physically, she was about as average as one might find. Late thirties, maybe, clothes simple and casual but obviously expensive. It was her way of moving, her air of confidence, that one noted.

"This is Ted Carrol," said Jean, "and my niece Sally."

"Theresa Carver," she said, taking my hand. "Call me Terri. You, too," the woman said to Sally. "It took me a while to hunt you down, Miss Stuart. I have heard things about you. Both of you."

So this was one of Sally's bosses, daughter of the law firm's founder. She took a seat on the bamboo-print sofa next to Sally. "Is it all right if I call you Sally? Okay then. You have done a great service to *Carver, Carver and McGee*, Sally."

"Some would say I had done damage to the the firm," murmured Sally.

"You have prevented damage to the firm," was Terri's reply, "at personal cost." Her eyes went to Sally's cast, but did she know of her relationship troubles as well? That sort of thing would be inevitable gossip at any work place.

"She helped save my boss and friend, too," stated Jean. Then she chuckled, "Even though she got him into trouble in the first place."

"So I have heard. It was astute of you to notice what was going on, Sally. Have you been told who was behind the whole thing?"

"My aunt filled me in." She turned to me. "Just the man you suggested I watch, some time back."

"Blair Rainey," said Miss Carver. "One of the junior partners."

"He's pretty much going to take the fall for this," said Jean. "The evidence against Rouse may not be strong enough to arrest him. At least we forced him to resign!"

Terri took up the narrative. "Rainey was working with the Burkhardts. Or Donna Burkhardt, I should say — her husband is a nonentity."

"We hope to indict her," added Jean.

Carver nodded. "Good luck on that. Naturally, we do not represent her anymore, despite my sister being a friend." She frowned. "I fear Rhonda might have had some idea what was going on and chose to look the other direction."

"Doesn't Marcus Bowes report to her?" asked Sally.

"He does. He's chosen to keep her out of it though, hasn't he?" Terri inquired of the Acting Chief. Or was she back to being Deputy Chief? I hadn't heard whether Bill had returned to duty.

"Yes. He's made a deal with our prosecutors. I would have thrown him in jail and left him there for running Sally down."

"Oh, he did that?" I hadn't heard this.

"He's not admitting to it and the DA isn't pushing it, as part of the deal, but, yes, he definitely was the one. Bowes was basically trying to clean up Rainey's mess."

"Which involved bribery of Rouse," I stated, hoping to get this all clear in my head.

"Starting, apparently, with Donna Burkhardt getting him a membership at her golf club," said Terri. "Then little favors led to bigger ones."

"And finally that contract I saw," stated Sally. "That would have been for getting the city land sold to Burkhardt, I would think."

To that I added, "Something that will not happen now, I expect."

"Of course, Bowes coordinated the frame-up of Bill Cotton," said Jean. "And getting those two rednecks to make trouble for you and Dave."

"Can I sue him for the surfboards?" I asked.

Terri laughed. "I'll represent you myself!" She turned to Miss Sally Stuart. "You plan to study law, don't you?"

Sally nodded. "Yes, ma'am. Er, yes, Terri."

"Then *Carver* will foot the bill for law school. Consider it a full scholarship."

Sally Stuart gasped.

Chapter 80

I was glad to see the Bells had not invited the whole neighborhood. This baker's dozen was enough.

It did not remain at that number standing about in their backyard. Who should drive up but Dave Blake?

"Who invited him?" asked Charlie, decidedly too loudly.

"I did," said Jan. "We're going to give this a try." She went and escorted him to a picnic table, where the two sat and conversed much of the afternoon.

When I managed to get the young fellow alone, I asked, "What became of the policewoman?"

"Anna and I didn't last beyond two dates. She thinks I'm too serious."

Which was kind of what Jan liked about him. I silently wished them luck.

"So we are celebrating new arrivals and new additions," announced Pat, having appointed himself master of ceremonies. "Miss Patty Singer. Mr. Alvaro Guzman and his lovely daughter. And the acquisition of a house by Michelle and Ted."

"And me too," called Charlie. "My name is on the deed!"

"Yes. We could even include Miss Karrie Goodpaster, currently squatting on your property." Laughs. I wondered if she were observing us from afar. I wondered if she would come over if I waved in her direction.

I decided not to.

"We need to celebrate Ted's birthday too," declared Pat. Darn him.

"When?" asked Michelle. "Why don't I know about this?"

"We've known him eight years and we couldn't tell you when it is," said Kay.

"A week from today," Edwards reported. "April Twenty-eight."

Patty nodded. Her memory had been jogged. And just when was her birthday, anyway? Heck, when were Michelle's and Charlie's? I would have to learn and write them down.

That was only fair if they were going to know mine.

"Most of all," I announced, preempting Pat, "I, at least, am celebrating an end to all this unpleasantness with crime and corruption!"

"And getting beaten up!" added Dave.

"You deserved it," muttered Charlie. I think only I was close enough to hear her that time.

From there, it became a normal gathering, people sitting and gossiping. Cold beer, food from Rick's grill — fortunately, no veggie-burgers. My date for the evening seemed to be Marty, as everyone else ended up in pairs and groups.

"I think my dad likes Miss Singer," she told me. They certainly were spending a lot of time in each other's vicinity.

"That's not something I would ever have expected," I replied. "Has it been long since your mother passed away?"

"I was only three. He has never dated."

A new home, Marty getting older, an end to thirty years in the service. I could see Al making one more change in his life. But with Patty?

Time, as they say, would tell. Tell of many things. Of Jan and Dave, of Charlie and John.

Of Michelle and me.

It was near dark when we too wandered back across Al's lawn toward the shop. "I hope he does put in a walk," Michelle whispered. "It would be so convenient."

"We could extend it right on to our new place," I said. I had just thought of that but immediately considered it a brilliant idea. Enough wine will do that to one.

Charlie and John had driven off someplace. Everyone had driven off. Okay, some walked. Al walked to his house while Patty drove. Nothing of interest going on between those two.

Nor would there be with Marty in the house. I already knew Alvaro well enough to realize that.

Maybe we could do something of interest in our house tonight, however. Michelle and I kissed before going in. Then we kissed again in the kitchen.

Michelle started down the hall. "Wait," I called. "I have something to show you first." I stepped into the utility room. The former utility room.

"I know you gave me ten years," I said, reaching into the stall and turning on the shower.

Michelle came over and put a hand under the stream of warm water.

"That's great, Shaper." She rarely called me Shaper. Then she came and put her arms around me.

"So, which day are we going to get married?"

Afterword

WAVES is the second novel about Ted Carrol and Cully Beach by Stephen Brooke, the followup to SHAPER. The author is himself a surfer and has shaped a few boards in his time. He has also turned out novels of fantasy and realism, illustrated children's books, nonfiction, and volumes of poetry, all available from Arachis Press, a small publisher dedicated to presenting meaningful literature for readers of all ages. Visit http://arachispress.com for our catalog.

Cully Beach is quite mythical. This does not mean it has no resemblance to certain towns on Florida's Atlantic coast. All we are willing to say about it is that Cully Beach would lie somewhere between Daytona Beach and Jacksonville.

The text of this book is set in Dihjauti, a typeface by T. Christopher White.

www.ingramcontent.com/pod-product-compliance
Lightning Source LLC
Chambersburg PA
CBHW060421030726
47495CB00003B/673